LOVE IN MAGIC

IN MAGIC
BOOK FIVE

KJ WARAWA

MYSTIC
CITY
PRESS

*R*eece Williams glanced at the clock on the wall and froze. Six forty-five p.m.—the exact same time as when he opened his eyes after coming out of the magically induced coma.

The time was an unpleasant reminder, but it also meant he had to hurry. He put the finishing touches on the tray of cupcakes so he wouldn't be late for the weekly family dinner.

As he put some of the items in his bakery's freezer and packed up the rest to take over to The Magic Plate, his family's restaurant, the image of a certain fiery brunette entered his mind. He couldn't wait to see her—she had an armor around her that he suspected protected a scarred soul that spoke to something within him. Her beautiful olive complexion and the brownest eyes he'd ever seen didn't hurt either. He could get lost in them forever if their owner didn't absolutely hate him.

Isabella Garcia Flores had arrived with his cousins just over two weeks ago... and immediately decided she didn't like him. He didn't get it. He was a likable guy. The likableest, in his opinion, and he didn't care if it wasn't a word. It was true—anyone who knew him would agree.

The bakery had closed for the night an hour ago, but he double-checked that the doors were locked before turning off the rest of the lights. Stacking the three portable bakery holders he needed to take with him on the counter, he picked them up easily and used his magic to open the back door. Sweet Magic was in the bottom of the first of the three Williams's buildings and hadn't been opened long when he'd been spellbound for the second time. He'd be forever thankful that his family and staff ran it while he couldn't, and now he was making up for lost time.

In the alley, he turned back to the door and put a spell on it that would last for a few minutes until he had his hands free to arm the alarm system from his phone.

A good majority of magic people—magics—needed to use their hands to direct their magic, but he didn't—not anymore. With just a thought, he could control most objects. When he'd been healthy enough to practice magic and learn everything he'd missed out on, it hadn't taken him long to realize that manipulating objects was his specialty. He was especially thankful for the skill at times like this, when his hands were full.

A year and a half ago he'd still been spellbound and hadn't even known he was magic. During the ceremony to break the spell, he was bound again with another spell, one meant to kill him. He'd wasted away for months until he'd been put in a magic coma while he waited for an ancient spell to be found to cure him. His sister Jo and her now boyfriend, Simon, had been his saviors.

While on his deathbed, he had made a vow to himself that he would never be physically or magically weak again. It was the first vow he'd ever made.

When the spell was broken just over four months ago, he'd been too weak to even hold up his head. But he had determination on his side.

Every day, he pushed his body to get physically stronger and his mind to learn everything there was to know about magic. Ancient spellbooks and free weights were his constant companions now.

He shook off the thoughts and plastered the expected smile on his face as he used his magic to open the back door to The Magic Plate.

"Hey, Jennifer," he called out to the chef, ready with a joke as he placed the containers on the back counter. "Why did the chef have to stop cooking?"

Jennifer turned around, a spoon still in one hand as she chuckled. "I don't know and I'm not sure I want to, but okay, I'll play. Why?"

"He ran out of thyme." Reece grinned and looked around at the rest of the kitchen staff as they groaned good-naturedly.

"That's so bad," Jennifer said, but she laughed again before turning back to the stove.

All the kitchen staff were magic, but it wasn't always that way. It just depended on who was most qualified for the positions when they were hiring. Currently, the serving staff was a mix of magics and non-magics.

He was grateful the kitchen staff were magic because it meant he didn't have to worry about slipping around if he used his magic. Non-magics had no idea magics existed and it was best that way. There weren't as many magics, and they didn't need non-magics fearing them, or worse—trying to control them.

Reece used the app on his phone to set the alarm before chatting with the staff for a few minutes as they finished the meals and prepared to leave. They shut the restaurant early every Thursday evening for the family and close friends who'd been invited to gather. It was his favorite night of the week.

"Jennifer, are you ready for us?" Isabella asked when she pushed through the doors at the front of the restaurant. He knew the moment she'd seen him—her pupils dilated as her anger surfaced and she gave him a death glare.

"Oh hey, Isabella, yes, everything is ready," Jennifer said as she smiled and pointed over her shoulder to the counter where his cupcakes sat. "You guys can start taking the dishes and we'll all be gone in a few minutes."

"Thanks." Isabella directed her smile at Jennifer and then let it fall from her face as she walked past him.

He saw the moment her armor locked into place. There was something about her that called to him, and he just couldn't let Isabella go without saying something. He walked up to the back counter, purposely standing right beside her, and pulled out the cupcake stand from the cabinet below. "How are you tonight, cupcake?" he asked as he opened the containers.

He smiled when her shoulders visibly tensed. She hated the nickname, but she hadn't told him not to use it after the first time and he thought it was perfect for her.

"I'm fine," she said as she grabbed two dishes and gave them to a server who had come to help.

One of his signature cupcake recipes was orange creamsicle. It was made with sour cream and orange zest, which added a bit of a sour taste that was incredibly refreshing. Just like Isabella.

He'd caught her eating one while all bundled up in a sweater and scarf as she sat on the restaurant's back patio. The look on her face as she took a bite and closed her eyes was pure bliss. He wished he'd been the one to put that look on her face, not his cupcake.

A few days later when she'd come into the bakery, she discovered that the cupcakes were his and she'd stopped eating them. If she'd meant it as a dig, it had worked. He could still feel the sting. But now he was on a mission to get her to eat another one and enjoy it even more while knowing he was the baker.

While placing his cupcakes on the stand, he watched her out of the corner of his eye. She put serving spoons into dishes and passed them to the servers as they came in. Not once did she glance at him.

He finished setting up the display and turned toward her with his sexiest smile. At least, that's what a past girlfriend had called it. "Aren't you going to ask me how I am?"

Her shoulders tensed again, and she passed off the last dish before turning to him. "No. I'm sure all your muscles—I mean, you—I'm sure *you* are just fine," she said as a blush stained her cheeks and she rushed out of the kitchen.

He barked out a laugh as his eyes followed her out the door. Now he knew that she'd noticed him and not just in an annoyed way. That was progress. He picked up the cupcake stand, careful not to jostle any of the three dozen cupcakes, and pushed through the swinging doors into the restaurant.

"Reece's Pieces!" His sister's screech was loud enough to pierce his eardrums, but he didn't care. He quickly put the stand on the table with the dishes and turned, bracing himself for the attack.

Jo launched herself at him, her petite body not enough to knock him over. Enveloping her in his arms, he breathed in her natural scent, peppered with hints of coffee, and felt like all was right with the world.

After a full minute, he let her go and got a good look at

her. She looked happy. "Hey, Pinky Pie, it's good to have you home." He'd started calling her by the nickname when she was in college after she first dyed her hair purple and it wouldn't matter if she wasn't still dying it. She'd teased him that Pinky Pie was pink, not purple, but the name had still stuck.

"Hey, Reece. Good to see you up and healthy," Simon said as he walked up to them and extended a hand.

With practiced ease, he gave Simon the jovial smile everyone expected from him and shook his hand. It wasn't that he didn't like Simon; he did. And he was perfect for his sister. He just hated being reminded of his once-withered state. "Yeah, I'm doing well."

Jo and Simon talked about their travels to find more of the ancient magic books, and then Meredith told everyone to get in line for food. Tonight's dinner was being served potluck style.

Reece got in line right behind Isabella but didn't say anything as she filled her plate. When she got to the cupcakes, he watched her pause. She reached out to grab one and then pulled her hand back.

He leaned closer to her. "It's okay to take one," he whispered in her ear.

She jumped back and shook her head before walking away.

As he took a seat across from Jo and Simon, he wondered if Isabella really did hate him. That wasn't something that sat well with him. He wasn't the kind of guy who needed everyone to like him, and yet he was easygoing enough that most people did. But with Isabella, it was more than that. More than just wanting her to like him—he wanted her to get to know him. To figure out what to do about it, he'd need a plan, but at the moment, he wanted to enjoy being surrounded by family and friends.

There were more people than usual at the dinner tonight,

some who only showed up once in a while, as well as the regulars. The din hovered just below what was probably the safe decibel range when all conversation suddenly stopped. Reece turned toward the door to see what had everyone's attention.

Out of the corner of his eye, he saw Connor Davis, his cousin Rowena's new boyfriend, push his chair back and slowly stand. Then his eyes caught movement at the restaurant's front doors. Ben and Stella Davis came in with their two sons, Nate and Travis. They often joined them on Thursdays, so that wasn't anything new.

It was the woman standing between Ben and Stella who had everyone's attention. She was rescued a few weeks ago. When his cousin Morgana's spell had been broken, she remembered where her friend was likely to be and had gone to Mexico to find her. There'd been a lot of spells going around lately.

She had been given the name Sam in captivity, but her real name was Julia Davis, and her cousin Connor thought he'd been responsible for her supposed death over twenty years ago.

Connor walked slowly up to Sam and then stopped. Reece couldn't imagine what the two of them must be feeling. But he wanted to experience the feeling for himself. His brother Dylan had been taken with Morgana and two of his other cousins only a few months before Sam. Morgana was safe, though they'd discovered his cousin Taren had died. Yet no one knew anything about his brother Dylan or his other cousin, Mirek, but he had hopes they were still alive. Dylan was two years older than him and Jo was two years younger. Being the middle child had always felt right to him. Then, on the day of the fire, he became the oldest. He'd also become the only boy in his family when up until that day there had been four, but if they found Mirek and Dylan, he wouldn't be anymore.

Connor held his arms out and Sam walked right into them. There was an audible exhale around the room. Then, as if by a collective, unspoken agreement, everyone turned back to their dinners and let the Davises catch up.

Reece dug into his meal and joined in the conversations around him. He was considering going up for seconds when he realized Simon was staring at him. He'd been doing it on and off all through dinner, but it was getting a little intense.

He leaned back in his chair, going for a relaxed look, and smiled at Simon. "Hey man, since you're with my sister, I know I'm not your type, so you've got to let up on the lustful stares."

For the second time that evening, all conversations ceased. This time all eyes turned to him and Simon.

Simon didn't laugh or seem bothered by Reece's comments. "I've been trying to figure out all evening who you look like, and I finally did," Simon said, a frown marring his features.

"Who?" Jo leaned closer to her boyfriend. "A movie star?"

"No. He reminds me of Rocky."

Reece heard several people curse but didn't look to see who had made the exclamations; he was too focused on Simon. "You're talking about the guy who worked for Snake and helped capture you and Jo?"

He felt a hand on his shoulder and glanced over to see Morgana. Meredith, her twin, and her husband Jack were standing behind her. Out of all the people who had been involved, only Simon had seen Rocky.

"Are you sure?" Jo asked Simon. "You think Rocky could be our brother Dylan?" Her eyes went wide and she didn't wait for Simon to answer. "Holy shit! He knew I was his sister. That's why he didn't let me see his face."

Isabella gasped and he finally looked down the tables. Her fingers covered her mouth. Her brother Mateo was missing, but not thought to be dead like his, and he'd been working with Rocky. Knowing where Rocky had been recently was likely the first clue she'd had in a long time to finding her brother.

"Yes." Simon wrapped his arm around Jo, pulling her into his side. "Rocky and Reece could be twins."

"Then why didn't you say anything before?" Jo asked.

"The other times I saw Reece, he didn't look anything like he does now."

When he'd first met Simon, Reece had been frail—just skin and bones. Pale, and not bulked-up like he was now.

"I didn't know." Jo blinked rapidly, clearly fighting tears.

Simon turned and kissed Jo's forehead. "Of course not. You already said that Rocky didn't show himself to you." He turned and met Reece's gaze. "When he helped me, I asked him why he didn't leave. I even told him I'd help him escape when I did."

A horrible feeling gutted Reece. If Rocky really was his brother and he'd chosen not to leave, maybe he wasn't the same person anymore. "What did he say?"

"He said he couldn't leave, or he would have done it years ago and never looked back. I asked him if it was because of the healer, but he didn't answer."

Jo turned to Simon. "Do you think the healer could be our cousin Mirek? That he's the one Dylan was staying to help?" He heard the break in his sister's voice and he started to stand to go comfort her when Simon held out his hand to stop him—the hand that was missing a finger because he'd lost it saving Jo's life.

Simon pulled Jo's chair back and then picked her up and walked out of the restaurant. The action made him smile. Jo hated anyone thinking she was weak because she was so petite, but Simon was her world and could get away with it.

"Let's finish dinner," Jack said to the group.

Reece looked at Isabella again but couldn't catch her eye. Her head was bent over her plate and she looked like a huge weight had descended upon her. Right then, he made another vow to himself, the second he'd ever made in his life. He'd find his brother and help Isabella find hers.

2

*I*sabella flashed directly to her apartment after dinner. Flopping down on the couch, she stared out at Blue Mountain's skyline in the distance, not even bothering to turn any lights on. It was so corny, but she'd heard comments in movies about people looking up at the stars and wondering if their loved one was looking up at the same stars. She wondered if it was true for Mateo.

She couldn't imagine Mateo being a star gazer, at least not as she remembered him as a teenager. He was always on the go and wanted to be where the action was. But maybe he was different now. She'd been told he was. Told he was mean and hurt people, but she couldn't picture it. Mateo was still locked in her mind as a young teen. He'd been sullen at times, and she could admit his behavior hadn't been perfect back then, but whose was? All teens needed to act out and figure out who they were while they were growing and learning their way in the world. His behavior had been typical for his age. Even she'd had some non-stellar moments while growing up, but she'd matured, just like everyone else did.

Regardless of what people said, she couldn't give up hope

for her baby brother. Some part of her believed that he was still the same person she remembered. She just needed to find him.

Pushing off the couch, she walked over to the sliding glass door and opened it. As soon as she stepped onto the balcony, she shivered against the cold and thought about going back inside. Now that it was late October, the temperatures were dropping below freezing most nights, something she wasn't used to.

Closing the sliding door behind her, she conjured a hoodie and shrugged into it. Taking a deep breath of the crisp and fresh night air helped settle her. She needed it, especially after everything she'd learned at the family dinner.

She snorted and then looked around out of habit before she caught herself. It wasn't like anyone would be lurking about on the building's eighth floor. Leaning on the railing, she looked at the apartments on either side of her. Rowena's was on the other side of the building and the rest on this floor were empty, so there'd be nothing to see. But being surrounded by vacant apartments was another thing to get used to.

When Meredith had given her the apartment, she'd said that each family member was on a different floor from the eighth to the twelfth and that they'd only just started renting out some of the lower floors.

Her modern and spacious apartment had come furnished. It was nicer than anything she'd lived in since she'd left home nine years ago to start the search for her brother.

But now, even her parents' house wasn't home anymore. When she'd first started searching for Mateo, she went home at least once a year to update her parents on what she'd learned, but then they'd asked her to stop. They said they'd moved on with their lives and considered themselves childless.

Not wanting them to see how deeply their comments cut her to the bone, she'd given them a nod and left. That had been six years ago. She hadn't been back to their house or even stepped foot in San Diego in all that time. It was pointless since there wasn't anyone there who would be happy to see her.

But from then on, the task of finding her brother had sat even heavier on her. A never-relenting burden of knowing she was the only one who cared about Mateo.

It also meant that no place was home anymore. Now she went where she needed to go to find things for people and earn a living, traveling all over. Not being tied down to a nine-to-five job in one place also gave her the freedom to look for clues to Mateo's whereabouts.

While she was in college and picturing her future life, it had been vastly different from her current reality. She'd just earned a bachelor's degree in kinesiology and was working as a fitness trainer, about to begin earning her master's degree, when Mateo went missing.

In her dreams growing up, she'd thought that by the time she was in her thirties she'd have a successful career, a loving partner, a couple of kids, and maybe a house in the burbs. Never in her wildest imagination did she think that most of her worldly possessions would fit in a backpack and she'd be traipsing around the country, living out of hotels and borrowed apartments.

She had or could conjure most of what she needed but satisfying her needs alone didn't make for a fulfilling life. Being surrounded by family and friends were what rounded it out, except Isabella didn't have that. It was one of the reasons she both loved and hated the Williams's weekly family dinners. They were a painful reminder of everything she thought she'd have by now and didn't. Everything she'd given up because of her search for Mateo. Yet she liked being included and having human connections, even when they showed her what she was missing. She liked everything about being with the Williamses and their friends. Every week she helped with the family dinner and several times she'd filled in at The Magic Plate when a server had called in sick. When Meredith had asked for her help finding a lost item—as a friend, not a client—she'd been filled with a sense of pride.

When she came to Blue Mountain, Colorado, with Morgana and Damon three weeks ago after helping rescue their friend Sam, her sole purpose had been to find clues that would help her locate Mateo. For years she'd shoved down feelings of loneliness and missing her family, hiding them so deep in her soul she could no longer feel them. The Williams family had dragged those wants right to the surface and now they had a hold on her heart, squeezing it tight as a reminder of everything she'd given up.

But she'd made some progress since arriving—she found a clue about Mateo. He went by the name Eddie now. Learning that would help her, but with that bit of intel came the knowledge that he'd tried to kill Rowena. He'd forced her car over the side of a cliff; luckily, she was found in time and healed. At first, she couldn't believe her little brother would do such a thing, that they must have gotten the wrong guy. Then she'd been told that he'd almost killed Javier Cano, an FBI agent. That gave her hope that maybe they did have the wrong guy because her brother wouldn't have done something so heinous. Yet, if they had the wrong guy, she was back at square one with no clues.

Mateo had always been headstrong as a young boy, but he'd also been sweet. With him being ten years younger than her and their parents being the absent type, she'd had to be more of a mom than a doting big sister. Having almost raised him was another driving force for her—she felt responsible for him. It also raised a question: could something she had done or taught him be the reason he left?

Pulling away from the railing and burying her hands in her hoodie's pocket, she stared across the skyline. Mateo could be in one of those buildings right now. For the first time in years, she knew her time to find him was running out. Sam's recent rescue proved that. The building in Mexico had been destroyed and all the loose ends of that time were being tied up. People were also dying, and she didn't want her brother to get caught in the crossfire.

She wanted to believe that he felt trapped and just needed her to rescue him. That he was doing all the horrible things she'd heard about because he didn't have any other choice.

It wasn't out of the realm of possibility as something similar had happened when he'd been seven. Steven had been Mateo's best friend since they'd met in kindergarten. They'd hit it off from day one and spent all their free time together. One day, during the summer before they went into the second grade, Isabella had been in the house while the boys played in the backyard. She'd heard shouting and a dog yelping, as if it was hurt.

Without taking the time to put shoes on, she'd sprinted outside. Mateo was kneeling on the ground, holding the collar of the neighbor's dog while Steven kicked the poor animal. Breaking them apart, she rescued the dog and sent it home, then called Steven's mom to pick him up. When she'd sat Mateo down and asked him why he'd hurt the animal, he'd looked up at her with tears in his eyes. Her heart broke for him when he sobbed and said Steven told him he wouldn't be his friend anymore if Mateo didn't do what he said. Steven didn't like the dog because he'd scared him. Mateo sobbed in her arms when he said he couldn't live without his best friend.

A knock on her sliding glass door startled her out of her

thoughts. Spinning around, she saw Reece standing there in all his muscular glory and smiling at her. She ripped open the slider and pushed into the room, forcing Reece to step back. "What the hell are you doing in my apartment?"

The smile on his face faltered for a split second before he put it firmly back in place. "Don't get mad, cupcake. I just wanted to see how you were—it was a lot at dinner tonight. When you didn't answer my knock, I worried."

She opened her mouth to say thank you and then shut it. He'd been thoughtful, but he wasn't what she needed in her life. He wasn't serious enough—he made everything into a joke, and she didn't have time for that with her time running out. She had to keep her brother as her top priority and not get distracted by someone who didn't have the same priorities she did.

Which meant not aligning herself with anyone, as she was Mateo's only hope. "I could have been in bed! Were you just going to barge into my bedroom if you didn't find me out here?"

His smile turned into a sly grin. "Not without an invitation, cupcake. I'm not that kind of guy."

"Right." She put her hands on his chest to push him backward toward the apartment door, but he didn't budge. Then her fingers betrayed her and kneaded the thick muscles through his T-shirt.

She gasped and stepped back, shoving her hands back into her hoodie's front pocket. "I'm fine. You can leave."

He took a few steps back, but not toward the door. Instead, he let the couch hit the backs of his legs and he dropped onto the cushions. The light on the side table turned on without him even waving his hand in its direction. That wasn't a skill most magics possessed. She'd have loved to ask him about it, but he might think of it as an invitation to chat.

"I thought we could talk," he said

Crossing one leg across the other knee, he looked up at her. Not that he had far to look up. There were a lot of giants associated with the Williams family, all of them over six feet, but Reece was probably just under. It was the breadth of his shoulders that made him seem so big.

His presence was so distracting she had to rewind his words in her mind to figure out what he'd just said. Talk. Right. "What do you want to talk about?"

"Our brothers."

Normally she'd jump at a chance to talk about Mateo, but he'd already been running through her mind all night. She couldn't see the point in talking to Reece about her brother—he didn't know Mateo like she did. He'd probably be biased too. Not to mention that he joked about everything.

Talking about something to distract her from Mateo sounded like a better idea. Isabella's stress had been mounting for weeks—from helping with Morgana's rescue to coming to Blue Mountain and learning about her brother. And now, after spending time remembering Mateo and wondering where he was, she needed a mental diversion, if only for a short while.

She'd wondered more than once what it would feel like to have Reece surround her with his body, even though he wasn't right for her. Maybe she could have him just once. Since he was a happy-go-lucky type of guy, this type of distraction might be right up his alley.

From the first time she'd seen Reece, he'd been driving her to distraction. She hoped sleeping with him would get him out of her system. A good romp in the hay would also help her relax. Then she'd be able to focus again. One night would give her what she needed without distracting her from her plan.

"I don't want to talk." She stepped forward and pushed his foot off his knee. It fell to the floor, leaving his knees spread in front of her. She walked between them and leaned forward, putting her hands on his shoulders. It had been a long time since she'd slept with anyone, but maybe that's what she needed—a quick sexual interlude. "I'd rather do something else."

WHEN ISABELLA STEPPED between Reece's legs, his hands moved to her hips as if they had a mind of their own. Seeing his hands spread across her small frame was sexy as hell, but he'd come to her apartment with a purpose. "Yes, cupcake. We should talk."

She leaned forward, her hands still braced on his shoulders, and touched her lips to his. It was light as far as kisses went, but it sent a spark straight to his groin. She smelled like apricot and vanilla, sweet and fresh, a contrast to her prickly and tart persona. He made a mental note to create a new cupcake recipe—apricot and vanilla with maybe swirls of lemon rind as a garnish. It was only the start of an idea and needed work, but it would encapsulate all of Isabella. Shoving the recipe to the back of his mind, he focused on the now.

It took all the willpower he possessed, but he pushed on Isabella's hips, and she stepped back, breaking their connection. "I'm attracted to you, cupcake, but I really did just want to talk." He hoped the nickname would throw her off balance. Standing up, he took a step to the side. Yes, sex was fun, but a roll in the hay wouldn't lead to a long-term relationship. And that was what he wanted. He hadn't been with a woman since before the spell that had almost killed him, but it wasn't for a lack of offers. In his early twenties, he'd have soaked up the attention and enjoyed just sex, but now, inching closer to thirty, he wanted more. Someone he mattered to, more than a sibling or a cousin, and someone who mattered to him. Someone to grow old with.

"Well, muscles, I don't want to talk. I want to fuck." She puffed out her chest and faced him head-on. He smiled but didn't enlighten her that it was because she was so cute standing there with her hands on her hips and her sweatshirt almost swallowing her.

It was ironic that the one woman he'd been attracted to in over a year didn't even like him. There was no doubt in his mind that all she wanted from him was a temporary way to get her mind off her troubles. He could be anyone right now; all she wanted was a warm and willing body.

"Really? That's it? No talk? No cuddle time? You're not going to buy me dinner first?" He hoped irritating her would be enough to get her to back off so he wouldn't cave and grant her wish.

"You've already had dinner. And you've been flirting with me since I got here. Are you nothing but talk?"

Throwing his head back, he barked out a laugh. It was the second time that evening that she'd elicited that response from him. She was thrilling to be around. "Oh, cupcake, goading me like that won't work. I see right through you, but I'll tell you what…" Lifting her chin, he bent down and softly trailed his tongue along her lips and then pulled back just enough to look into her eyes. "I'll give you what you want. Not because you're egging me on, but because you're the sexiest woman I've ever seen," he said, keeping his voice low, with a sexy drawl. He wanted something meaningful, but that didn't mean he couldn't convince her he'd be good for her too.

He grabbed her hand and tugged her toward the bedroom. The apartment had the same layout as his, so he knew his way around. When she pulled back on his hand, he stopped and turned. "What's wrong? Change your mind?"

"No. I just don't want to go to the bedroom. Let's do it here." She pointed to the couch with her free hand.

He manipulated the small lamp on the side table, dimming the light, but not so much that he couldn't see every expression running across her face. There was lust and anticipation, but not an ounce of fear or regret.

This wasn't what he'd had in mind, but maybe it would still work in his favor. If he gave in, she might realize that he was eager to please her. She was going to use him, and he was going to let her. He wanted her that much, but maybe they could both use some connection. Afterward he'd have to work to get her to like him. And he would.

Standing in front of her, he lifted the hem of her sweatshirt slowly, revealing her T-shirt and the curves it showcased an inch at a time. He tossed the sweatshirt on the arm of the couch and dropped to his knees. She might be using him for his body, but he was going to take his time and explore hers. Lifting his hands to her waist, he snaked them under her T-shirt and slowly moved them upward. His lips followed his hands, kissing her beautiful, soft skin.

"No."

He looked up at her. "You change your mind? It's okay if you have."

"No." She pushed his hands away. "Stop asking that. I already told you I haven't changed my mind. But I don't want all this." She waved her hand between them.

A warning went off in his head as he figured out what she meant, but he wanted her to spell it out for him anyway. He needed her to be clear. "Cupcake, it's kind of difficult to make love if we don't use this," he said, mimicking her hand-waving gesture.

Isabella stepped back and waved her hand at herself and

all her clothes disappeared. Still on his knees, he sucked in a breath as he looked at her naked form, soaking in her natural beauty.

"Reece, you're not getting it. I don't want to 'make love.'" She used finger quotes and her face squished up as she said the word *love*, as if it was distasteful. "I don't want you to kiss me all over. I just want you to fuck me."

He stood up and it was his turn to take a step back. Using him was one thing, as long as he could still make her feel good and cherish her. Being asked to treat her like a cheap trick by not allowing him to pleasure her was something else entirely. It didn't matter that she was asking for it. He expected that she was hurting inside because of everything she'd learned about her brother in the past few weeks. A distraction he understood, but he couldn't use someone the way she was asking him to. He would still respect her after, but he wouldn't respect himself.

Using his magic, he had her dressed in seconds.

"What?" She looked down at her fully clothed self and then up at him, her eyes wide. "I thought you wanted me?"

He leaned down and kissed her softly on the lips. "I do. All of you." He kissed her once more and flashed to the foyer in his apartment. Leaning back against the door, he took a deep breath and blew it out slowly to steady his breathing.

When he had himself under control, he used his magic to turn off the lights as he walked toward his bedroom to get ready for bed. He was too wound up to focus on anything else.

Lying in bed, he pictured Isabella right before he'd dressed her. She'd been beautiful, standing in front of him naked and offering herself to him like the tastiest cupcake in the world.

His first thought when he'd realized what she wanted was that he'd be disrespecting them both if he followed through.

But now he realized he'd have broken his vow to himself as well. He would have been weak. Allowing himself to be used would have been a decision made out of weakness and he would never put himself in that position again.

Now, he had to find a way to make her want him—all of him and everything he could offer her. All while keeping his second vow—to find their brothers.

3

*I*sabella left the bright early morning sunshine behind as she walked two buildings over. She kept her head down and hurried past the bakery on her way to the building's main entrance, daring herself not to look through the bakery's large windows for Reece.

She hadn't ventured out of her apartment even once yesterday to avoid accidentally running into him. When she thought back to his rejection, embarrassment still flooded her. For the first time in her life, she'd been brazen and had asked for something she wanted just for herself and it had backfired. In a big way.

She'd replayed the scene in her mind so many times and knew that she'd been trying to use Reece. He'd been right to refuse her, but that didn't lessen her embarrassment any.

When someone knocked on her door late in the afternoon the day before, she'd been tempted to ignore them. Her humiliation had been too strong and raw to face Reece, but she'd pulled up her big girl panties and opened the door.

Jack and Meredith stood there, asking if they could speak

23

with her. For a split second, she had imagined that Reece had sent them to kick her out because she'd thrown herself at him. She caught herself before she'd blurted out an apology. Instead, she had offered them some coffee and learned that they wanted her to come talk to the council about using her skills to find something for them.

Now, here she was walking into one of the Williams's buildings that housed newly finished office spaces with boardrooms. Not familiar with the building, she chose not to flash and took the elevator to the fourth floor. She was checking the numbers on the doors, looking for the right room, when she heard voices.

Squaring her shoulders and cloaking herself with an air of nonchalance that she'd perfected years ago to protect herself against her parents' disappointment, she walked into the large boardroom.

Scanning the people sitting around the large table, her gaze traveled from couple to couple. Jack and Meredith sat at one end with Morgana and Damon at the other end. The scars on the right side of Damon's face were a stark reminder of what they'd gone through in Mexico and how her time to find her brother could be slipping away. Giving into her physical attraction to Reece for more than a quick fuck could mean the difference between finding her brother or not, and she couldn't let that happen. She was afraid she could too easily become addicted to Reece and want to spend all of her time with him instead of looking for Mateo.

Jo and Simon sat on the far side of the table with Rowena and Connor on the side closest to her. Reece sat next to them, and beside him was an empty chair.

Another empty chair sat across the table near Jo, but she didn't want Reece to think she was bothered by his rejection and avoiding him, even if she was. He smiled at her as she sat down, but she didn't acknowledge it as she looked at Jack and Meredith.

Jack cleared his throat and all conversation stopped. "Isabella, thank you for joining us."

"I hope I didn't keep you waiting." She desperately wanted to look at her watch to make sure she wasn't late but didn't want to seem rude. When she'd gotten on the elevator, she'd still been ten minutes early.

"No, you're fine. We had a council meeting so we were here for that first. Now we're ready to talk about what we'd like you to do for us."

Meredith put her hand on her husband's arm as if stalling him. "Jack, I think we should fill Isabella in on the council first so we aren't just springing it on her."

"Right." One corner of Jack's lip turned up in a semi-smile. In the few weeks she'd been around him, he'd rarely smiled, unless he was looking at his wife. Isabella took the partial smile as a good thing. "You probably know there are seven councils in the world…"

"Yes. While growing up, I was told that councils work with magics within law enforcement agencies, like the local police and the FBI, to make sure magics are staying within the laws because magics could get away with a lot if they wanted to. Councils act as a justice system for magics. They are also there to support all magics in the areas they govern, providing support when needed."

Jack gave her a single nod. "Correct. We are—"

"Excuse me," Isabella said interrupting Jack and leaning forward to avoid seeing Reece out of the corner of her eye. Seeing him wasn't the only problem, as trying to ignore how good he smelled, citrusy as usual, was another distraction. "I just realized that yesterday you mentioned a council, but I don't think it really registered with me. And earlier you mentioned a council meeting...I thought North America didn't have a council anymore."

"That was true until about a year ago. You may know that many of the council members on the last council were corrupt." He paused and picked up his wife's hand from where it rested on the table and put it in his lap.

Isabella didn't know what that was about, but she decided it was probably a gesture of support as she'd heard rumors that both their fathers had been on the old council. None of that affected her; she just wanted to get on with the task they wanted to discuss.

"Anyway," Jack said as he continued. "We are now forming a council of fourteen members. The other councils in the world are doing the same thing. I didn't get into it yesterday, but Meredith and I are co-leaders of the council, and everyone else at the table, except for Reece, is a council member."

She glanced at the couples before turning back to Jack. "There's only eight of you. What about the other six?"

Meredith gave Jack a nod and picked up the conversation. "We're hoping we will have all fourteen members soon, but we don't choose who is on the council. Jack gets told who to induct into the council."

"By who?" she asked and then forced herself to keep her air of confidence and not shrink into herself the way she wanted to for being so forward. This group had done so much for her but they were also some of the most powerful magics she'd met in a long time. She didn't need to piss any of them off.

Jack smiled a full-blown smile this time, and Isabella was completely taken aback by how it transformed his entire face. "That's information only for the council leads, and if I told you..." He paused and looked at the group as if waiting for their response.

"He'd have to kill you," everyone said at once, and then there were chuckles and scoffs around the table. She guessed it was an inside council joke.

When the laughter quieted down, he turned to her once more with a serious expression. "When Meredith and I spoke with you yesterday, we said we wanted you to look for a magic object. What we didn't say was that we don't know how dangerous the object could be. We know from the objects we've found before that it will be spelled, but that's about it."

Jack lifted his chin toward the side of the table and Isabella turned in that direction. Everyone was looking at Jo and Simon—they were historians, or something like that, and looked for magic objects.

"Simon and I have been looking for some ancient books, but the process is lengthy, and we don't have that kind of time now," Jo said and turned to her boyfriend, as if wanting him to continue.

"Jo's right. The way we search for the books is methodical and time consuming. We're hoping you'll be able to take a more magic approach."

Isabella turned back to Jack. "What's the rush to find this object?"

Jack frowned, his face becoming even more serious than before. "A magic box was opened and we need the object—a particular piece of metal—so it can be formed into a lock to close the box."

"That's the box that Maverick was talking about in Mexico?"

"It is. The box contained magic that has the potential to corrupt or destroy whatever it comes in contact with, at least from what legends tell us, and the person wielding it wants to control all magics. We..." Jack gestured to the group around the table. "Are trying to figure out how to contain the magic. Once we do, we'll need the object to lock the box."

"Okay, I'll help you, but I won't stop looking for my brother to do it."

"We understand. We'll give you everything we have on the object so far. As well as your brother's last known whereabouts."

She leaned forward. "You know where my brother is?"

"No." Jack shook his head. "But we know where he's been recently, so that might help."

For the first time in months, Isabella felt a small amount of hope bloom inside her. A tiny voice in her head wanted to remind her of all the horrible things she'd heard Mateo had done, but she ignored it. She'd find her brother and then worry about everything else. "Can you give me everything today so I can start right away?"

"Yes," Meredith said, "but we need you to work with someone." She looked at Reece and Isabella felt a sudden sense of dread.

She wasn't willing to think the worst yet and asked. "Who?"

"Me, cupcake," Reece said and shifted in his chair to face her.

"No offense, since he's your cousin," Isabella said, ignoring Reece and looking back at Meredith. "But, but he's just a baker and a… a… himbo! What can he do to help me?"

Her last words were drowned out as laughter broke out in the room.

"She's got you pegged, Reece's Pieces!" Jo said through her laughter.

Isabella looked around the room and saw everyone was smiling but Reece. For a split second, she thought she saw hurt on his face, but then he smiled—a smile so big he could have been a poster child for a toothpaste ad.

"Okay, that's enough," Jack called out and pushed his hands down in the universal sign to calm down before turning to Isabella. "We need you to work with Reece for a couple of reasons."

Although still not wanting to offend them, she needed to speak up. She opened her mouth to protest but shut it when Jack continued. "We appreciate all the help you gave us in Mexico, but we really don't know you. Yes, we've given you a place to stay, but that doesn't mean we haven't been cautious as well."

Isabella interpreted Jack's statement to mean they'd been watching her. She should have known they wouldn't let a stranger into their lives without keeping an eye on her until they knew more about her, but it still stung.

"Also," Jack continued. "We don't know what you're going to come up against, and as charming as Reece is..." Jack paused and gave Reece one of his almost-smiles before becoming serious again and looking back at her. "Reece is extremely knowledgeable about all things magic and has a specialty I haven't seen very often. I'll let him explain it to you when he's ready, but it might come in handy. He's also physically strong, which will likely be helpful as well."

"And if I say no?" She wanted to help this group and she needed the information about Mateo, but she didn't know how she'd work with Reece. Even ignoring her shame from the other night, she couldn't have him get her off course. And she suspected he could because her attraction to him grew every time she was around him. If she gave into that attraction, she could waste time she didn't have.

Jack stood and gave her a pointed stare. "Then we'll send Reece on his own. Meet me and Meredith here at three this afternoon to let us know your answer. If you decide to help us, we'll hand over everything we know, including the information about your brother."

If Isabella was playing chess, she'd say this was check-mate. He'd won. She would get exactly what she wanted, but only if she did it his way. She didn't move as everyone filed out of the room.

"You dislike me so much that you won't work with me. But you were willing to fuck me?" Reece asked quietly.

4

Reece maneuvered the piping bag across the cupcakes, decorating each one with the ease that came with years of practice. When he finished with one color, he changed piping bags. Adding tiny touches, like different shapes and colors, and delicate sprinkles, could mean the difference in whether or not his creations elicited a smile from someone. Having so much taken away from him when he'd been sick had made him appreciate the little things in life, and he wanted to give that to others.

Once he knew what he wanted for a batch, it didn't take much thought. That left him with lots of time to think about Isabella. Maybe too much time. She was getting under his skin, and he would have much preferred to be running his hands across hers instead.

After he'd voiced his question to her in the boardroom, she'd looked at him, startled, as if she had forgotten he was still there. Her face lost all color before she stood, shoving her chair back so quickly it flipped backward. When he reached for the chair to right it, she pushed past him as she stormed out of the room.

That was two hours ago during which time he'd tried to work off his frustration in the make-shift gym he'd set up on the second floor above his bakery. He'd pushed himself on the treadmill until his T-shirt was soaked through and his legs shook when he'd stepped off it. Then he hit the weights, but even complete exhaustion wasn't enough to get the images of her out of his mind. Nor was the cold shower.

As he shifted to the next tray of cupcakes and effortlessly moved the piping bag, competing images of Isabella moved through his mind like snapshots in a digital frame. Only, there were just the three, each so vivid as they repeated over and over again.

The first was his favorite—the joy on her face as she bit into a cupcake and closed her eyes, licking icing off her lips. As much as he wanted to keep that sole image in his mind, the second one pushed the first out of the way. In the second, utter shock filled Isabella's face. Her beautiful eyes had gone wide, and her luscious lips parted as the realization of his rejection sunk in when he'd dressed her.

That image had played in his mind a thousand times in the last two days, and one part of him wished he could go back and replace it with a look of pleasure. But another part of him—the part that had made the vow to himself—knew he'd made the right choice.

It was the third image that cut him the deepest. He'd never forget the look of absolute disgust on her face when she said he was just a baker and a himbo. She hadn't been putting down his profession, he got that, regardless of what it had sounded like.

Her 'just a baker' comment meant he couldn't help her magically, or maybe she thought that with his choice of profession he didn't have any useful skills at all. He loved being a baker and bringing people joy. But it didn't mean he didn't have other skill sets. True, he didn't advertise them.

Yet being called a 'himbo' was a new one. If he was looking on the bright side, he'd be flattered that she found him attractive, even if unintelligent.

"Hello, my favorite baker!" Morgana called out as she pushed through the swinging doors into his kitchen.

His smile was genuine as he looked up from his work; no need to pretend or exaggerate with Morgana. His cousin was one of his favorite people and someone he could be himself around. "Hello, beautiful! What brings you in today? A cupcake or convo?"

She kissed the cheek he presented to her since his hands were busy and he couldn't hug her. They were all huggers, and he wouldn't have it any other way.

"A little of both," she said as she moved to face him across the workbench. She picked up one of the cupcakes he'd just piped with fall leaves. She was already peeling the paper off when she stopped with a sheepish look on her face. "Oh… can I?"

He laughed at her. "A little late to ask, but yes." Morgana's spontaneous and happy personality had come back more and more in the weeks since the spell on her had been broken. As she'd learned who she was, she was becoming an adult version of the seven-year-old she had been when she'd been taken. He expected Damon loving her had a lot to do with it and it was good to see.

It made him pause and wonder if Isabella was prickly because of what she'd been through. Was it her real personality or an armor she'd adopted because life had forced her to protect her emotions? Maybe he needed to approach things with her a bit differently.

"Deep thoughts?" Morgana asked. He looked up to see her shove the last of the cupcake into her mouth and chew like she was in food heaven. "Yum. You make the best cupcakes ever."

"Thanks." Putting down the piping bag, he braced his hands on the workbench and gave her his full attention. "Now that you've had a cupcake, tell me what's happening with you."

"Actually, I wanted to talk about you."

He wasn't sure he wanted to, but he knew her concern came from a good place. "About?"

"No playing dumb with me, Reece. I know you're way smarter than you let most people see. You know exactly what I'm talking about."

And he did. Everyone had laughed at the 'himbo' comment, but he and Morgana had had a lot of long talks over the last year and a half, minus the time he was in a coma. She knew better than most that he didn't want to be seen as a player. He'd never been one, but he was a flirt, and with that came assumptions about what type of person he was. "You're talking about Isabella's 'himbo' comment."

She picked up a cloth and wiped icing off her fingers. "Ah, yeah, that one. Why didn't you say anything?"

"Why bother?"

"Oh, come on, Reece. That's a cop-out. I know you like her. And when she volunteered to help the chef, you suddenly decided you needed to tag along to learn that recipe?" Morgana gave an inelegant snort. "Yeah, right. But she's got you pegged wrong. You're not a himbo."

"I know." And he wasn't just saying it. He loved to flirt and make people happy, but he was smart too. Besides having a college degree in business, he knew more about magic than most other magics. It gave him pride when Jack came to him with questions, and Jack was the most powerful magic Reece knew.

"Are you going to say something when you work with her?"

Morgana could be like a dog with a bone and didn't easily

drop things. Too bad he was the bone in this scenario. "I'll play it by ear. Having to tell someone how smart you are kind of defeats the purpose. But before I can even go there, she has to agree to work with me."

"She will," Morgana said, and then bit her bottom lip. It was a gesture he'd noticed she adopted when contemplating things. She could contemplate all she wanted this time, but it wouldn't do any good. The decision was up to Isabella.

Looking down at the cupcakes on the workbench, he made some quick calculations in his head before boxing some up. "Want to give me a hand?"

"Sure." She grabbed some flat boxes that needed assembling and they worked together seamlessly.

"Tell me about your driving lessons. Is Damon being patient with you?"

She laughed as she picked up another box. "Well, that's a story. After day two, he hired a driving instructor for me. So... he decided..."

Reece listened and laughed as Morgana told her story. For a short while, images of Isabella weren't in the forefront of his mind. But he'd see her again soon and then he'd have more images for his memory bank—but he hoped they were all good ones this time.

THE BOARDROOM WAS empty when Isabella showed up before three. She chose a seat on the far side of the table with a clear view of the door. Jack hadn't told Reece to be here, but she knew he would be. He wouldn't miss an opportunity to flirt with her.

In another lifetime, before her brother went missing, she would have loved to have attention from someone like Reece.

Someone who was kind and had a career, was self-confident and went after what he wanted, especially if it was her. Flirtation and attention were things she'd been missing in her life, even back then. She would have lapped it up like a cat with cream, but that was then.

Now she needed to be serious and focused. If Mateo had done the things he'd been accused of, she needed to find him soon. Convince him that she could help him before he had a chance to do any more damage. With everything coming to a head, her time was running out to save him. And she *would* save him.

Saving Mateo wouldn't change her parents' thoughts about her, but it would make up for some of the mistakes she'd made in her life. Her brother was her last chance at having her family back, or at least some of it, and she wouldn't fail him. She loved her brother and had sacrificed years of her life looking for him, but she'd been selfish too. Turning around Mateo's life path would absolve her of some of the guilt for feeling responsible for his current outcome, that she'd carried for so long.

She glanced at the time on her fitness tracker and saw that it still wasn't three. Fiddling with the strap, she watched the door. Her nerves were fired up, but they shouldn't be. All day, she'd hidden in her apartment, weighing the pros and cons of Jack's offer, and she'd come to a decision.

She looked up as a shadow fell across the table.

"Hello, Isabella. How are you this afternoon?" Reece glanced around the empty room before he pulled out a chair directly across from her and sat.

"I'm fine, thank you." She waited for some teasing. Instead, Reece looked down at his phone, as if in the last three seconds he'd forgotten she existed. It was then she realized that he'd called her by her given name. An old feeling, one she hadn't felt in a long time, swamped her—disappointment. For so long, she'd cut herself off from hope, mindlessly pursuing her goals without thinking about them too deeply. If you didn't hope, you could never be disappointed. Her parents had taught her that lesson well. They'd also shown her that if she hadn't been having fun and only been concerned about herself, Mateo might never have strayed.

Nicknames were juvenile, and cupcake was a ridiculous name for a grown woman. For weeks she'd convinced herself Reece was too much of a jokester, a sign of immaturity. Yet, when Reece didn't smile at her and call her by the silly name, she realized that deep down she'd grown used to it. It made her feel like she mattered to someone.

"Thanks for coming," Jack said as he walked into the room holding Meredith's hand.

Meredith gave Reece's shoulder a squeeze as she walked by and took a seat beside her husband. "Hi."

Isabella directed her gaze at the couple and took the plunge. "I've decided to accept your offer. I'll work with Reece to find the magic object you're looking for in exchange for the information about my brother."

Jack gave a single nod. "Good. Reece will keep us updated, but you can come directly to us if you have any concerns. As I said this morning, we'll be working on trying to contain the evil magic." His lips ticked up and he paused. "Well, we don't know exactly was it is. Evil magic is a bit of a silly name, but it works. Right now it is inside a former council member, Forest Sharpe. You probably know him as Maverick since you were unfortunate enough to meet him in Mexico."

Isabella nodded. She'd never forget the man.

"No one has seen him since he consumed that magic just over three weeks ago." Jack nodded toward the table and file folders appeared. One landed in front of her and the other in front of Reece. "That's what we have right now." He stood and reached for Meredith's hands. "We'll leave you to it."

They flashed away from the head of the table without another word.

She looked over at Reece, expecting him to say something, but he was already flipping through the file. After a few moments, he looked up. "Aren't you going to read it?"

"Ah, yes, of course." She opened the file but couldn't focus on any of the words. Reece was constantly throwing her off balance. She'd finally come to anticipate his joking and flirtatious advances and now he'd become as serious as a scholar.

Taking in a deep breath, she forced herself to read the first page. It was a detailed accounting of everything they knew about the magic object. No one had ever reported seeing it, but a few weeks ago a seer mentioned it. According to the seer, it was a piece of metal, magically enhanced, that could be forged into a lock to close the magic box.

She looked through the notes and blinked when she got to the information about the seer. The seer, Helen, had died in the late 1990s.

During the family dinners and while hanging around The Magic Plate, Isabella had heard that Rowena and Connor could talk to ghosts. They must have been the ones to talk to Helen.

Isabella went back to the file and read through the next several pages. It listed the places that Maverick and his now dead cohorts had been seen during the last two years. There were also comments about their activities during that time.

When she scanned the next page, she felt her world start to close in on her. Her vision blurred and she took in a long slow, breath before she could focus on the words in front of her.

The page detailed all the dealings and crimes that Mateo —Eddie to them—had been involved with. Her little brother was a criminal, and a vicious one. There were mentions of him hurting numerous people as well as several murder attempts.

She closed the file and squeezed her eyes shut.

"You alright?"

Flinging her eyes open, she looked across at Reece. His eyebrows were drawn down in concern. "Yes, just processing the information."

He opened his mouth as if to say something and then shut it again. She knew he didn't believe her, but he let it drop and continued. "Do you need more time to read or are you ready to brainstorm?"

She raised her brows. "Brainstorm? You mean together?"

He conjured a pen and a piece of paper. "Yes, that's how brainstorming works. We throw ideas back and forth to figure out where we want to start."

Closing the folder, she picked it up and stood. "I know what 'brainstorming' means!" She pushed her chair into the table. "I'm going to check some things out. You do that too, and then we can touch base. Tomorrow, maybe." Too afraid to look him in the eyes and possibly see more rejection, she flashed to her apartment.

Reece walked up to the front of the room with the pretense of studying the information on one of the whiteboards. Jack had suggested they whiteboard what they knew. Now, two large whiteboards on wheels stood side-by-side along the longer wall of the rectangular-shaped room. They'd set up in a small boardroom on the third floor of the same building as his bakery, leaving the larger board-room available for the council.

There was one board for the magic object and one for Mateo, giving them a visual of any overlapping information. Notes, pictures, and comments littered the white surfaces, but they were no closer to finding the metal object or Mateo than when they'd started.

Keeping his back to Isabella, he put his hand on his hips and let his gaze roam over the various notes and sticky notes they'd plastered on the board over the last two days.

He needed an immediate solution to a problem, but it wasn't the location of the object or their brothers' whereabouts. It was what to do with the infuriating brunette sitting behind him. The images blurred in front of him as he let his gaze wander over them, hoping that from the back he looked to be deep in concentration.

Isabella had gotten under his skin somehow. At first it might have been lust because she was a beautiful woman and watching her eat his cupcake had been pure torture. But little by little, even with her armor in place, he'd come to see a different side of her. Not only was she kind and thoughtful by helping others, she also had a sense of loyalty that was truly rare. Even if her little shit of a brother didn't deserve the sacrifices she'd made for him.

The 'himbo' comment the other day meant he'd have to adopt a new approach with her. His new strategy had been to show her he was more than just a muscular body. Being physically strong may have been one of the keys to keeping his vow to himself, but it didn't completely define him.

The serious approach hadn't worked at first since she'd refused to brainstorm with him. But he'd given Isabella a few hours to calm down and then had Morgana deliver a note to her. Requesting her presence in the boardroom had been more formal than the situation required, but he knew she wouldn't be able to refuse if it meant she would have to tell Morgana no. And he took a chance that Isabella would have abhorred other people finding out she'd refused his request when she'd promised to help.

He'd become the epitome of business-like, even biting his tongue to avoid calling her cupcake. For two days he had talked about nothing but their tasks to prove to her that he was more than just a player. But the play was backfiring because she'd clammed up even more and was shutting him out. The only reason he was standing at the boards now was to come up with a new plan.

Behind him, Isabella studied the notes they'd compiled

and then occasionally she would quietly add items to the whiteboards without saying much. Only when she wanted to compare notes would she ask him a question. Brainstorming and collaboration were nonexistent.

This morning, when he'd been working in his bakery's kitchen alone, Jack had flashed in for an update. Reece had little to report, just that they were still putting the information together. When Jack had asked if they'd had any luck using Isabella's specialty of finding things, he'd put Jack off, saying they hadn't yet but would soon.

That brought him full circle to his current strategy. The serious and studious approach wasn't working, so it was time to change things up.

He studied the two boards for a moment, looking for just the right connection, and looked over his shoulder, projecting a casual air. "Cupcake?"

Isabella's head shot up. "What?"

Her instant response to the nickname made him want to fist pump the air, but he kept a neutral expression on his face. "Come here, please."

When she was standing beside him, whiffs of vanilla and apricot floated up to him. Before Jack had arrived to talk to him that morning, Reece had been experimenting with his idea for an Isabella-inspired cupcake. It still needed more work, just like his strategy with the woman herself, but it had potential.

While he'd been playing with ingredients, he'd realized that Isabella had been playing him. He suspected that she wasn't really committed to finding the object, only her brother. She was using him again, but instead of his body, she wanted information. And once again, he'd been ready to give her what she wanted with no benefit for himself, but no more.

It was time to call on everything he'd learned about

strategies and tactics in his business classes. Showing his serious side hadn't worked, which led him to come up with his new strategy—soften her up. If he could break through the hardened shell she'd erected around herself and get her to trust him, she might see that by fully collaborating, they'd find both the object and her brother, and hopefully his brother and cousin as well. The stakes involved for all of them were high, and she wasn't seeing them all yet.

He placed his hand at the small of her back to pull her a bit closer as he angled his body toward the second board. Pointing to some sticky notes, he pressed more firmly into her lower back on the pretense of guiding her to what he wanted her to look at. She tensed for a minute and then leaned into his side.

He did another mental fist pump before explaining what he found. "I think we need to go to the apartment where Morgana was held."

Isabella leaned in a bit more as she reached to take a sticky note off the board. "This one says Copeland. I had the unfortunate pleasure of meeting Maverick and Snake in Mexico, but I didn't meet Copeland. He was the guy working with Snake and Maverick who hurt Meredith, right? Morgana was found in Copeland's apartment?"

Reece's hand warmed as Isabella's heat seeped into him. He wanted to pull her flush against him but kept with the plan to soften her up. Though that didn't mean he couldn't deploy different tactics when executing his strategy.

Using his free hand, he reached for a sticky note on the opposite board. The movement angled him toward her and brought their faces within inches of each other. Her eyes widened and she licked her lips. Mimicking her, he licked his lips as well before snatching the note off the board like nothing had happened.

"I don't know who owned it before Jack bought it, but

yes, Copeland was there." He held the note up for her to see. "This is the address of the apartment where Snake held Simon and Jo. We know for sure that your brother was there."

Her eyes went wide for only a moment before her armor fell back into place. Rubbing his hand in a slow, subtle movement on her back, he gave her a moment to process the information. Reece had no idea how he'd feel if he knew where his brother and cousin might be. He knew they'd been in the apartment where Jo and Simon had been kept, but they'd be long gone from there now.

After a minute, he dropped his hand and stepped back. "I think we should check both of them out. It isn't much but it was the last location, besides the building in Mexico that blew up, that we have for Maverick and your brother."

Isabella moved back against his side and pointed at the note. "Rocky and the healer were at that building too, right?"

"Yes."

"Then let's check that one out first. Maybe I'll be able to feel something."

Reece leaned toward her to put the note back on the board on the other side of her and grazed his lips across her temple as he moved. He felt her tense at his touch, but once again, he acted like nothing happened. "Sure. Do you know where it is?"

She seemed almost frozen in place for a moment as she brought her hand up to her temple. Then her eyes widened, and she dropped her hands. "Uh, what?"

"The apartment. Do you have the address?"

"Yes, I've got it."

"Great. I've been there before so I know there's a small alley between the building and the next one that will hide us. Flash to the south side."

"Now?"

He smiled. "Sure, why not?" She nodded, but before she could flash, he laid his hand on her arm, and she looked up at him. Something he was starting to crave. "It's cold out, so it might look strange with you walking into the building in just a T-shirt. Maybe you should conjure a sweater or something."

"Right." She conjured a hoodie similar to the one he'd stripped off her the other night. "Okay, see you there." She flashed away, and he conjured a sweatshirt as well before he followed her with a smile on his face.

Isabella arrived in the alley only seconds before Reece, not even giving her time to think about what he'd done in the boardroom. She was sure the brush of his lips on her forehead was accidental. It couldn't have been on purpose because he'd stopped flirting with her since that night in her apartment. Maybe he'd finally realized she wasn't worth it. Another pang of disappointment shot through her, even though she was getting what she wanted. She'd have to dissect that feeling later, way later.

While walking together to the front of the building, she turned to him. "How are we going to get in?"

He put his hand at the small of her back to guide her while he used the other to open the main door. "We're just going to walk in. Jack bought the apartment, so there shouldn't be an issue. He also bought the one where Morgana was held."

"Why?"

"I'm not sure what he plans to do with them, but I think he wanted to preserve evidence and energy signatures. And right now, that works well for us."

He didn't drop his hand as he turned to speak with the door attendant and gave his name.

"Yes, Mr. Williams, I see you on my list. You can go right up," the attendant said.

"Thank you." Reece gave the woman one of his killer smiles and a feeling far too close to jealousy joined Isabella's disappointment. Her brain was becoming a little too crowded with emotions for her liking.

Pushing the feelings aside, Isabella let him guide her into the elevator. He pressed the button for the penthouse floor and they both looked up, watching the digital numbers as they ascended.

She looked away from the numbers and faced him. "Did Jack put your name on the visitor list?"

A sly grin spread across his face. "No, I learned that handy little trick from Damon. The attendant was non-magic so I added my name to the list when I walked up. It took me a while to perfect that little maneuver, but I figured it might come in handy someday."

He flashed his pearly whites at her, and she thought his smile faltered for a moment, but it was so fast she wasn't really sure. He was always smiling and joking— except for in the boardroom earlier. It was the main reason she knew they'd never be any good together, no matter how much she might like to use his body for a while.

There wasn't any room in her life for fooling around—a lesson she'd had to learn the hard way. In the first year she'd been searching for Mateo, she met a guy and let him persuade her to hang out for a few days. A few days turned into two weeks before he'd had to go back to his real life. At least, that's what he'd told her. When she picked up Mateo's trail again, she discovered she'd missed him by only four days. That was the closest she'd ever been to finding him, and she'd thrown it all away for a little fun.

Now, if she wasn't earning a living while traveling all around the continent, then she was searching for Mateo. A tiny part of her brain nudged her, saying that Reece was helping her look for her brother. Luckily, she was getting good at shutting down that little voice.

When the elevator reached the penthouse, Reece again placed his hand at her lower back to guide her. She wasn't sure how to take the gesture. On one hand, she didn't need someone to guide her—she was a grown-ass woman and had been finding her own way for years. On the other hand, that tiny part of her brain that wouldn't shut up, said it liked the feel of Reece's large, warm hand and that it was nice to have some help.

"This is it," Reece said, and the apartment door swung open.

She turned toward him and his hand dropped from her back, taking away his warmth. "How did you do that? I didn't see you even direct your magic… ah… I mean, not everyone has to, but I thought you'd only had use of your magic for less than two years."

Damn. Now she was back to insulting him again. But she'd heard all about the spell that had almost killed him and how weak he'd been after the coma. It would have been the first time he'd been fully unbound since he'd been a child and could use his magic. The Reece she saw now was so big and confident in his abilities that she couldn't imagine him any other way, but his magic still shouldn't have been so powerful.

"I can do lots of things." He winked at her and guided her into the apartment. "Now, what do you need to do your thing?"

When she faced him again, he dropped his hand and she took a step back. "My *thing*, as you call it, is more of a sense than something I do."

She looked around the massive, empty apartment. What she could see was far larger than the entire main floor of her parents' home. She walked over to the floor-to-ceiling windows and closed her eyes to the late afternoon sun.

Pulling on her magic, she ran images of her brother through her mind. She'd been told Mateo had been in the apartment, but it still surprised her when she sensed his presence. For years her search for him had been fruitless. She'd run into endless dead ends and had become used to the never-ending disappointment of being too late.

Holding onto a memory of Mateo, she opened her eyes and slowly walked down the long hallway. All the doors were closed, so she stopped at the first one, turned the doorknob, and stepped into the room.

Her hands flew to her chest and she squeezed her eyes shut, taken aback by the sensations bombarding her from all corners. Mateo's signature, what she sensed of him, was in layers, like he'd been in this room a lot. It was also faint, which meant it had been a while, maybe months, since he'd been there.

Placing her hand on the wall, she closed her eyes and soaked in the sensations in the room. Using the wall as a guide, she slowly walked around the room, pulling in its energy. Hope died within her when she learned no more than Mateo had been there.

"You okay?"

Isabella opened her eyes and faced Reece, who was standing in the doorway. "Yes. Mateo was here. Usually, I can get a sense of where a person went next, but I'm getting nothing, as if this part of his signature had been erased."

Reece held out his hand. "Let's check out the rest of the place."

She laid her hand on his and he closed his fingers around hers, then brought it up to his lips. He kissed her hand softly before leading her out of the room into an open-concept area.

"I think this was the formal dining room. Jo and Simon were..." Reece's voice trailed off as he turned around in the space. When he finally faced her, his eyes held sadness. "They were hurt here, forced to do Snake's bidding."

Isabella nodded and crouched down, laying her palm on the floor. Besides the walls, there wasn't anything else for her to touch. She squeezed her eyes shut as an emotion hit her—despair. Her magic usually connected her only to objects and people. She'd felt emotions before, but it was so rare that she remembered each of the eight times it had happened. Each time, a death had occurred.

Mateo had been here when someone had died, but she had no way of knowing what his involvement had been. There had been five times over the years when she'd felt his presence alongside a death. The first two times she'd convinced herself they'd been coincidences. Then at the last three she'd told herself that he'd been held against his will and hadn't been able to prevent the deaths. That Mateo was just waiting for her to find him. Now doubts were creeping in.

"Cupcake?"

Isabella opened her eyes to see Reece crouched down in front of her. "I don't think there's anything more here." He stood and held out his hand for her, pulling her up and into his embrace. The hug was so quick she didn't have time to protest before he let her go and put his hand on her lower back.

Neither of them spoke as they left the apartment and made their way to the back alley. Reece made a point of saying goodbye to the attendant to show they'd left. The woman waved, telling Reece to come back soon. Isabella didn't have any emotional energy left to even be jealous.

As they flashed back to their apartments, Isabella promised herself that nothing would stand in her way of finding her brother. Not even herself. Even if that meant separating herself from her growing attraction to a sexy, caring, muscle-bound man.

6

*R*eece was getting frustrated with Isabella's lack of cooperation. He'd tried being serious, and when that hadn't worked, he'd tried softening her up. It had seemed to be working because she'd leaned into him, and he'd thought they'd made a connection at Snake's old apartment.

Once more, he'd been wrong, and she'd used him. Isabella flopped between treating him like he wasn't serious enough or using him for her own gains. It was time for that to end. She was either going to help or he'd find the object and his brother and cousin on his own. He needed to take matters into his own hands—no more being weak and pliable.

You around? He telepathically threw the message to Jack, knowing if Jack was in any of the family buildings, he'd get it. Playing into Jack's and Meredith's enhanced abilities was even easier than texting.

In the restaurant, Jack responded immediately.

On my way, Reece answered Jack before popping his head into the front section of the bakery to get the attention of

51

one of his staff members. "I'm heading to the restaurant. You okay to lock up?"

"Sure. It's almost closing time anyway. See you tomorrow?"

"Probably not, but I'll let you know." Whether or not Isabella decided to cooperate, Reece couldn't waste any more time. They needed to find the object.

"Sounds good, boss."

Reece said goodbye and left through the bakery's back door. When he walked into The Magic Plate's kitchen, the staff was busy preparing for the dinner rush. He gave them a wave but didn't have the energy for any jokes and headed straight through to the front of the restaurant. Jack was sitting at the family's usual table in the corner with Meredith, Jo, and Simon.

"What's up?" Jack asked as Reece pulled up a chair at the end of the table.

"Isabella." That one word carried enough weight that Jack raised his eyebrows in question.

"Has she figured out you're not a himbo yet?" Jo teased.

Reece let out a huge sigh but didn't smile at his sister. "Probably not. But that's not the problem." He turned to Jack. "I think she's playing us."

"You think she took the information only to find her brother and isn't serious about helping us?"

Reece wasn't surprised that Jack figured it out; besides being a powerful magic, he had good instincts because he was an FBI agent. "Yes. I've tried to work with her, but she hasn't been forthcoming. And I haven't seen her since we went to Snake's old apartment two days ago."

"Did she find anything there?" Simon asked, massaging the finger stub on his right hand. Reece had seen him do it before and knew it wasn't pain that was bothering Simon—it was memories. The apartment didn't hold good ones for him or Jo.

"I don't think so. I know she could feel that her brother had been there, but I don't think she found anything else. I'm still not sure how her magic works, although she might not know either." Reece looked at Jack for confirmation.

"Could be true. Most don't know how their magic specialties work, but she should be able to tell you what she can and can't find. I take it she hasn't even said that much?"

"No, she hasn't. I think I'm going to have to work without her," he said, once more looking to Jack for confirmation, even though he hadn't asked a question.

"Could you hold on a bit longer? We were just talking about what we'd learned and were going to fill you in once we finished here, but now is as good a time as any."

Meredith looked at Jack and then picked up the conversation. "Connor called just before you contacted Jack to say that Linda, a seer we know, reached out to him. Linda believes that something is going to happen tonight. Something involving the evil magic Maverick consumed."

"That's it? Just 'something'? No other details?" Reece looked between everyone at the table.

"That's it," Meredith said.

"Either she doesn't know any more, or she can't tell us, which is sometimes the case," Jack said. "We instructed the other council members and all the FBI agents with the magic task force to be on alert."

"What are you guys going to do?" Reece asked.

"Meredith and I are going to our apartment and the other council members are prepared to flash there if needed. The same with Ben, Frank, and some of their agents." Jack let out a long breath. "There isn't much more we can do. We're operating blind."

Reece stood and put the chair back where he'd gotten it

from. "Keep me in the loop. I'm going to go lift some weights."

"Will do. I'll reach out to you telepathically if we have any news."

Nodding his goodbye, Reece headed to the back of the restaurant to the stairway that led to the walkway between the buildings. Instead of taking the stairs, he looked around to make sure he was alone and flashed to his gym.

After some stretching, he loaded the bench press bar and laid down. Frustration with Isabella had a definite advantage —he was in the gym constantly to work it off.

An hour and a half later, he was drenched, his muscles ached, and he still didn't know what to do about Isabella. His plan to soften her up wasn't a bad one, because she'd physically responded to him. But if he didn't see her, he couldn't keep executing it.

And therein lay the problem. Yesterday morning he'd knocked on her apartment door before seven a.m. and she had her sweater on and looked all ready to head out.

"Can I talk to you?" he asked when she'd answered the door.

"Uh, not now. I'm heading out."

"At seven in the morning?"

"I'm following up on something."

"I'll go with you. I just—" He cut off his words when she'd said goodbye and flashed away.

This morning he'd knocked on her apartment door at six and she wasn't there.

He put the weight on the rack and grabbed a towel from the stack he'd conjured and wiped the sweat dripping down his neck.

The stack of towels made him smile. Conjuring towels was another one of those little things he appreciated and would never take for granted. When almost everything you loved, including your freedom, was snatched away, it put life into perspective.

Coming out of the coma and learning to use his magic had been a long slog. There had been days when working on becoming physically stronger and practicing magic consumed all his waking hours. Pushing through the weakness and pain from months of being left to atrophy was the hardest thing he'd ever done.

Disappearing the towel, he threw off his thoughts of weakness and decided he'd run on the treadmill for a while. He conjured a water bottle and smiled as he put it in the treadmill's cup holder and hopped on, then punched in his preferred settings.

The rhythm of his feet hitting the belt mixed with the sounds of his breathing were the only noises in the room. He realized he hadn't even turned on the sound system he'd built that included speakers in all corners. He'd been too distracted by thoughts of Isabella to even notice the absence of music until then.

Picturing the sound system in his mind, he turned it on. Moments later, the raucous crooning of Social Distortion's lead singer was bouncing off the walls. Reece loosened his shoulders, looked out at the skyline through the large wall of windows, and let the music surround him as he forced his mind to go blank.

An hour later, he slowed down the machine and walked to cool off, his legs feeling rubbery, but Reece was more relaxed than when he'd entered the gym. Shutting the machine off, he slugged back the rest of his water and disappeared the water bottle.

After he shut off the treadmill, he jumped off, turned around, and felt his breath hitch. Isabella was doing shoulder presses with free weights, her back turned to him. He hadn't put up any mirrors in the gym yet so she couldn't see him, though he had unfettered access to watch her. She looked fit and toned, the muscles in her shoulders beautiful as they contracted with her movements.

When she set the weights down, she turned and her eyes jerked up to meet his. The music was still too loud for conversation so he debated for about zero point two seconds about whether he should leave it on. He could just wave goodbye and leave or turn the music off and talk to her.

In the end, he couldn't pass up an opportunity to talk to her. She'd occupied his thoughts so often, he wanted to be close to her. He shut the music off abruptly in the middle of a song. The silence was deafening after the loud music. "Hello, cupcake. How was your workout?"

7

Isabella stared out at the skyline from her balcony and wondered where she'd gone wrong. She'd honed her magic ability over the years, allowing her to find almost anything and anyone. Yet her brother continued to elude her.

The last two days had been a complete waste of time as she'd wandered around the places the reports said Mateo had been. She'd picked up traces of him in each place but no clues as to where he could be now.

Isabella wished she knew how strong Mateo's power was. Not because she could do anything with the information, but maybe it would give her clues as to where to look more in depth. She'd never considered the strength of his power before, at least not until she'd been at the apartment with Reece. Someone had erased traces of Mateo's signature, preventing her from following it. Maybe Mateo's magic was strong enough to do that.

He hadn't come into his full power when he went missing because he'd still been too young. Yet she knew his power was similar to hers because she'd seen glimpses of what he could do.

For the first time that day, she smiled as she remembered how proud Mateo had been as he'd shown her how he found an old action figure. He'd buried it in the backyard when he'd been smaller and had used his magic to find it.

If Mateo's power was much stronger than hers, then he could be doing something to block her from finding him. Or erase it, like at the apartment. That thought sent a shiver racing down her back. It meant that everything she'd done for years had been for naught.

Then that small voice of hope inside her spoke up. If he had been blocking her, maybe it wasn't what he truly wanted. He could have been brainwashed by Snake and Maverick and led to think something that wasn't true. It didn't matter, she decided; she was going to find her brother and reason with him.

She just didn't know how to find him. Nothing she'd done had worked, and if he was working with Maverick, she had to hurry before Mateo was harmed, or worse—killed.

Looking at the skyline one last time and sending up a prayer for her brother's safety, she went into her apartment. Since there wasn't much else she could do tonight, she decided to work out.

It was one of the things she missed most now that she was always on the road. Sometimes she'd luck out and find an excellent gym close to her hotel, but most times she had to make do. When she'd arrived in Blue Mountain and Meredith was showing her around the buildings, she'd learned of the temporary gym. Meredith had explained that she had grand visions for the three buildings, including adding more businesses. Her hope was to make it a small community with almost everything someone would need once they'd left work. A gym was in the plans, but further down on the list of priorities.

On the buildings' tour, Meredith had brought her up here to show her the setup. She'd explained that it was haphazard because they weren't ready to open a professional gym yet, so when someone in the family wanted a piece of equipment, they either bought it or conjured it. There weren't any mirrors in the room yet and the placement of some of the equipment was awkward. But Isabella had worked out in far less equipped places and was just thankful to have access to the gym.

Isabella changed into workout clothes and flashed to the hallway outside the gym. The loud music reverberated through the still space, and she debated whether or not to leave.

In one of Reece's early attempts to get to know her, he'd said he liked the early punk bands of the era. So unless someone else liked the Sex Pistols, Reece was inside. Her urge to work out warred with her thought that she'd have to explain to Reece what she'd been doing for the last two days.

When the need to work out won, she stepped inside the large space and looked around. Reece was on the treadmill facing the windows and didn't notice her. Skirting around the edge of the room to avoid being spotted, Isabella made her way to the machines and free weights at the back of the room.

Looking around at the weights, she decided to do a simple full body workout with free weights. Picking up the first weight, she exhaled and let her mind get into the zone.

She switched out weights as she worked through different exercises, doing four sets of each and working up a sweat. After returning the weights from her last set, she turned and froze. Her eyes met Reece's but the music was too loud to talk. They both stood staring at each other as if waiting for the other to make the first move.

The wait wasn't long as a Clash song cut off in the middle and Reece grinned at her. "Hello, cupcake. How was your workout?"

Reece's muscles looked bulked up and they glistened with sweat in the bright florescent lights. She wanted nothing more than to walk up to him and see if his lips tasted as salty as the rest of him probably did.

He was back to being charming. The sound of his nickname for her in his deep voice made her ovaries want to burst, but she shut that feeling down. If she gave into his charm, he could distract her and she'd miss a clue to finding her brother, just like she'd done before. "I'm fine, thank you. How was your workout?"

"It was great. Just working out some frustrations." He walked toward her until he was close enough that she could smell a mix of sweat and something citrusy. It was a heady combination of man and lust.

He lifted her chin so she was looking directly into his eyes. If any other man had done that, she would have ripped her chin out of his grasp and given him a piece of her feminist mind. But with Reece, it was different. He wasn't trying to control her, just see right into her soul. Maybe that was worse.

"Did you have a good day, cupcake?" His voice was soft and didn't hold any recriminations when they both knew she hadn't looked for the magic object like she'd promised.

She couldn't look away from his gaze. "I didn't find anything." Her words were raspy, even to her own ears, and she swallowed against the sudden dryness in her throat.

"I want to kiss you, cupcake."

She wanted that too but didn't know if they should. After the night when Reece had rejected her, he'd never brought it up again. He could have used the situation to embarrass her and didn't. Now, he was waiting for her permission.

Her body didn't seem to care what was best for her. It moved as if it had a mind of its own and lifted her onto her tiptoes and tipped her chin higher.

She wet her lips just as his mouth descended to hers and he wrapped one hand around the back of her neck, pulling her closer. Their bodies lightly touched as they kissed. Opening her mouth, she invited him in, and she practically melted as he kissed her in the most sensual way she'd ever known. The taste of salt on their lips and the mix of their scents heightened every nerve ending in her body.

This was more than just foreplay to sex, and she wanted it. She emptied her mind of all thoughts but the feel of Reece making love to her mouth.

When he pulled back and looked down at her, she wanted everything he was offering. For the first time in years, she wanted something for herself. She opened her mouth to tell him as a powerful energy entered her brain and she dropped to her knees.

Just before her eyes forced themselves closed, she saw Reece drop to his knees as well.

Isabella slammed her hands on the sides of her head out of instinct, as if that would release the pressure.

Hello, my magic children. I am Maverick, chosen by the ancient to rule all magics. Hear my voice to the depths of your soul and know that together we will unveil the true power within. It is a frail illusion that the magic council will protect you and bring order to our kind; they will only keep you in the shadows. The time has come to unite, which can only be done under my command. Defy me and you will be cast into obscurity. Unite with me and you will see true power. The choice is yours: rise and join me or your magic will waste away and you will die.

8

Reece felt the energy leave as quickly as it had arrived. He heard Isabella suck in a huge breath and he stood, pulling her up. He magically scanned her to make sure she wasn't hurt. "You heard Maverick?"

Her eyes were wide, and when she nodded, he wrapped her in his arms, needing to feel her against him.

"I've never heard of someone being able to telecommunicate from such a distance before," she whispered against his chest and then shivered.

The movement pushed him into action as he realized he was cold too. After their shock of hearing Maverick in their heads, he wasn't surprised they were cold. Reluctantly, he let her go and conjured a hoodie like the one she normally wore. "Raise your arms," he said softly. She did as he asked and he slipped the warm garment onto her. Then he conjured another and did the same for himself.

What happened? He threw the thought to Jack, knowing he'd get it if he was still in the buildings.

Isabella opened her mouth to speak, and he held up a finger.

Meet at our apartment. "Sorry, I was just reaching out to Jack. I don't know what's up, but he said to meet at his and Meredith's apartment." Isabella nodded again but didn't say anything. Instead of asking her to flash, because he needed a couple of minutes to steady himself, he took her hand and gently guided her out of the room. They didn't speak as they walked over two buildings to the one that housed their apartments.

Meredith and Jack's apartment was on the floor below his, and he heard a quiet hush of voices as soon as they approached the door. He didn't bother to knock and walked in. Isabella dropped his hand as soon as they were inside, and as much as he wanted to continue to touch her, he had a bigger priority.

"Reece's Pieces, are you okay?" Jo asked as she flung herself at him. He hugged her and couldn't help himself; he had to do the same for his sister as he had Isabella, and magically scanned her. Simon and Jo had probably already checked each other out, but he had to make sure for himself. He would always be her protective big brother.

"We're good, Pinky Pie," he said and kissed the top of Jo's head before letting her go and looking at the others. "I'm guessing you all heard Maverick?"

Everyone chimed in that they had and that no one was hurt.

"Let's move into the living room. Conjure a chair if you need one; I've called in more than just the council."

As if scripted, the rest of Connor's family arrived—his uncles, aunt, dad, and Sam. Then Damon's mother, Fiona, and his sister Kate arrived, followed by two of Ben's FBI agents who Reece had become friends with, Javier and Lisa. Isaac, the tattoo artist who had broken the spell on Morgana, came in next. Isaac conjured a chair next to Kate and she visibly prickled. At any other time, he would have loved to razz her for her reaction.

Reece squished in beside Isabella on one of the couches and she moved over to make room for him. Another thing he'd celebrate if the situation was different.

"Everyone is here now," Jack said, and the room went quiet. "Let's make sure we're all on the same page." Jack turned to Simon. "You ready?"

"Yes." Simon stood and walked over to the sliding glass doors leading to the balcony. He waved his hand and solid white paper covered the glass, blocking out the view of the outside. Then Simon faced the paper and said something too quiet for Reece to hear. A bubble appeared, and inside it floated the words Maverick had spewed into their minds.

Simon turned around and stood to one side of the paper. "The words will stay floating in the air, but can everyone see them clearly?" When consents echoed around the room, Simon gestured to Jack before going back to sit with Jo.

Jack stood where Simon had and looked at the group. "Did anyone hear anything different than this?"

Reece quickly scanned the words and pulled up the memory from the gym, seeing the words in his mind, and confirmed they were the same. "Exactly the same," he said, and others confirmed as well.

"I called Mary—the magic Emissary, for those of you who might not know," he said, looking at Sam and Isabella and giving them a nod. "The seven councils each have two co-leaders, and one person is elected from the fourteen to be the Emissary, or chairperson of the leaders. That's Mary right now. She said she hadn't heard Maverick but would reach out to the other leaders to see if they'd heard anything. So, right now it seems to be concentrated in North America. Frank, what did you confirm?"

Connor's dad, the head of the Colorado division of the

FBI, stood to the side of the room so he could face the group. "Ben and I reached out to magic agents in other states and a few contacts we have in Mexico. Maverick's message reached them all. I've come across a lot of magic in my years, but never have I heard of someone being able to communicate like this. The power that Maverick consumed from the box must be giving him the ability."

Frank paused as if gathering his thoughts and everyone waited. Reece had known the man his entire life and he never spoke without carefully considering his words.

"As fucking scary as it was, the fact that Maverick could communicate with all of us over great distances and simultaneously is not my biggest concern. I'm sure Maverick's message will have invoked widespread panic that you're going to have to deal with..." Frank nodded at Jack and Meredith. "But my biggest worry is that Maverick will be able to do more than communicate. What if he can control people through their minds?"

Everyone started talking at once. Reece looked over at Isabella, and she met his gaze. He took her hand in his, loving that she didn't resist, and held it on his leg. "Jack," he said, raising his voice above the chatter in the room.

"You've got something?" Jack asked him.

Pride filled Reece that Jack had confidence in him. "Not to stop Maverick, but something that might help. When I was studying the spellbooks, I came across a spell that might prevent Maverick from getting inside our heads." Reece gave Isabella's hand a squeeze and let go as he stood.

Holding out his hands, Reece retrieved one of the magic spellbooks he had in his apartment. It landed on his palms and he turned the pages with his mind until he got to the one he wanted.

"Did the book turn the pages or you?" Simon asked, curiosity in his voice.

"I did." Confirming he had the ability to turn the pages without touching them had revealed some aspects of his magic specialty that not many people knew about. He would have told Simon and Jo eventually. They'd been out of the country when he'd discovered it and he hadn't had a chance in the short time they'd been back. Now everyone in the room knew some of what he could do. A few butterflies swirled in his stomach at the thought that the more people who knew what he could do, the more chances there were for him to be used and weakened. But he reminded himself that these people were family and he could trust them. He was also placing his trust in Isabella.

He glanced around the room as he spoke. "I found this spell a couple of months ago and couldn't imagine what it would be used for, but now I do. It should allow people we know to still communicate with us but prevent anyone unknown to us from being able to. Simon, could you put it on the paper like you did the memory?"

"Sure." Simon walked over to the sliding doors and waved his hand, clearing Maverick's words. "Read it aloud?"

Reece nodded and turned back to the book in his hands.

"Persons unknown, my mind is charmed, hidden from harm.
Thoughts concealed, magic steeled.
Sealed from illusion, sealed from intrusion.
No trespass, no breach, no wrongful intent,
with this spell I cement,
I lock, I guard, I defend my mind,
all uninvited I turn blind."

When he looked up from the book, the words he'd spoken were written in black, floating in front of the paper.

"Thanks, Reece." Jack turned to face the group. "Now, how do we test it?"

"It will take several people," Sam said quietly. "The way it's written means the person doesn't need to have evil intent, just be unknown to us." She turned to Ben, her father. "Do you have enough contacts that you could find several people who don't know everyone? The person doesn't have to be unknown to everyone here, only the person the spell is being tested on."

Ben looked over at his brother, Frank. "Between us, we should know enough magics, don't you think?"

"I agree, and from there, we can continue to spread the spell, passing it off to people to use and test."

"Uncle Frank, I don't think everyone would need to test it. We can select a sampling of people. Considering how big the magic population is, we'll have to consider the sample size." Sam looked over at her other uncle. "Uncle Joel, will you work with me on the sample size?"

"Of course," Joel said.

Reece closed the book in his hands and turned to Jack. "I think we might need to add one more line to ensure Maverick can't breach the spell. He does have harmful intents, but he's also no longer unknown or a stranger to any of us."

"Good call. Do you have a suggestion?" Jack asked.

Reece had read dozens of spells in the last few months and knew the best ones were always simple. He'd also practiced making up spells, knowing he might one day need one quickly. If he ever needed to counter a spell against himself or his family, he wanted to be able to create one without much thought.

For this spell, all they had to do was add something to the spell so it could recognize evil. "We could try something like: *No matter the source, if evil in question, deception believed, our minds be secure.*"

"Thoughts?" Jack asked the group. Some back-and-forth

discussion followed before everyone agreed and Simon added the line to the spell.

"Now, let's talk more specifically about Maverick." A silence fell over the room with Jack's mention of Maverick, everyone's attention captured. "The council will work on getting the spell together and also on a plan to close the box. But since we've got such a large group here, I thought we could brainstorm about what Maverick's end goal might be. If we can come up with some possibilities, we might be able to get one step ahead of him."

"Jack, I wasn't able to foresee Maverick getting into our heads, but I've seen wisps of something that might be worse than Maverick," Fiona said. "I don't think Maverick will be able to control what's inside of him for long."

Jack nodded. "Agreed. He's merely a vessel, and if the legends are true, the magic is more powerful than one person can handle."

Reece took his seat beside Isabella and let the conversation float around him. Once more, a sense of pride settled inside of him—all his studying and being magically strong had paid off.

His next step was to convince Isabella that she was the one who needed to get serious now or he'd look for the object on his own.

THE SMALL BOARDROOM was empty when Isabella arrived the next morning. When the meeting broke up the night before, she'd asked Reece to meet her this morning. Maverick's message had been a wake-up call. She'd been selfish by only looking for her brother. People were depending on her to find the magic object because now it was urgent. And it could be her fault that it had gotten this far. If she hadn't screwed around and had found the object already, maybe they could have prevented what happened last night.

Sitting in the same chair she'd sat in before, she watched the door. Reece would show up; he was too professional not to, even though he liked to joke around. How ironic that she had thought he wasn't the serious one when she'd been the one wasting time. Not that looking for her brother was a waste of time, but she'd made a promise to the council. A promise she hadn't kept.

The realization had sunk in the night before when she'd laid in her bed, unable to sleep. It had been a tough pill to swallow, but it hadn't been the only epiphany. If it hadn't been for Maverick's message, she would have continued to kiss Reece. Probably even gone to bed with him. That's what she'd asked him for before, but now things had changed. If she slept with him now, it wouldn't be just sex. And even though he was helping her find the object, what would happen after? What if they didn't find her brother at the same time? Would she let him distract her from her task?

"Good morning, cupcake."

"Morning, Reece." She returned his smile and waited. Would he mention the kiss? She no longer knew what to expect from him. He could be joking around and calling her "cupcake" one minute and acting serious the next. Perhaps she'd underestimated him. She certainly hadn't expected his knowledge of spells that he'd demonstrated the night before.

Reece leaned with his hands on the back of a chair and focused his beautiful blue gaze on her. "Are you ready to actually work this time?"

"Yes." There was no point in denying what they both knew. She hadn't been looking for the metal object. She pushed back from the table and walked to the whiteboards as she spoke. "Why don't we go over everything we have and see if we can find another place to start? Although I could feel that Mateo had been at the apartment, I didn't feel anything else."

"Sounds good." Reece walked up to stand beside her, and they were quiet as they stared at the boards.

After a few minutes, she turned to face him. "Why don't we concentrate on finding the object and maybe that will lead us to our brothers and your cousin?"

When he turned to give her his full attention, she locked her knees, forcing herself not to swoon. It wasn't just his looks that she was attracted to. It was also how he made her feel like she was the most important person in his life when he spoke to her. And that's where the danger lay—he could help her repeat the past.

"What do you have in mind, cupcake?" Reece lifted one hand, pushing her hair behind her shoulder. His fingers brushed across her cheek before he dropped his hand. The contact made her want to melt. Instead, she focused on the board. "What references to the object do we have?" Taking another step closer to the board, she moved a sticky note off to the side. "Let's group all the references and see if we can find a pattern."

Two hours later, they hadn't found a clue, but they had a place to start looking for one—the library. While they'd been organizing the sticky notes on the boards to see if they could find a pattern, she'd touched one and her magic told her to follow it. The note listed a book Simon and Jo had found, which had eventually led them to the ancient spellbook.

She didn't know what she'd find at the library, but it was a place to start.

9

"Hey, man. Good to see you," Reece said, extending his hand to Viktor. The older man shook with a strong grip.

"I apologize that Catherine and I have not been able to make it to dinner recently, but we hope to soon."

"Sounds good. We all like seeing you both." Reece turned to Isabella and placed his hand at the small of her back, loving it when she sunk into his palm. "Isabella, this is Viktor Szabo. He helped Jo and Simon find the ancient book. And Viktor, this is Isabella Flores. She assisted Morgana and Damon in Mexico."

"Good to meet you," Viktor said.

Isabella shook his hand. "It's nice to meet you too."

Reece chatted with Viktor for a few minutes before turning to Isabella and nodding as a cue for her to take over.

"Reece told me you might be able to help us find something."

"I guess that depends on what you're looking for." Viktor looked between them. "Should we go in the back where it's quieter?"

"Good idea." Reece kept his hand on Isabella as they followed Viktor. The massive library in Blue Mountain was busy as usual. Before they arrived, he'd filled Isabella in on what he knew about it from a magic standpoint. Unknown to non-magics, it housed the biggest collection of magic books in the world. To the general public, Viktor appeared to take care of one section of the library, and he did, but he also took care of all the magic books. If a non-magic picked one up, the book would appear as something else, like a history book.

"Tell me," Viktor said when they were seated in a back room with floor-to-ceiling bookshelves. Reece could sense power emanating from some of the books. He'd already studied many of them in his quest to learn everything he could about magic.

Reece would have preferred to explore the magic books instead of getting into the seriousness of why they were there. But he'd made a vow to find their brothers, and along with that came the promise to find the missing object. "You heard Maverick in your mind?"

Viktor rested his hand on the table and conjured a pen, twirling it in his fingers. "Yes. I reached out to some friends in Europe and they did not know what I was talking about, but everyone I contacted in North America heard Maverick." He stilled the pen and his expression saddened. "There is widespread panic and fear among many senior magics. They remember the old council and the corruption that eventually took it over. They will not trust Maverick because he was part of the old council, but they will not easily trust Jack and the other new council members either. I fear they will create factions, and already I have heard rumors that it will happen. Divisions amongst magics could mean that our kind is outed to non-magics or that other magic leaders will try to rise up and control others. Similar to what Maverick is already doing."

Reece hadn't thought about that possibility. Political parties or organizations weren't his thing. "Have you told Jack?"

"Yes, and I promised to update him when I heard more. In the meantime, I have been passing on the spell he gave me." Viktor twirled the pen again, spinning it rapidly in his fingers, and then suddenly he disappeared it. "That is enough of that. Jack and Meredith will figure out what to do. Now, what can I help you with?"

"We're looking for an object that is reported to be able to lock the box Maverick opened." He gestured to Isabella to continue.

She hesitated for a moment, and just as Reece was about to jump in to say she could trust Viktor, she met the older man's eyes. "Yes, I think there is a clue to the object in this library, but I don't know what it is."

Viktor's expression turned thoughtful. "You are a finder."

Isabella's eyes widened and she sat back in her chair. "How did you know?"

"I have met hundreds of people with magic specialties over the years, including a few finders. What you said about a clue was similar to what I've heard other finders say." Viktor smiled and gestured as if it was nothing. "How do you figure out where to start?"

"That's the tough part. It's not always the same. Sometimes I can sense something as soon as I walk into a room, but other times I need to walk around." She stood and pointed at the far wall. "Do you mind if I look?"

"No. Go ahead. But first... we must practice how to fight."

Reece laughed. "What?"

"These are crazy times and you are looking for something others want. Jo and Simon were taken off guard when they were attacked. You need to be prepared in case someone comes after you."

At first Reece thought Viktor might have recently knocked a few screws loose. But after ten minutes of practicing how to get out of someone's hold without using magic, he felt good and confident and Isabella said the same. He still thought it had been a crazy idea, but a crazy good one.

"Now you can look," Viktor said, once the training session was over.

Isabella walked up to the books and ran her hand gently along a row of them.

"I feel something," she said quietly, still facing the shelving. Reece didn't know if she'd been talking to herself or him. She continued to run her hands along the spines. Every so often, she'd stop and flatten her full palm against one before moving on. He had nowhere else he needed to be, and he could watch her all day—the expressions on her beautiful face, the way she moved with purpose, the tough persona she projected when he expected she had a caring soul underneath her façade. He'd seen it before when she helped in The Magic Plate's kitchen.

A few minutes later, she pulled out a book and brought it over, placing it on the book stand in the middle of the table. "There's something in this book we need to look at."

"That is the same book Jo and Simon found their first clue in." Viktor chuckled. "It was a d..." He paused; one eyebrow lifted as he looked at Reece. "What is the short word for defective?"

Reece grinned. "A dud?"

"Yes. A dud. It did not work. Later they combined part of the spell with one from another book and it led them to the next clue." Viktor winked. "Let us hope we have better luck this time."

Isabella hesitated, her hand over the book. "I don't know

what I'm looking for. I just felt something strong, but I don't know what it's leading me to."

"Let us try something." Viktor came around the table to stand beside them, facing the book. He turned to Reece. "Dim the lights."

Reece imagined the lights in his mind and dimmed them to forty percent. "Now what?"

"Isabella, open the cover and then step back. That worked with Simon." Viktor joined Reece a few feet away and they watched as Isabella lifted the book's cover. She moved a step to the side so they all had a clear view. Within a few seconds, the pages were flipping back and forth.

Isabella turned around, her eyes wide as she looked at him. "Are you doing that?"

Reece raised his hands and gave her his perfected grin. "No, cupcake, that's not me."

"It's the book," Viktor said.

Isabella glared at Reece before looking back at the book and he heard her quick intake of breath. "Shit. It's not in a language I can read."

"It's Latin," Viktor said. "Let me." He walked up to the book and waved his hand over the page. Words hovered in the air, like they were floating on an invisible cloud.

Reece glanced at the words. "They're in English. Viktor, did you translate them?"

"No, the spell did th—" Viktor stopped talking as the words in the bubble moved, as if changing and rearranging themselves. "That is a first," he said in awe. "I think the words are updating themselves."

"Updating? As in, they have knowledge of the object since the spell was first created centuries ago and they're updating the information so it's current? Like where the object may have been moved to?" Reece couldn't remember if he'd read anything about that in the magic books.

"Yes. I think so."

After a minute, the words stopped moving and stayed floating in the bubble.

Isabella walked toward the bubble so she stood facing the words. "It looks like a prophecy," she whispered, and then read the words aloud.

Looking glasses with secrets they confide,
Reflections of fate, they must abide.
Hidden from all eyes,
Thrice divided under safety of skies.
Entwined they decree,
Unveil what's meant to be.

When Isabella finished, she looked up. "Looking glasses. Thrice divided—we're looking for three mirrors. I thought we were looking for metal that could be forged into a lock?"

"That's what I thought too, but we're dealing with magic, so answers are rarely clear and simple." Reece smiled. Magic could be frustrating when there were spells and riddles involved, but he loved the challenges that came with it. "Maybe the mirrors will lead us to the object or the metal on the frames is what we actually need and the mirrors are used as a disguise."

"Isabella," Viktor said, handing her a piece of paper. "I have transferred the spell here. I think the words will disappear soon." As if the spell could hear Viktor, the words dissolved and the book closed with a *soft whoosh.*

Using his magic, Reece brought the lights back to full strength. "Isabella, can you feel where the mirrors are?"

"Not yet. Let me sit for a moment." She pulled out a chair and sat facing the closed book.

"I will go back to my desk. You know where to find me," Viktor said. He patted Reece on the shoulder and left.

Reece sat across from Isabella and waited. It gave him another chance to study her as she placed her hands on the closed book and shut her eyes. Her hands looked small and delicate on the large book. She was petite compared to him and he loved that. Yes, he could admit that it was a bit neanderthal-like of him to want to be able to envelop a woman in his arms. It'd been a long time since he'd been with a woman, but besides making love to Isabella, he'd like to sleep with her and be the outside spoon. He could imagine holding her, being protective and keeping her safe. And be there for her at other times too, so she didn't always feel like she had only herself to rely on.

Her forehead wrinkled as her eyes remained closed. He'd seen that expression on her face before as she worked out a problem, like when they were standing at the whiteboards. But it was the image of her from last night just before he kissed her, when she'd wrinkled her forehead and licked her lips, that he pictured now. The kiss had surprised him. His hand on the back of her neck had been a protective gesture and a way to bring her closer, but he hadn't expected her to melt into it like she had. He wanted to see what other ways he could make her melt.

Isabella's eyes popped open. "I know where to go."

"Where, cupcake?"

"The first mirror is with a wealthy magic. It's at his home."

Reece raised his eyebrows. "You felt all that from the book?"

She reared back in her chair and tugged at her hoodie's neckline. "You doubt me?"

A red flag reared up in him when she hesitated, as if she wasn't going to tell him. They'd worked well together this morning, but he wasn't naïve. A few hours of cooperation didn't erase years of mistrusting other people. And Isabella didn't trust. Reece wasn't an expert at reading body language, but Javier was. As an FBI agent, he was taught how to read people, and he'd taught Reece a few of those things. Her expression, her answering a question with a question, and her tugging at her clothes told Reece she was hiding something.

Working with Isabella was a bit like taming a wild horse. He had to be gentle, but not a pushover, and show that she could trust him. He raised his hands, palms facing out. "I'm not doubting you. I just don't know how your magic works. I don't know if you can visualize a place or get an address or what. You know where we need to go?"

"You want to go with me?" she asked as she pulled down the cuffs of her sleeves.

"Yes, cupcake, I want to go with you. Where are we going?"

"Ah, it's in San Francisco."

Reece pulled out his phone and checked his map app. "That's about twelve hundred miles from here. A little long for one flash, but we should be able to do it." He met her gaze. "You want to go now?"

Isabella frowned and straightened her sweatshirt as she stood before pushing the chair back against the table. "Now?"

Reece picked up the book and shelved it in its original spot and joined her. "Yes, let's go now. It's still early in the day, so we've got lots of time. We can walk to the back alley and flash from there."

They said their goodbyes to Viktor and walked out to the back alley. In between two buildings with the stench of a dumpster wafting over to them, they waited until a lone car passed. When they were alone, Reece turned to Isabella. "You going to give me the address, cupcake?"

She spewed out an address and flashed away. Reece shook his head and called up the address on his phone. Flashing was still new to him, and he didn't like flashing somewhere he'd never been before. The address showed a street in San Francisco. Using the street view, Reece found a place he could flash to. Isabella had been even cagier than usual, and as he pulled on his magic, he wondered if she'd even be there waiting for him.

10

Isabella flashed to the public garden in the Back Bay neighborhood of Boston. Several of her past clients lived in the area so Isabella was familiar with it. She'd used the garden to flash in and out of before, knowing where there were enough bushes and trees to hide her from sight.

She glanced at her pedometer slash watch to check the time. The average magic person could only flash about a thousand miles at a time so she'd been forced to make a stop halfway. She'd stopped at an old strip mall that she used before on the outskirts of Indianapolis. After an hour's rest and a meal, her magic was charged enough to flash the rest of the way.

Walking down the street toward her destination, she felt a slight twinge of guilt for misleading Reece. The comedy club she'd sent him to in San Fransico was owned by a really nice elderly magic woman she'd done some work for the year before. And the club was near the water, so Reece would have a nice view as he waited for her and it wouldn't be a complete waste of a trip for him. Hopefully he wouldn't wait too long before he realized that she wasn't going to show.

She crossed the street and headed toward the address and wondered how angry Reece would be. He'd been upset, frustrated, and likely disappointed with her in the past, but never really angry. Reece almost always had a smile on his face, but she was beginning to think that sometimes it was an act. Like when she'd called him a himbo—not one of her finest moments. At first she could have sworn he looked upset, but then he'd smiled as the others laughed.

When she'd first met him, he'd joked so much she wasn't sure he could ever be serious. Joking was a distraction she couldn't afford. But now, she'd seen his serious side. Her guilt climbed the more she thought about him, but she told herself she was right in what she'd done and why she'd misled him by sending him to a different city. It was the man himself—not just the joking side, but all sides—that she needed to be wary of. If she wasn't careful, she'd find herself waiting for him to call her cupcake and kiss her. She'd be too busy focusing on when the next kiss might come instead of focusing on her goal.

Looking up at the addresses as she passed, she guessed the one she wanted was in the next block. She loved the look of the brick in different shades of orange and brown with iron railings on the steps and surrounding small, well-kept gardens. The neighborhood spoke of wealth, so different from the one where she'd grown up. Her parents had good jobs and, like all magics, they could conjure so many things they needed, which saved money, but this area was in a class by itself.

Stopping in front of a home with large, black lacquered double doors, with eight steps leading up to it, she checked the address. This was it.

She used her magic to make sure her breath was minty fresh and her hair didn't look like a windblown mess. Changing her clothes on the street would draw too much attention, so jeans and a hoodie were going to have to be good enough.

At the top of the steps, she rang the doorbell and heard a deep sound peal inside the house. When the door opened, she looked up to a tall man, whose head nearly brushed the doorframe, probably in his late sixties or early seventies, staring down at her. His completely gray hair was impeccable, as were his clothes.

Isabella put on a serious face. "Sir, my name is Isabella Flores and I believe you have a mirror that is needed by the new North American council. May I come in?"

He moved forward, pulling the door closed behind him, forcing Isabella to back down a step. But not before she sensed that the object she was looking for was inside. Her magic was calling to her like it had at the library. Already short, she felt even shorter after going down a step and she had to crane her neck to look up at the man.

He frowned and pursed his lips. "Did Maverick send you?"

Hadn't he heard what she said? "No, sir. I'm looking for an object for the new magic council."

"Maverick was a council member and now he thinks he can control everyone. He will not control me or my family." He turned to go back inside, and Isabella knew her chance to get the mirror was closing fast.

"No. No, please don't go. I'd like to talk to you about your mirror." She held up her hands in protest and realized too late what she'd done. He wouldn't know that she was using simple body language to get him to stop—but he did know she was magic, and raising her hands could be seen as a threat.

Before she had a chance to drop her hands or say anything further, the man flicked his hand toward her and rushed into his house. The sound of the door slamming was deafening.

That didn't go well. Maybe she could come back and try a different approach. Or maybe she should have given Reece the correct address and let him do the talking.

Isabella turned around and jumped when she felt something on her neck. She slapped her hand against her neck and felt a crawling sensation on her hand.

She pulled her hand away from her neck and saw an ant on crawling on her. Shaking her hand to get rid of it, she had to catch herself on the railing before she tumbled down the stairs. Still feeling the ant, she looked down. A tiny yelp tore from her when she saw dozens of ants crawling up her arm.

As fast as she could, she ripped off her hoodie and pulled at her T-shirt, hoping to knock off the rest of the ants, but they wouldn't let go. She ran down the steps and called on her magic. Creating a wind, she circled it around her to fling off the remaining ants. The little creatures flew in all directions. Wind was the first thing she had thought of in her moment of terror that could get rid of the ants, but it hopefully wouldn't be noticeable to a passer-by.

At the bottom of the steps, she shook out her hoodie and watched two more ants fall to the pavement and scurry away. Isabella had heard some of what Morgana had gone through with spiders and was thankful the man had only thrown ants at her. And non-biting ones at that.

Bending at the waist, she flipped her hair over and carded her fingers through it to make sure all the ants were gone. She couldn't see any more, but could still feel them crawling on her. The thought sent a shiver skating down her spine.

Standing next to a tree on the boulevard, she called up some more wind. Her hair batted around her face, stinging like little needles, but no more ants flew out.

Isabella sat on the curb and hung her head. She'd royally

fucked up. For so long, she'd been on her own with a laser-sharp focus on finding her brother. The thought of Reece distracting her had blinded her from the fact that maybe he could have helped.

Now she'd have to explain to Jack and Meredith that she didn't get the first mirror. At least they'd already given her all the information they had about Mateo if they asked her to leave. What she had wasn't much, but maybe if she went over it again she'd find something she'd missed the first time.

But getting the information meant going back to her apartment. No, it wasn't her apartment, she told herself, and she couldn't forget that. She'd gotten too comfortable in Blue Mountain. The Williams had let her use the apartment and then she'd messed up by not following through on her promise to work with Reece. If they kicked her out, she'd have to find a new place to live. For years she'd been moving from place to place for work and to look for Mateo. But in the last few weeks, she'd felt like she finally had a home—the first time since college.

She shivered again, but this time from the chill in the air and not ants. Turning her hoodie inside out, she shook it again, inspecting the hood. Those six-legged little buggers weren't going to sneak up on her. When she was satisfied she didn't have any more of them on her sweatshirt or her person, she put the hoodie back on. Leaning forward, she balanced her elbows on her knees and placed her head in her hands. She needed to figure out what to do next. Go back and admit what she'd done? Or attempt to get the man to talk to her again?

Not being a fan of having egg on her face, she'd sit a bit longer and think of a better argument for the man to let her in.

WITHIN FIVE MINUTES of flashing to the San Francisco address Isabella had given him, he knew he'd been had. He stared up at the sign on the front of the comedy club and realized the joke was on him.

He threw back his head and laughed at the irony. She knew exactly what she'd been doing. Looking around, he took in the tourists wandering about. The wharf was only a couple of blocks away, and he'd need to get something to eat to fuel up or he wouldn't be able to flash home. Since he was still so new to using his magic, he hadn't yet flashed a long distance, but he'd heard Damon and Jack tell stories about pushing it too far and having to stop halfway. Reece didn't want to have to land in Utah to get a bite to eat and rest—not that Utah wasn't a great place, but it was easier getting some lunch here.

Instead of pulling out his phone to check for possible restaurants, he turned toward where the crowds were coming from and walked toward the wharf. The day was beautiful and warmer than in Blue Mountain, so he'd make the most out of this unexpected little jaunt.

"Thank you," Reece said, smiling at the woman as he took his order of fish and chips through the food truck's order window. A couple was just vacating a table at the small patio and Reece smiled at them before sitting down.

Taking a bite of the succulent fish, Reece had to hold in a groan as the subtle flavors coated his tongue. He couldn't remember the last time he'd had fish and chips and almost wanted to thank Isabella for the detour. Almost.

He looked around at people as he ate, soaking in the sun and the atmosphere. But he also thought about his next steps. Going home was his only option because he didn't know where Isabella had gone. Once back at home he'd be able to look up the locator spell he'd found when studying the spell-books and track Isabella.

When he had come out of the coma and had first started studying, he'd been overwhelmed with the amount of information he'd found. It hadn't taken him long to learn that many magics never used spells. They stuck with the innate magic within themselves, such as flashing and conjuring, and if they were lucky, they had a specialty. His family was unique because they came from a powerful magic line and almost all had specialties, but not every magic person did.

He could have chosen, like so many others, not to worry about spells. Instead, he'd decided to learn everything about them he could. Twice in his life a spell had taken away his freedom and he had promised himself it wouldn't happen again in the future. Weakness wasn't an option. Not only had he studied every magic book he could get his hands on, but he'd kept a database of the spells. And one was a locator spell. It wouldn't enable him to sense an object or person's location like Isabella's magic could, but with something of hers, he'd be able to locate her.

After he finished eating, he sat for another twenty minutes, drinking his soda and watching the crowds. Guessing that the meal and short rest had recharged his magic enough to flash home, he got up and threw away his trash. Strolling back to the same place he'd used when he arrived, he flashed home.

He landed in his apartment's foyer and felt at full strength. Staying to eat and rest had been the right choice. If Isabella was still where she'd originally flashed to, then good. If not, he'd find her sooner or later, because he refused to weaken himself by flashing too far or too often.

In his spare bedroom, he sat down at the desk in the corner and pulled up his spreadsheet of spells. Checking his table of contents, he pulled up the document with the spell he needed. When he'd first started the database, it had made sense to him to write down each spell in case the spellbook was one he couldn't keep.

The night before had been an anomaly because the spell was from the ancient magic book that the new council had kept. The only time Jack and Meredith had let it out of their possession was when his cousin Rowena had needed to find the key to the magic box.

Reece sighed and sat back, running his hands through his hair. Everything bad in his life seemed to be connected to that box. First it was the deaths of his father, brother, uncles, and cousins, although they hadn't been what they seemed. Then his aunt Lillian had died, followed years later by his mom's death and his aunt Elise's. His sister and his cousins, along with their partners, had almost all died as well, all in different scenarios. Then there was the spell that had almost killed him.

He hit print on his computer and turned off the screen. It was time they put an end to the magic box, and to do that, he needed Isabella's help. One way or another, he was going to convince her to work with him instead of against him.

Grabbing the piece of paper off the printer, he flashed up three floors to Isabella's apartment. Just in case she was home, he knocked on the door and waited. After a minute with no answer, he pulled on his magic to see if he could detect a spell on the door.

Not detecting one, he smiled. No spell meant she was starting to trust at least some of his family members, if maybe not him. Using his magic, he opened the door, walked in, and listened—all quiet.

Glancing around, he looked for a personal item he could use with the spell. He didn't want to be an ass and invade her space, but he needed to locate her. There wasn't anything in the kitchen or living room so he walked to her bedroom. At the door to her bedroom, he hesitated, but only for a moment, before pushing it open.

Her bed was made with enough pillows for a girls' sleep-over stacked neatly on top. He never got the pillow thing. Turning in a slow circle, he let his gaze wander over the room. On the dresser was a necklace. Picking up the silver chain, he looked at the small pendant—a butterfly. He'd seen Isabella wear it before. It wasn't an expensive necklace, but it must have some sentimentality to it. If the necklace didn't work, he'd look for something else.

Performing the spell in her bedroom without her there seemed too invasive, so he went to the kitchen. Holding the necklace in one hand and the spell in the other, he recited the words aloud.

> *With this piece, seek and find*
> *Provide the ties that bind*
> *A soul stolen or lost*
> *Show the place*
> *Of where I seek the face*

Looking down at the paper, he watched as an address appeared as if he'd typed it out with the spell. When he'd first found the spell, he'd tried to locate his sister as a test. He hadn't been holding a piece of paper then, but it hadn't mattered. Jo's address had appeared on the open document on his computer.

"Shit." The address was in Boston. That was almost double the distance to San Francisco. Even with rest and food, he wouldn't be able to flash there in one go. His elation from earlier vanished as fast as his cupcakes did at a children's birthday party.

Leaving Isabella's apartment, he locked the door and was about to flash to his own when he had an idea.

Flashing up two floors to the floor below his, he knocked on Meredith and Jack's door.

"Come in," Meredith yelled from inside.

"Hey, Mer," he said as he walked in and over to the kitchen island where she was working on a laptop. "I need a favor."

She smiled. "Sure. What?"

Some days he was still taken aback by how relaxed she looked. With her business and her prominent place on the council, she was probably busier than she'd ever been, but accepting her magic and marrying Jack had settled her. He was happy for her, like he was for his sister and his other two cousins. But he wanted that for himself too.

Shaking off the thought, he gave her his most impish grin. "Can you flash me to Boston? It's too far for me to flash at once on my own."

"What's in Boston?"

"Isabella."

A puzzled expression crossed Meredith's face. "I don't get it. I thought you two were working together. Why is she in Boston?"

Telling Meredith the truth could make Isabella look bad, and he didn't want to put her in that light. Sure, she'd taken off, and as much as he disagreed with what she'd done, he understood why. She had a need to find her brother above all else. Others might not understand that like he did. But he still hoped he could convince Isabella to cooperate with him. He shrugged. "I think we found a clue to the magic object, but we got our wires crossed."

Meredith stood. "Sure. Just flash you there? I don't need to stay?"

"Yes, just get me there. I don't know how long I'll be there, so I'll get back on my own."

"Okay. What's the address?" Reece read off the address and the name of the garden he thought would be a good place to flash to. "Ready?"

He just hoped Isabella was still there… Shit, he didn't even know who she'd met with. "One more thing… can you tell me who lives at that address?"

Meredith gave him a skeptical look. "You don't know who you're going to meet?"

"No, but Isabella does. I just want to be prepared." It wasn't a lie.

"Hold on." Meredith's eyes glossed over and she became silent. He figured she was talking telepathically with Jack. Cool trick, and if Reece had been able to do that, he wouldn't be going through all this to find Isabella.

"May I?" Meredith asked, gesturing to the paper in his hand. When he handed it over, she placed it on the kitchen island and hovered her hand about six inches above the paper. "Allan Pantenburg. He owns Pantenburg Group, one of the largest hedge fund companies in the country."

"Wow." He might have his work cut out for him convincing the man with that amount of clout to just to hand over something in his possession if Isabella hadn't already done it. "I'm ready."

"Let's go." Meredith clasped his hand and flashed with him.

"Holy shit," he said, steadying himself on the ground where they were hidden amongst some bushes. "Can you always flash that fast? And with someone else?"

Meredith's eyes sparkled. "Yes, but it's all because of the power bestowed on me for being a council co-leader." She shrugged. "It comes in handy. You good?"

"Yes, I've got it from here."

With a wave, Meredith was gone. He chuckled and headed out of the garden. In the months since he'd come out of the coma, he'd learned to not just accept his magic, but love it. Yet sometimes he was still taken by surprise by how much his life had changed because of it.

It didn't take him long to get to the address where he hoped Isabella would still be. When he was a few buildings away, he saw her sitting on the curb, her elbows on her knees and her head in her hands. She looked dejected.

He didn't wish that feeling on anyone, but maybe he could use it to his advantage. Covering the last few steps, he crouched down beside Isabella, who was so lost in her thoughts she hadn't noticed him yet. "Hey, cupcake. Need some help?"

11

Isabella's butt was numb from sitting on the curb, but she still hadn't figured out how to convince the man with the mirror to listen to her.

"Hey, cupcake. Need some help?"

She startled and would have fallen sideways onto the pavement if Reece hadn't caught her. "What... what are... how'd you get here?"

Dropping her arm, he perched on the curb beside her, his knees almost hitting his chin. "After I finished my wild goose chase, I thought you might need some help."

His eyes were questioning and he hadn't yelled at her, which made her feel guiltier than she had before. She stood and brushed off her pants. "I have it under control."

Reece stood as well and raised his eyebrows as if issuing her a challenge to defend her statement. "Cupcake, do you really have it under control? Or were you worried I wouldn't be able to handle it?"

Isabella shrugged because she didn't want to tell him the truth.

The silence hung between them for a moment.

"Did you talk to Mr. Pantenburg?" Reece asked.

She finally looked up at him. "Who?"

"The man who lives at that address," he said, pointing over his shoulder. "Allan Pantenburg. Isn't he the one with the mirror?"

"My magic doesn't usually reveal a name, just a location." The fact that Reece knew the man's name made her feel like a bit of an idiot for leaving him behind. Nothing was going like she'd planned.

"So, did you talk to him?" Reece repeated.

"Yes. I haven't just been sitting here the entire time." Well, the entire time minus the about two minutes it took for the man to turn her away. "He wouldn't let me in." She purposely didn't mention the ants.

Reece nodded and then turned to the house's front steps.

"Wait!" she called, hurrying to catch up with Reece. "I said he didn't want to talk."

At the top step, Reece turned to her. "I heard you, cupcake, but it doesn't hurt for me to try."

"Fine." Although anyone knew that *fine* didn't really mean fine, she stood beside Reece anyway. He knocked on the door, and less than a minute later, it was opened by the same man as before.

"Mr. Pantenburg?" Reece asked, extending his hand. "I'm Reece Williams. I believe you probably knew my father, Griffin Williams. And my uncles, Thomas and Evan. May I come in and speak with you?"

The man shook Reece's hand and then stepped back from the doorway. "Yes, of course. Please come in. I'm sorry about what happened to your father and uncles. I heard your mother and Elise passed away last year as well. My condolences."

"Thank you." Reece put his hand on Isabella's lower back and propelled her into the tiled foyer with him. "I believe you already met my colleague, Isabella Flores." Reece chuckled, sounding genuine. "She was a bit eager to meet with you and didn't wait for me."

"Yes, I thought Maverick had sent her." He didn't apologize for dismissing her, not even for the ants, and since she didn't want to get kicked out, she let it go.

They followed him into an elegant room that could have housed her entire apartment. A fire was crackling away in an enormous stone fireplace, big enough for Santa to easily slip down. One wall was covered with floor-to-ceiling bookshelves, the kind with a ladder that slid along a rail. Isabella would have loved to cuddle up in a room like this—she'd read a book and let the outside world fall away.

When they were seated, a woman in pleated black pants and a crisp white shirt walked in carrying a tray with a carafe of coffee and cups and saucers. Setting the tray down on a sideboard, she nodded to the homeowner and left.

Mr. Pantenburg stood and walked over to the sideboard, pouring himself a cup. "Would you care for some coffee?"

"No, thank you," Reece said. "I know you're a busy man and we don't want to take up too much of your time. We just have a question—"

"No, no. It's alright, Reece. I used to be quite good friends with your parents and aunts and uncles. We must catch up. Please," he said, gesturing to the coffee again.

Reece smiled and stood. "As long as we're not putting you out." He poured two cups of coffee and brought them back to the couch, giving one to Isabella before sitting beside her.

Mr. Pantenburg took a sip of his coffee and then balanced it on his knee. "Tell me what your family has been up to. I heard that Meredith was restoring the buildings and creating quite a community." He huffed a soft laugh. "Your uncle Thomas had such grandiose plans for that area."

"Like father, like daughter," Reece said, chuckling. "I think Meredith's plans are bigger than our dads' ever were."

Isabella sat and listened for the next fifteen minutes while Reece chatted with Mr. Pantenburg. They laughed and told stories about Reece's dad and uncles like they were besties. She stayed quiet, and just when she thought they might be winding up their little tête-à-tête, one of them would launch into a new story.

She gripped her cup in both hands and had to force herself not to squirm. Letting out a small breath, she loosened her jaw, an ache setting in from grinding her teeth.

After his most recent bout of laughter, Reece's expression sobered. "I appreciate all the stories. It was great reminiscing because there has been so much heartache in my family. It's good to remember we had so much to laugh about."

Mr. Pantenburg took in a deep breath and closed his eyes for just a moment before looking at Reece. "Yes, unfortunately, the old council had quite a few bad apples. Your father and uncle excluded, of course." He paused and set his cup down on the low table in front of him. "I'm assuming that's why you're here. Your friend here, ah—"

He looked at her as if he'd forgotten her name. "Isabella Flores," she supplied, hoping her attempt at a smile didn't come across as a grimace.

"Yes, Isabella. Well, when she arrived, I thought that maybe Maverick had sent her. He's caused quite a stir, and panic is spreading amongst magics. I didn't believe him about the new council, but many will. What is it you're looking for and why?"

"It has been foretold that a magic object, most likely a piece of metal, has the ability to close the magic box forever."

Mr. Pantenburg snorted. "A bit late for that, don't you think?"

"No, sir. Jack and Meredith and the rest of the new

council members believe that they can get the magic back in the box, and when they do, they need to be ready to lock it." Reece waved his hand between himself and Isabella. "We've been tasked with finding that object."

"And you think I have it?" He raised his brows, a skeptical look on his face.

"Yes. The object has been divided and embedded into three mirrors. We believe it's in the frames," Reece said.

Isabella watched a look of disbelief flitter across Mr. Pantenburg's face before something more calculating replaced it.

"I do have an old mirror. I've never thought much of it, and I'd be happy to pass it along."

"Thank you, sir," Reece said.

"For a trade." Mr. Pantenburg sat back like he had just won the lottery. From the looks of his home and his obvious wealth, money couldn't be his objective.

"Of course," Reece said, not missing a beat. "We wouldn't expect you to just hand over something of such importance. What would you like in return?"

"Rumor going around is that there's a spell that can protect me and my family from Maverick's, ah... intrusions."

Isabella bit the inside of her cheek to stop the smile pulling at her lips. The council would have gladly given the spell to the man. In fact, they were trying to get it to as many people as possible and asking for nothing in return.

"The spell..." Reece paused as if he had to consider the request. "I'll have to ask. Is that all?"

"No. Now that I think about it, I'd like some physical protection for my family as well. I've heard there are spells for that too."

"I understand. Of course you want to keep your family safe." Reece stood and walked around the couch. "Let me reach out."

Reece turned to face the window, although she knew he hadn't needed to. He could have reached out to Jack in seconds since the council leader was powerful enough to receive a telepathic message even from this great distance.

Two minutes later, Reece turned around and walked back to the couch, taking his seat beside Isabella. "Your request was approved. It shouldn't take long."

The look on Mr. Pantenburg's face was so smug, Isabella itched to wipe it off. He stood and looked toward the room's entrance. "I've just messaged for someone to get the mirror," he told them.

"Hello, Allan," Jack said as he stepped into the room, extending his hand to shake. "Thank you so much for parting with the mirror for such a great cause."

Everyone in the room knew who had the upper hand here, and it wasn't Mr. Pantenburg. Jack's use of the man's first name established the pecking order as soon as he'd walked in.

A moment later, the same woman who had delivered the coffee walked in with a rectangular mirror, obscuring most of her from view. It looked like the kind of mirror you'd buy at a home building center to hang on the back of a bedroom door. Instead of a wooden frame, it was metal, but it was still nothing special to look at.

Jack smiled at the woman. "Thank you." Then the mirror disappeared.

"Hey—" Mr. Pantenburg stepped forward, his face red.

Jack held up his hand. "No worries, Allan. I just wanted to get the mirror some place safe." He turned to Reece and Isabella. "Why don't you two head home and I'll make sure Allan has the protection he needs?"

Isabella nodded at Jack, knowing his question was really a direction, and walked to the front door.

Reece said goodbye to the two men, and he walked

outside with her and down the steps. She felt like an idiot for the second time that afternoon. Reece's easygoing character and joking ways had been the answer when she'd feared he wouldn't be taken seriously. If Mr. Pantenburg could be charmed by Reece, Isabella didn't stand a chance of not being sucked in by it.

All along she'd been worried about Reece distracting her with his joking ways but it wasn't him, it was her. She'd become an old cliché–it's not you, it's me. She liked him—maybe too much. Fulfilling her promise of finding the magic object—all three mirrors—was one thing, but doing it with Reece as she let him suck her into his orbit, was something else. He was becoming more than just a temporary diversion.

At the bottom of the steps, she turned to him, hands on her hips. "I would have figured it out, you know. You didn't have to come to the rescue with your dentist-worthy smile and all your charm."

Reece smiled and then looked like he was going to say something. She couldn't stay mad at him as he'd managed to retrieve the mirror when she hadn't. Even after everything she did to derail him. And he was smiling about it.

Her earlier guilt magnified ten-fold and then a healthy dose of shame piled on top like a cherry on a guilt sundae. Once more she had failed to do the right thing. And this time she couldn't even say she had the best of intentions because she knew she'd done it out of selfishness. "I'm heading home." She flashed away before he had a chance to stop her.

"Hey, sorry we're late," Jo said as she rushed into the room. She squeezed Reece's shoulder and took a seat beside him at the large boardroom table while Simon sat on her other side. "We were just following up on a lead for a book and dealing with a time difference."

"No problem. I know it's early," Jack said, standing at the head of the table.

Reece focused on Jack and Meredith while still remaining hyper-aware of the intriguing and frustrating woman sitting across the table. Isabella's chair was about a foot back from the table, as if she was trying to distance herself from everyone.

Her hands were locked together in her lap and the muscles on the side of her jaw jutted out. Reece was worried Isabella would crack a tooth with how tightly she was clenching her jaw. He'd seen her do the same thing before. It made him want to walk up to her and kiss her until she was a pile of goo. Besides the room full of people, it might get a bit dicey because she wasn't currently speaking to him. At least not since she'd left him standing on the sidewalk in Boston yesterday. Whether it was because he'd gotten the mirror or because she hadn't, he didn't know.

"…sounds good, keep us posted." Reece caught the second half of Jack's comment to his sister and Simon and realized he'd missed something. Since it was probably about the books Jo and Simon were looking for, it didn't pertain to him so he didn't bother asking him to repeat it.

"Thanks for coming," Jack said, addressing the entire group. "We've had too many of these emergency meetings lately, but things are moving too fast to chance someone not being in the loop. Reece, you want to fill everyone in on your progress?"

Reece nodded at Jack and let his gaze wander from person to person as he spoke. "Isabella was able to find a clue in an old book—" He turned to look at his sister and Simon. "The same one you found your first clue in, actually."

"Shit, imagine that," Jo said, and Reece looked back at the group.

Reece explained how they'd found a prophecy and its update, which led them to a magic's house in Boston and the deal Jack assisted with. He left out his little side jaunt to San Francisco. "Now the mirror is at Kate's forge, but we don't have a clue about the other two mirrors yet. We'll let you know when we do."

"Thanks, Reece," Meredith said. "We've set up a kind of hotline—er, email line, I guess—for magics to report in. Before, most just reached out telepathically since Jack and I can be contacted over great distances. But with the spell in place, they can't reach us telepathically if we don't personally know them. We've been spreading the news about the hotline as much as we can, and Fiona has been helping. Fiona, do you have anything to add?"

Reece looked over at Damon's mom. He'd known her for as long as he could remember. She was like a second mom to him, and a social butterfly with some ability of sight. Since she seemed to know everyone, she was a natural for helping with the hotline.

"Thanks, honey," Fiona said before addressing the group. "The number of magics using my consulting business has grown substantially in the last ten years, and I've made other contacts through those people. Damon helped me set up an encryption system years ago in case anything magic was mentioned in an email, so I sent an encrypted email blast the other night after our meeting. It went out to forty-three hundred magics and most of them will have extensive contacts lists as well. As of right before I came here, ninety-two percent of the recipients had opened the email."

"Thank you, Fiona. That should help to get the word out." Jack faced the group again. "Unfortunately, Maverick has worked faster than us. Ben?"

The meeting had the feel of a board meeting with everyone giving updates, and Reece supposed that's what it was. Their lives had changed so much since the spells on them had been broken. Jack had taken the reins of the new council, bringing so many of Reece's family into the fold. He expected this would be the new normal for all of them.

Ben nodded and stood at the opposite end of the table from Jack, standing back as his gaze swept across everyone. "Panic is spreading among all magic people. We've heard it from some older magics we trust, like Viktor Szabo and Allan Pantenburg, but panic isn't the only thing. It seems that Maverick can control minds as well."

Curses and questions blew up in the room until Ben held up his hands. "Let me explain." When the room quieted down, Ben turned to his brother. "Frank was alerted by a magic in the bureau who isn't one of my agents."

Frank stood and, like his brother, looked around the room, meeting everyone's gaze. Reece figured it was an FBI thing, because Jack did it as well. Or maybe it was the seriousness of the situation. "A young magic, fresh to the bureau and assigned to the field office in Chicago, started acting erratically. Luckily, his dad had asked him to stop by the house to give him the spell we created. His dad was able to subdue him. And because his dad is a retired agent and we had worked together many times, he got ahold of me."

Reece leaned forward. "What did he do that alerted his dad?"

"Nelson, the young agent, hadn't hugged his mom or sister like he normally would have and seemed aloof and on edge, which was apparently out of character for him. Nelson Senior had just asked Junior to read the spell when he pulled out his service weapon and aimed it at his younger brother." A few more curses blistered the air and Ben held up a hand to quiet the room.

Frank paused and carded his fingers through his hair. "Junior had been out of town at his family's cabin with a bunch of his buddies. I feel responsible because he was one of my agents and I hadn't gotten to him yet."

Ben, still standing, patted Frank on the back of one shoulder. "Because of that, Frank and I were up a good portion of the night contacting every law enforcement agency we have contacts in. Nelson Senior and others we contacted were doing the same, and we ended up with an enormous phone tree. We've passed it on to Jack and Meredith, and we've agreed to create a database of magics, including Fiona's contacts. We'll keep it encrypted and confidential and it will only be used in situations like this."

He couldn't imagine another situation where they'd need such a list, but then, no one had predicted this either. Since Isabella's brother was working with Maverick, that meant he could be controlled too. Reece glanced across at her to see how she was taking the news.

Her head was bent down, and she was avoiding all eye contact. She held a piece of cloth, twisting it around her fingers, causing the tips to turn white. Then she'd release it and start over. She must have conjured it and he hated that she needed it to combat her stress.

"Ben, Frank, thanks," Jack said. "Everyone, thanks for coming. That's all we've got for now. If anything strange happens, no matter how small, check in."

People started to stand when something occurred to Reece. "Jack, wait." Everyone in the room stopped and all eyes turned to Reece as he looked at Frank. "Frank, once Nelson Senior subdued Junior, what did you do? Subduing him didn't stop the mind control, did it?"

Frank's shoulders dropped. "Unfortunately, no. With Jack's help, we put Junior in a magically induced coma. It should prevent Maverick from accessing his mind. All we can do now is hope that we'll be able to pull the magic out of Maverick and lock it away, which will permanently stop the mind control."

"What if you can't?" Rowena asked from where she'd stopped by the door. "Pull it out of Maverick, I mean. Then what?"

"If it comes down to one versus many, we'll lock Maverick in the box, magic and all," Jack answered.

Rowena gave an inelegant snort. "Usually I want to save everyone, although in Maverick's case, I won't lose any sleep if he dies. He should pay for his crimes. But, Jack, you do know the magic box is just the size of a shoe box, right?"

"Magic, Rowena, magic." Jack winked at Rowena, and there were chuckles and laughter as everyone began to exit the room.

Reece stood and walked over to the door, waiting as everyone filed out. Isabella had been on the far side of the table, near the end. She was the last person to walk around it and head for the door.

As soon as the person ahead of Isabella cleared the doorway, Reece pulled on his magic and slammed the door shut.

She stopped short, just avoiding getting hit by the door. "What the hell, Reece?"

"Sit down, Isabella. It's time to talk."

Isabella looked at the closed door and debated what to do. It wasn't like she couldn't open the door or even flash away. She had been hoping to walk out of the boardroom with the others and avoid talking to Reece. Just like she'd avoided him yesterday when she'd flashed, leaving him on the sidewalk. She'd even taken her time getting back to Blue Mountain so she wouldn't run into him.

She'd become a coward.

As much as she didn't want to admit it, maybe Reece was right and it was time they talked. She turned and walked back around the table directly across from where he stood and sat.

Coward or not, she needed the physical distance between them or she'd grab him by his shirt and kiss the ever-loving hell out of him.

Just because she knew he was right didn't mean she had to capitulate right away. "What would you like to talk about?"

Reece didn't comment on her choice of seats and pulled out the chair closest to him and sat. His expression was neutral, so she couldn't read him.

"I want to know what game you're playing, Isabella."

That was the second time he'd used her full name. When had she started yearning to hear his nickname for her pass his lips?

"I'm not playing a game. We found the first mirror." It was the truth, even if it happened in a roundabout way and the charming Reece was the one who saved the day. Ugh, she was even starting to sound like a bitch in her own head. This wasn't her. She was the one who had put her life on hold for years to find her brother and please her unpleasable parents. The one who went above and beyond to please her clients.

"Yes, but we've also wasted a lot of time. We don't know where the second mirror is yet and we haven't even started looking."

He leaned forward on his forearms. His very muscular forearms with his sleeves rolled up, showcasing said muscles. She had to rip her gaze away from his arms to look him in the eyes as he continued. "If you don't want to help me find the objects, Isabella, then say so. I'll ask Jack to find me someone else who can help."

That made three times now—the third time he'd used her full name. "I do want to help. I was just worried about you distracting me from finding the mirror and I thought I could get it by myself."

"Bullshit," he spat out. His eyebrows were drawn together; it was the first time she'd noticed him get angry. "Why the hell would you think I'd distract you?"

"Because you're distracting." Her excuse sounded lame even to her own ears. She looked down at her hands for just a moment to avoid his tense stare. When he didn't say anything, she lifted her gaze to his. "I'm sorry."

"For what?"

"You're not going to give me an inch, are you?" Now she was getting angry. She'd sincerely apologized and he wanted more. Ever since she realized years ago that she would never please her parents, she'd become extremely stingy with her apologies as they'd never gotten her anywhere before. She still felt responsible for her brother's disappearance, and she wouldn't stop atoning for her mistake, but she no longer apologized for it.

"It has nothing to do with me giving you anything. People could die because of what Maverick is doing. That young agent's brother almost did die. We have the ability to find the object to lock up Maverick and you've been wasting time. Even when we find the mirrors, it will still take time for Kate to forge the lock. I want to know that we're on the same page."

She breathed in slowly through her nose before letting it out. "I truly am sorry that I misled you and sent you to San Francisco."

"And what about taking off yesterday so we couldn't look for the second mirror? Or for trying to take off today?"

"Yes, I'm sorry for those things too," she said, looking him directly in the eyes. Apologies didn't mean anything if they weren't sincere, and she hoped he could see that she was. "I won't do it again."

Isabella gasped when Reece was in his seat one second and gone the next. Before she could even look around, Reece was standing at her side. She shoved her chair back, knocking it to the ground as she stood.

Reece looked down at the chair. It righted itself before he took a step toward her, coming close enough she could smell his familiar citrus scent. She didn't know if it was his body wash or a cologne, but she could become addicted to it. Maybe when Maverick was gone and she and Reece went their separate ways, she'd have to hang out in the produce section in the grocery store every now and then to get her fix.

"Isabella, can you please look at me?" he asked softly.

Jerking her chin up, she took a step back to see his eyes since she was so much shorter than him. She hadn't realized that she'd been staring at his chest.

"Okay." He nodded. "I believe you."

It took her a moment to remember what he was talking about... her promise. That she wouldn't take off again. "Thank you." That almost felt too easy. He hadn't berated her or gone on about her poor choices. But then, he wasn't her parents. Maybe it was okay for both of them to move on, but she didn't know if he really had. He said he forgave her, but either he didn't believe her, or he'd decided to be strictly professional, because when he asked her to look at him, it was Isabella number four. She should be happy to have no distractions, so why wasn't she? He brought out emotions in her she hadn't felt in a long time, and that confused her.

"Do you know where we can look next?" he asked.

Reece was right; people might die if they didn't find the mirrors, and soon. Maybe she was the one who needed to get serious. "My magic is still calling me back to the library. Maybe there was something else in the book that I missed."

He gripped her wrist lightly and turned it, looking at her watch. "It's not even lunch time yet, so Viktor should be there. Let's go."

With her skin still tingling from his touch, she flashed as soon as he did.

REECE SAT BACK in his chair and rotated his head from side to side, stretching out his neck. They'd been in the library for hours and hadn't found a single clue to lead them to the next mirror.

"Ugh." Isabella thunked her head down on the table before lifting her chin just enough to look up at him through her lashes. "I had no problem finding out where to go for the first mirror, so I don't understand why I can't find something now." She flopped her head back on the table and closed her eyes.

He wanted to haul her out of her chair and call her cupcake before he kissed the fuck out of her. But he wouldn't. The softening her up strategy hadn't worked, so he was back to being serious. The approach had gotten her to apologize and work with him, so he'd stick with it for a while longer. "You'll find something. Viktor said there are books in a different room we could try."

She sat up and focused her beautiful brown eyes on him. Their warmth was almost enough to make him want to change his strategy back to softening up. Instead, he sent some magic throughout his body to cool himself off and get rid of the almost permanent hard-on he had around her.

"I think whatever I'm feeling is in this room. It seems to be strongest here." She got up and walked over to the shelves on the back wall. "It's even stronger on this wall."

Reece looked down at the books scattered across the table, doing a quick tally. "We've looked through nine, but I think only three were from there. We can look through the ones here again in case we missed something, or you could try seeing if something else calls to you."

"I'll check again." Isabella walked to one end of the wall and raised her arm, stretching it above her head to reach the books on the top shelf. Slowly, she dragged her fingers along the books' spines. She would stop occasionally and flatten her hand on the book, like she'd done when they'd found the prophecy, before moving on.

"Nothing," she said over ten minutes later when she'd reached the end of the top row. She shook out her arm before turning around to use her other hand and going back the way she'd come, checking the next row.

By the time Isabella got to the bottom row, she'd been at it for almost an hour. She looked defeated, and her shoulders sagged with what had to be exhaustion. He wished there was something he could do, but it was her specialty that was going to find the clue, not his.

"Ow." She was on her knees trying to rotate her arm so she could drag her fingers along the books while scootching forward. "This is awkward."

Finally, something he could help with. He walked over to her and extended his hand to pull her up. "Let me help." When she stood to the side, he directed his magic to the shelf and carefully pulled the books from their perch. An entire row of books now floated in the air, their bindings still perfectly aligned. Raising the books to waist level, he rotated them all at once so their spines faced up. "How's that?"

She clapped her hands like a little schoolgirl, albeit a tired one. "That works."

Reece felt a sense of pride for making something easier for her, but he wanted to do so much more for her. He kept his focus on the books as Isabella did her thing, brushing her fingers over the spines. It wasn't much of a strain on his magic, but he didn't want to lose concentration and have all the books tumble to the floor.

When Isabella was halfway along the row, she stopped. "This book is calling to me." She turned sideways to look at him. "Can I pull it out, or will all of them fall?"

He chuckled. "Good question, and one I don't know the answer to. Can you take note of the book and finish checking the rest first? Then I'll put them back and we can pull out whatever you need."

"Okay, but just curious, is that all you can do? Move an

object? Ah… I mean, it's cool, I just wondered if you can do anything more with objects."

"I'm very skilled," he teased. "You'll just have to wait and see."

By the time Isabella was finished she'd found two more books she thought were worth checking.

Reversing his earlier movements, Reece flipped the entire row of books until the spines were facing forward. Once he lowered the row, it was easy to slide them all back onto the shelf. Not a single book fell out of place.

Isabella grabbed the three books she'd identified and brought them to the table, pushing the ones they'd already checked to the side. She handed one of the new books to him and started on another. They'd decided earlier that she would still check each book to see if it called to her magic, but he could at least look through them for anything that might stand out.

"Come and look at this," Isabella said.

They were each on their second of the new books and hadn't found anything yet. Reece walked around the table and peered at the book over Isabella's shoulder.

"Look at this," she said, pointing at a verse on the page. "Does it move when you read it?"

He leaned closer and forced himself to ignore Isabella's apricot and vanilla scent and focus on the page. As soon as he concentrated on the words, they moved as if rearranging themselves. But it was more than that. "They're updating, just like the prophecy."

"Exactly. Do you see a reference to New Orleans?"

Reece read the passage again, this time to the end, and saw what she was talking about. "Now I do. It's referring to an antique store in New Orleans." He pulled out the chair beside her and sat and picked up his phone that he'd left lying on the table. "There's more than eighty," he said after doing a quick Google search on antique shops in the city. "And that doesn't mean the list I checked was even up to date. Do you think you can narrow it down?"

Isabella laid her palm flat on the page and closed her eyes. When she opened them, she was smiling. "Yes, I think I know which one it is."

Reece lifted his hand to cup her cheek, remembering his new approach at the last minute. Slapping his hand on the table, he said, "Excellent, Isabella," and hoped she bought the switch.

The smile on her face drooped a little before she busied herself with tidying up the books.

When they'd put all the books away, Reece shoved his phone into his back pocket and gently grasped Isabella's wrist like he had earlier in the day to look at her watch. He knew he could have easily checked his phone for the time, but he wanted an excuse to touch her. His new serious approach just might kill him. "It's almost dinner time. Want to head home and grab a bite to eat? The shop will probably be closed so we can wait until tomorrow morning." Not having a reason to keep holding her wrist, he finally let it go.

"Sure."

Reece didn't see Viktor but waved at the person manning the desk and headed upstairs to the main entrance. They were both quiet while they walked along the outside of the building toward the alley in the back.

If it wasn't dark, Reece would have thought it was just like the day before when they'd flashed to find the first mirror. "Will I find you at home when I get there or am I going to have to hunt you down in a distant city?" He grinned as he teased her. He couldn't help it—he could only be so serious.

"Haha, Mr. Williams. Yes, I'll see you at home. Want to meet at The Magic Plate?"

"Sounds good. Do you know about the back hallway near the kitchen you can flash into?"

"Yes. I've used it before."

"Great. I'll—" Someone flashed in front of Isabella, and he heard her gasp just as a hand clamped around Reece's upper arm, preventing him from flashing.

*U*sing her magic, Isabella pushed it through her arm and shoulder, temporarily giving her extra strength, and ripped her arm from the guy's hold.

She was about to flash when Reece spun, taking a guy out by the legs. Another man grabbed Reece's arms from behind just as the first guy jumped up and plowed his fist into Reece's stomach. He doubled over, sucking in air.

"Now, now, Reece, we just want to talk," Mateo said as he walked out from the shadows. He ignored Isabella, not even glancing her way.

A heavy feeling settled in the pit of her stomach, and she shivered as a sudden cold spread through her core. She'd been searching for her brother for years and had imagined their reunion a hundred different ways. None of them were even close to this.

Since she hadn't seen him in years, she knew logically that he'd be older, but in her mind, he was still shaggy-haired and barely a teenager. The man standing in front of her looked hardened and dangerous. His hair was cropped so close to his head it was barely a black shadow on his scalp, and the backs of his hands were covered in dark tattoos. Her brother's deep brown eyes that used to be so like her own, looked bottomless, as if all the life had been sucked out of them. "Mateo," she said in almost a whisper as he walked closer.

Mateo sneered at her. "Mateo is dead. My name is Eddie."

Isabella didn't know how to act around this person her brother had become. This was not the happy reunion of her dreams. Maybe he didn't recognize her. The thought created an ache deep in her soul as well as a small taste of hope. "I'm Isabella. Your sister."

He sneered again, the corner of his lip lifting like he was looking at someone far beneath his station. "I know who you are." He jerked his head to the man still behind Isabella and he grabbed both her arms. The thug tightened his grip and pulled her arms backward, straining her shoulders. She hissed from the pain but focused on Mateo. He turned away from her and faced Reece, who was standing upright now, flanked by two of Mateo's men.

"Reece, your family has become fucking annoying." Mateo kicked Reece's foot with enough force that he teetered sideways and would have fallen if Mateo's goons weren't holding him up. "How is your sister? Too bad her boyfriend Lucas had to die." He laughed at his own sick joke.

Her brother's dismissal cut Isabella to the bone, but she pushed it aside for now. She wouldn't give up on him, but she needed to help Reece and get both of them out of there.

Since being in Blue Mountain, she'd heard the stories of everything that had happened to the Williams's cousins. Mateo was talking about Jo and Simon, but Simon wasn't dead. Although she hadn't seen Simon's magic specialty in action, she'd heard he had the ability to transform into someone else. He'd been undercover as Lucas when he'd met Eddie. Lucas's death had been faked and apparently faked well since Mateo believed it. Maybe she could use that to their advantage.

Isabella watched Reece and tried not to focus on the person who had become a stranger as he taunted them. She needed a plan to help Reece.

"Jo was a cute little thing. It would have been great to tap that," Mateo said as he continued to goad Reece. But he wasn't taking the bait and kept his eyes aimed at the ground.

Her brother had changed but some traits were innate, and she knew it wouldn't be long before he lost his temper. Mateo had always hated being ignored and would expect Reece to respond to him. In all the years she'd been looking for her brother, she'd been so solely focused on finding him that she'd forgotten little things about him. Or maybe she'd figured he'd have matured and outgrown them. Like his temper. It could go off like a shot when his trigger was pulled, and she could see it about to happen now by the way his shoulders bunched up.

"You think you can ignore me, hijo de puta? Or should I say motherfucker? Your buddy Lucas liked that term better. But in the end, it didn't matter what he liked because he's dead." Eddie lifted his chin to his man on Reece's right. The goon let go of Reece's arm and raised his own elbow, plowing it into the side of Reece's head. He flung sideways into the other goon, who shoved him back upright.

"Ready to answer me, motherfucker?"

Reece's head hung forward and he was breathing heavily. Blood dripped into his eyes from where the blow had split the skin on his scalp, but Reece didn't react.

Needing to say something, she opened her mouth just as Mateo reared back and smashed his fist into Reece's stomach.

"Nooooooooo!" she screamed, but it was too late. Reece

doubled over, his shoulders rounding as the contents of the late lunch he'd had with her spewed onto the pavement.

"Fuck! You puked on my shoes!" Eddie yelled as he jumped back. Throwing out his arm, he waved low to the ground, magically cleaning his worn high tops with one sweep.

Isabella yearned to go to Reece and help him in some way as he struggled to suck in air. She squirmed in the goon's grip, but he wouldn't let go.

"Hold him the fuck up," Eddie said, directing one of the guys holding Reece. The goon on the right fisted his hand in Reece's hair and jerked him up.

Reece's eyes were just slits, his face covered in blood, vomit, and snot, as he faced Eddie.

Eddie snorted, but the laugh contained no humor. "That packed a punch, didn't it?" He made a fist and waved it in front of Reece's face. "Look, not even a bruise on my knuckles. That's courtesy of Maverick. He gave me a bit of juice to help me out. And see my guy here?" Eddie tilted his head to the guy on the left. "He said you used to play college football with him. Well, now he plays for me. Another nice little trick from Maverick. And don't try to reason with them because these two will do whatever I want."

Eddie paused as if contemplating what to do next. Isabella couldn't stand it anymore. In her mind, the guy standing in front of her wasn't her brother and she couldn't think of him as Mateo. She didn't care what happened to her; she didn't have people who loved her and who would miss her if something happened to her. Reece did. She couldn't let Eddie hurt Reece anymore, or worse, kill him.

She thought about what Viktor had taught her about getting out of a hold. Nothing was exactly the same as when they'd practiced, but she could use the principles. Pulling in as much energy as she could, she called up her magic. "Leave him the fuck alone!" she yelled at Eddie at the same time she sent her magic outward. The goon holding her screamed as an electrical current went straight through him, knocking him off his feet.

Isabella ran toward Reece and extended her arms. With her magic in her palms, she slammed a hand into the chest of each of the goons holding Reece. The impacts jarred her shoulders, but she didn't care. As they released their holds and flew backward, Reece crumpled to his knees, his hands jamming into the pavement.

She dropped to her knees beside him. "Reece, can you flash?"

A kick connected with Isabella's ribcage, and she cried out as she fell to the side, her head hitting the ground.

"You fucking bitch!" Eddie ground out as he grabbed a fistful of her hair and yanked her up to her feet. Her ribs screamed at the movement. She gasped for air, then hissed through her teeth as the action made it worse. "You're even more annoying than him and his fucking crew." Eddie pushed his foot into Reece's side, knocking him over. "You've been on my tail for years."

"I'm sorry," she said quietly. It was a lie, but she would have said anything in that moment to appease him.

He released her hair with a shove and she stumbled backward before catching herself. The goons were standing now and walked over to Eddie, joining the third man. All of them stood at ease, as if waiting for orders. Their eyes looked unfocused, and their expressions were neutral. She shivered at the thought of being under anyone's control like that.

Eddie crouched and laid his hand on Reece's shoulder, almost in a brotherly gesture. "Thanks for the fun," he said before standing and flashing away with his goons.

Isabella rushed to Reece, dropping to her knees. She blew out small pants to control her pain. Waving her hand over

Reece's face, she washed away the blood, snot, and vomit so she could check his head wound.

"Reece? Can you hear me?" When he didn't move, she put her hand on his shoulder to give him a small shake. "Reece?"

His chest was moving with his breaths, but they were shallow, like hers, probably due to the pain. A sense of panic started in her chest and rose. Swallowing against the bile rising in her throat, she touched his shoulder again.

"Reece, wake up. Please! I'm not a good healer. Please talk to me!" Shivering from the cold, she realized she was probably in shock, which meant it would be even worse for Reece. She conjured a blanket and laid it over him. He still didn't move, and she realized she needed help. Pulling out her phone, she called one of the only two people she knew who could flash with someone else.

"Knight."

"Jack, help Reece," she yelled. "Behind the library."

When he didn't say anything, she brought the phone in front of her face to see if the connection had dropped.

"What happened?" Jack said as he arrived on the other side of Reece and knelt beside him.

Gripping the phone in her hand, her next words rushed out. "Eddie and his goons beat him up, they punched him so hard in the stomach he threw up, and they hit him in the head, and they—"

"It's okay, we'll take care of him," Jack said, interrupting her word vomit. Then he scooped Reece up into his arms and was gone.

"Isabella, can you flash?"

She whipped her gaze up from where she was still kneeling on the ground. Meredith crouched beside her. Isabella had been so focused on Reece that she hadn't noticed her arrival. "I think so."

Meredith stood and offered her a hand. As Isabella was pulled up, she cried out, panting against the pain.

"Can I touch you?" Meredith asked softly.

Still panting, Isabella could only give a small nod. When hands landed on her ribs, she sucked in a huge breath at the pain that rocketed through her. But then the pain subsided and breathing became easier.

Meredith huffed out a small laugh. "I'm always thankful that we can heal, but that first bit is a bitch, isn't it?"

Isabella nodded again and tried to relax as Meredith continued to heal her.

"I think you're good now. You okay to flash?"

"Yes, thank you, Meredith. Where would Jack have taken Reece?"

"Probably to our apartment. You want to meet me there?"

"Yes." As soon as she'd answered her, Meredith flashed away and Isabella followed. She needed to know that Reece was okay.

Reece opened his eyes and looked around. He recognized Meredith and Jack's spare room and jerked to a sitting position. "No! Not again!"

"Oh, thank god!"

Reece looked to the side just as Isabella got up from a chair in the corner of the room. She walked over, sat on the edge of the bed, and laid one hand on his thigh. When she met his eyes, she removed her hand and put it in her lap with the other. Both hands twisted a cloth. Her version of a fidget device, he figured.

"How'd I get here?"

"I called Jack and he flashed you back here." She lowered her gaze to her fingers. "I'm not a very good healer. It's never been my specialty, and I was so worried you were going to die."

He reached out and put his large hand over both of hers, stilling her movements. "Ah... Isabella." The endearment "cupcake" almost slipped from his lips, but he caught himself just in time. The serious approach was kind of working, so he'd keep using it for now. "Please don't think you need to be a good healer. Lots of people can heal, but what you can do is truly special."

She looked up and he spotted tears rimming her eyes. It gutted him to see her like this. As always when he was around her, he wanted to haul her into his arms. Usually to kiss her, give her pleasure, and be enveloped in her scent. But this time, he just wanted to comfort her. There was still so much about her that he didn't know, but he expected that her life hadn't been easy.

"I'm okay. Don't cry for me," he said softly.

Her tears didn't fall, and when she blinked, they were gone and she focused on her fingers again. He wondered how often she'd used her magic to dry her own tears. If she'd let him in completely, he could be the one to dry them or make sure they didn't happen at all.

The afternoon's events came back to him, at least the ones from before he passed out. Eddie and his thugs had overpowered him. Once again, he'd been weak. Maybe he wasn't the right guy to dry Isabella's tears after all.

"Isabella? Can you look at me?"

She lifted her dry eyes to him. "I don't know why I'm crying. You're fine now."

"I am." Pulling up his legs, careful not to hit Isabella, he got out of the bed. He hated lying in bed. It reminded him too much of a time when that was all he could do. He moved from side to side and stretched, feeling for any pain. Standing upright, he looked at her. "I'm guessing Jack healed me because I feel great," he said.

"Shit, I didn't ask," he said quietly. Kneeling in front of her, he rested his hands on her knees. "You were hurt, weren't you?"

"Yes, I think Ma—Eddie broke my ribs, but Meredith healed them. She also healed the electrical burns on my arms and palms."

Reece felt anger well inside of him. "He burned you too? Breaking bones wasn't enough?"

She laughed and smiled at him. "No, I burned myself."

"How?"

"I got the burns on my arms from sending an electrical charge through myself into the guy holding me. I'm sure that was a big shock to him."

"Isabella, did you just make a pun?"

Her grin matched the one that was surely on his face, and he wanted to remember it for forever. She didn't smile or laugh often, and he suspected it was because there hadn't been much that was joyous or funny in her life.

"Yes, I did." Her pride was as bright as her smile and then she sobered. "I got the burns on my palms because I sent a ton of magic through them into the guys holding you. It got them to back off, but then it made it worse."

"Why would you say that?"

"Ma—Eddie's always had a temper. I was trying to stop him from hurting you even more. When you didn't respond to him like he wanted you to, I knew he'd start taking his anger out on you."

Reece knew from the others who'd encountered Eddie how evil he could be. Even Isabella had seen it, but he expected she was still holding on to the image of the little boy she used to know. It was so easy to ignore red flags when you loved someone. Not that he had personal experience with that—he'd been so lucky with the people who were in his life. But he knew from hearing stories from others that love could truly be blind.

He brought his hand up from where it rested on her thigh and rubbed his knuckles across her cheek briefly. "So instead you had him take his anger out on you?"

"No, I didn't… I mean, I wasn't trying to get him to do that." Her voice was so quiet, he leaned in closer to hear her, his lips almost touching hers. "I just wanted him to stop hurting you."

Rocking back on his heels, he stood and took a step back. If he hadn't, he would have kissed her. He also needed time to think. "Do you know what Eddie wanted?"

"No, he didn't say anything about wanting something."

"Don't you think it's strange that he met us in the alley only to hurt us? What could his end goal have been? To frighten us? But why?"

"I don't know." She wound the cloth around her fingers until they were white and then released it before starting again.

He wanted to go over to her and find a way to soothe her nerves, but he knew if he touched her again, he wouldn't want to stop.

"Oh." Her hands stilled. "I think I just assumed that Eddie wanted to know where the mirrors were, but he didn't ask. Do you think he knows that we have one of them?"

"He could, but then how would he have found out about them to begin with?" Reece paced in the small space for a moment before turning back to Isabella. After Eddie had punched him in the gut, he'd been so overwhelmed with pain that he'd stopped thinking about anything. Then he'd passed out. "I can't remember everything that happened, but did Eddie say that Maverick gave him power?"

She nodded. "He used the word 'juice', and I think that meant he has some of the power from the magic box. He even pointed out that his knuckles weren't bruised or swollen, but he could have healed them with his magic."

"I'm guessing you're right about the box." When he tried to remember details from the incident, all he could focus on was the excruciating pain. "Did he say something about the guys with him?"

"Yes, he said you played college ball with one of them. All

three of them looked like vacant zombies… oh, and he said that it was another nice little trick from Maverick. I'm not sure what he meant, but it was probably mind control, like Frank had talked about."

Reece paced in the small space again and the glow from the clock on the dresser caught his attention. It was the same clock that he'd seen when he'd first woken up from the coma. He looked up at the closed curtains, light from the street-lamps coming through the slit between them. "It's only seven forty-five, so I wasn't out for long."

"Ah…" Isabella hesitated. "It's seven forty-five in the morning. It took Jack a long time to heal you last night, and then he'd said you needed to sleep. He and Meredith said it was okay that I stayed."

The fact that he was out for so long and weak was a heavy pill to swallow. He leaned back against the wall as he digested the information. Eddie and his goons had over-powered him, though he knew four to one wasn't a fair fight. Reece hadn't even stood a chance. He'd bet Sweet Magic that he knew more about magic than Eddie did, yet Reece hadn't been fast enough to call up anything useful. Because of that, not only did he get hurt, but Isabella could have died.

"Thank you for staying."

She nodded and then stood. He straightened, pulling away from the wall. Awkwardness fell over them both. The need to pull her into his arms hadn't lessened, but now he needed to prepare for their trip to New Orleans.

He'd spend a couple of hours reviewing the spells he'd cataloged to see if there was anything he could have used. Then he'd hit the gym. Getting in an extra workout wouldn't make a difference to his physical strength, but it would tell him whether he was fully healed.

"I think we should head to New Orleans tomorrow

morning. That will give us today to prepare. You good with that?"

"Sure." She seemed hesitant but looked at the door and then pointed to it. "I… I'll just go to my apartment. Maybe we could meet for dinner to go over a plan?"

"Seven at The Magic Plate?"

"Okay."

"And…" He waited until she turned around and faced him again. "Thank you for saving me, Isabella."

She nodded, and instead of leaving through the door, she flashed away.

Reece slumped onto the bed. He needed to go back to his own apartment, but first he'd find Jack and Meredith and thank them for saving him. Again. Then he'd hit the books and the gym.

Yesterday he'd broken his promise to himself—he'd been weak. And what was worse was that he'd been not just physically weak, but magically as well. Now that they had a monumental and urgent task, he couldn't let weakness get in the way. If he did, it could possibly lead to someone's death. He had to do better.

ISABELLA SHUT the laptop and tossed it onto the couch cushions beside her. She'd been researching antique shops in New Orleans and she was pretty sure she knew which one to go to. She'd also responded to some clients, letting them know that she was busy, but she'd get back to them soon.

The searches and emails had wasted a couple of hours and kept her mind busy, but now she had too much time to think. She reached down to her backpack sitting on the floor and pulled out a journal with a plain brown cover.

She ran her fingers over the worn cover and then opened it, revealing a title page where she'd written her name. The girly-looking cursive writing made her smile. She'd been in her teens and so full of hope when she'd gotten the journal. At the time, she had planned to write down all her adventures and how she was going to change the world by helping one person at a time with their health goals. She'd written about wanting to go to college and then later about being accepted. It wasn't a journal she wrote in every day. Instead, she'd kept it for big news items, thinking that one day she would look back and see how many huge milestones she'd reached in her life.

Flipping through the pages, she stopped at the last entry. It was written nine years ago—the day she'd been accepted into a master's program. Her excitement practically leapt off the page.

The next day her parents had called to tell her Mateo was missing and she needed to come home and look for him. If she'd been home more and watching him, he never would have left. That's what her parents had said. They blamed her for Mateo's disappearance. In their eyes, it didn't matter that they were the parents; she should have done more.

Turning to the back, she came to the section where she'd taped photos to several pages. Mateo was in each photo, sometimes alone and sometimes with her or their parents. His hair was curly and shaggy and hung in his eyes but he didn't seem to care.

When she'd looked at the photos in the past, all she could see was his happiness. That hadn't changed, except for one photo. Maybe she was now looking at it through the eyes of a sister who had been beaten by her brother. The photo had been taken at Christmas time. There were gifts and wrapping paper strewn around in the background. She and her parents had spoiled Mateo, like they always had. Her mother had wanted a photo with Mateo, and Isabella had been tasked to take it. Standing on either side of Mateo, her parents had their arms around him as they smiled widely for the camera.

Isabella ran her finger over the image and wondered how she'd never seen it before. Mateo's expression was more of a sneer than an actual smile. He'd been upset earlier because he hadn't gotten the game console he'd wanted for Christmas. He'd asked for two, so their dad had picked out one and bought it. Mateo had wanted both. Her mom went to the sales the next day and bought the other console.

Mateo had been selfish and demanding, but perhaps that hadn't been his fault. If their parents hadn't always given in to him, he would have learned he couldn't have everything, just like she had. Being so much older than her brother, she'd lived a different life than he had. When she was young, her parents were still working on their careers and didn't have much money. Her parents had explained that there was an unspoken rule among magics that they didn't conjure money —it was serialized and like stealing. Instead, Isabella had learned to be thankful for what she had.

She closed the journal and put it back in the inside pocket of her backpack. Having a lightbulb moment that Mateo was selfish didn't change anything. He might not have turned out that way if she and her parents hadn't spoiled him. She had to keep her hope that she could still save him. Let him know that he was loved.

Yesterday he'd been under Maverick's influence, so maybe that cruelty came from being mind-controlled. Jack and the rest of the council members were looking into ways to reverse the mind control and lock away the evil magic. And when they did, she'd make sure that they helped Mateo. Her brother was not the man called Eddie who she'd seen yesterday. She'd make sure people saw that.

A quick glance at her watch told her she had enough time

to get in a workout and shower before she had to meet Reece.

When she was changed and ready for the gym, she flashed to it, landing in the hallway. Eighties punk rock was already blasting inside. Others used the gym, but she knew it was Reece inside. Sometime in the last few couple of weeks she'd built a connection with him and now she could sense him.

Pulling on the door handle, she was about to go inside but stopped. She needed to be honest with herself. Before she'd even changed for a workout, she knew where Reece was and she'd wanted to be with him.

Instead of a distraction, he was becoming the person she wanted to talk to. When she'd sat in the corner of Meredith's spare bedroom during the night and watched Reece sleep, she knew she wanted more with him. But she hadn't given up on rescuing her brother either. Sometime since yesterday, her goal had changed from finding Mateo to saving him. She didn't know if she could save Mateo and have Reece too, but she was going to try.

With her resolve in place, she pulled open the gym door and sent a thought out into the universe—a hope that she wouldn't ever be in a situation where she'd have to choose between the two of them.

Inside the gym, the music was almost deafening. Reece was sitting on a workout bench doing dumbbell curls. She wanted to just stand and watch him, but she couldn't even hear herself think.

She walked over and stood in front of him. It only took a moment before he looked up. She moved her mouth as if speaking, but didn't talk, hoping he'd get the not-so-subtle hint. A moment later, the music lowered a few thousand decibels.

"Thanks. It was a bit loud."

Reece put the weight down but didn't stand. When he

looked up, she wanted to brace her hands on his shoulders and lean down and smell him. Not in a creepy way, but to see if his combination of sweat and citrusy bodywash had the same effect on her that it had the other day.

"I'm glad you found me."

"I wasn't looking for you." It was true, she hadn't had to look for him, but she still wanted to be with him. Not that she'd say that out loud.

He chuckled. "What I meant was, I wanted to talk to you and say I'm sorry, Isabella."

"Why are you sorry?" He hadn't done anything to be sorry for, but that wasn't what she really wanted to ask him. If she had the guts, she'd ask him why he no longer called her cupcake. It was funny how a nickname that at first annoyed her was something she craved to hear now that it was gone. That was Isabella number nine. He'd called her by her full name twice this morning—numbers seven and eight.

"I was so lost in my own thoughts this morning that I didn't even ask how you're feeling."

She frowned and inched closer to him, letting his scent drift out over her. "I'm fine. I thought I told you that Meredith healed me."

"You did. I meant about your brother. It must have been difficult to see him."

"It was. He wasn't like I remember... I mean, I knew he'd look older, but I didn't expect him to be a stranger. I know he was being controlled by Maverick, but..." She let her words trail off; what else could she say? Should she tell him that even though Mateo almost killed him, she wasn't giving up on her brother? She couldn't say that because he might not trust her to follow through on finding the object. But she would; she just wanted to do both. "I'd rather not talk about him right now."

Going on pure need, she leaned over and braced her

hands on his shoulders like she'd wanted to. Standing, she was a few inches taller than him. She tilted her head down but didn't ask for what else she wanted. If he rejected her again, it just might break her.

"Ah, cupcake, you're killing me."

A warmth spread through her as he finally broke the Isabella streak, but he still didn't make a move. She froze, wondering if she should back up.

His hands landed on her hips, and when he pushed her back and stood, that warmth cooled off a little.

Lifting her chin, he looked into her eyes. "Cupcake, I want you, but I won't be used. You have to let me give to you like I wanted to in your apartment."

She nodded and went up on her tiptoes, brushing her lips across his. "Yes."

When he returned the kiss, she opened to him and felt herself melt a little inside. He wrapped one hand around the back of her neck and the other on her butt to lift her up. Winding her legs around his hips, she cupped his cheeks to bring him down to her.

He teased her with his mouth, nipping and licking with gentle caresses, but she didn't want that. She wanted him to let go and give her everything he had. She wanted him to possess her. "Reece," she said against his lips. "Leave tender until later. Right now, I want you too much for that."

Moving his hand from her neck to under her butt, he cradled her in both hands and walked over to the far corner of the room. "Nuh uh. I want to cherish you, remember? You agreed to accept what I give."

He turned his head, and she followed his gaze, seeing a weight bench move across the floor until it was almost against the wall. She looked over his shoulder and realized that they couldn't be seen from the door.

"I locked the door," he said as he lowered her to the bench

and dropped to his knees in front of her. Bracing his hands on either side of her on the bench, he leaned over and kissed her again. She forgot all about rushing as he devoured her mouth with his and then moved lower, trailing light kisses along her jaw and neck.

She squirmed on the bench, trying to get some relief from the tension building in her core. "Please, Reece."

"I'll get there, cupcake, just let me take my time." He moved back up and took her lips in another passionate but slow kiss. When he pulled back, he put his hands on her tank top. "Can I?"

"Yes, yes, take it off."

In the next second, her tank top and sports bra were gone, and her nipples pebbled at the feel of his breath on her skin. He sucked one nipple into his mouth while he pinched the other one, and she arched up, wanting more.

He teased her for ages until she couldn't stop squirming on the bench, aching for some relief. "You trust me, cupcake?"

"Yes!" She did trust Reece, but in that moment, she would have told him anything he wanted to hear.

A cool breeze washed over her, and she realized he'd removed her yoga pants and panties. Finally.

"Grip the bench with both hands," he ordered, and she didn't hesitate to follow his order.

He'd left several inches between the bench and the wall so she was able to lean back. Reece lifted her leg and draped it over his shoulder and then did the same with the other one. She was completely open to him and so vulnerable, but all she wanted was his mouth on her most sensitive parts.

It was like he could read her mind because he lowered his head and licked her slowly. He didn't touch her clit as he used his mouth to tease and drive her higher. At one point, she couldn't hold onto the bench any longer and gripped his hair instead. When he hit a spot just so, she tugged his hair. They developed a silent communication system, and he was a great listener.

When he finally inserted one finger and then two, she thought she was going to fly off the bench from the amazing sensation. Without missing a beat with his mouth, he placed one hand on her stomach and applied a delicious amount of pressure, keeping her in place.

Reece went on pleasuring her for what seemed like forever. Her groans and breathing competed with the music in the room, a heavy beat pulsing in her core. When he slowed down his movements, her breathing matched it, and then he gave her clit all his attention, as if he'd been waiting for just the right time.

Her body revved back up and then stiffened as the most intense orgasm she'd ever had ripped through her. She screamed his name as the orgasm took over. She'd never believed it when people said they'd seen stars behind their lids, but she could have sworn she came close.

"Cupcake?" She looked down her body to see Reece grinning at her. He lowered one of her legs to the ground but somehow supported her weight so she didn't ooze to the floor in a puddle. Next, he held out his hand and a towel appeared in his palm. Gently, he cleaned her with the warm cloth, and she closed her eyes. Everything he did just felt so intimate and tense, but in the most amazing way.

A moment later, she flung her eyes open as she felt material and realized she was clothed again. He'd dressed her and the towel he'd used was gone. Holding her by the waist, he lifted her up and waited until she was steady on her feet. Cupping her cheeks, he gave her a quick kiss. "Thank you for being vulnerable with me, cupcake. Now we should get going."

"What?" Reece was moving too fast. She was still coming

down from the best orgasm of her life and he already had her dressed and was thanking her and moving on.

Reece took her wrist and turned it so she could see her watch. She gasped when she realized he'd pleasured her for more than an hour; she'd lost all track of time. "Meredith and Jack are meeting us for dinner at The Magic Plate so we can talk about what happened yesterday. We'll need to hurry if we're going to have time to shower and change." He leaned down and brushed his lips against hers. Then the music shut off abruptly. "I'll meet you in the restaurant in thirty minutes."

He flashed away while she was still standing there trying to get her bearings. Reece had given her more than she'd ever asked for. Not just the orgasm, but his attention and care. As she flashed back to her apartment, she hoped once more that she'd never have to pick between him and her brother.

16

"Thanks again, Brandon," Reece said as he shook hands with his old college buddy. He put his hand at the small of Isabella's back and guided her out of the shop. What he really wanted to do was hold her hand, but she was back to her serious self this afternoon.

They walked out onto the sidewalk and headed toward Royal Street. He dropped his hand, not having a reason to keep it there anymore. Then he decided, fuck it, he'd go for what he wanted, and reached for her hand, grasping it in his.

She gave their hands a glance but didn't say anything.

This was one of the first times he'd flashed somewhere not within or near his family's buildings and that wasn't a back alley or a park. New Orleans didn't have many alleys, thus why Jack had connected him with his old college buddy. "Flashing into Brandon's was a welcome change because I think I've been in more back alleys in the last six months than I have in my entire life," he said as he chuckled.

"Oh yes, the glamorous life of a magic. I guess I'm used to it. But it was nice being able to flash into the back of a shop and not have to worry about who would see us."

"That's another thing that's new to me. Well… two, actually—flashing into someone's place so we're not seen and learning that a guy I used to play college football with is magic."

She squeezed his hand. "Two guys."

"Who's the other one?"

"One of the guys with Eddie who's under his control."

Parts of that event were still blurry, but he remembered talking about it with Isabella afterward. "Right. I wonder how many other magics I knew while growing up and they couldn't let me know because of the spellbinding." Magic people were able to recognize their own kind, as long as they weren't spellbound, like he had been for decades.

She shrugged. "Probably a few."

They'd been walking without paying attention to the direction when they reached a cross street. "Do you know where to go?" he asked.

"I think so. According to Google, there are four antique shops on Royal Street in the French Quarter that all start with the letter H. I think I've narrowed it down to one, but I should be able to know for sure when we get there."

Her hand still in his, Reece went in the direction Isabella headed. "We're only going to walk by today so you can get a feel for it. But we won't approach the shop owner until tomorrow morning."

Isabella stopped in the middle of the sidewalk and they had to move to the side to avoid being run over. She frowned at him. "Why? I thought we were going to today."

"We're not at full strength after the long flash and I have no idea what we're going to find. We'll check it out today, get some food, and then a good night's sleep so we're at full strength."

"Do you really think there will be a problem?"

He tugged on her hand and they started walking again. "I

honestly don't know. I didn't expect to be attacked behind the library either." After the dinner with Jack and the others the night before, he'd gone back to his apartment and stewed about the attack. He went over everything that had happened and what he could have or should have done. Then he'd spent another hour pouring over spells before images of Isabella lying on the bench in the gym, moaning with pleasure, took over his thoughts.

"Last night Jack said he hadn't heard about anything specific in New Orleans. Maybe Maverick hasn't been able to control anyone here yet. Or maybe this area isn't part of his plan," she said, keeping her voice low.

"I'm sure he's interested in controlling everyone; he seems like that much of a narcissist and megalomaniac. I just want us to be prepared."

When she hesitated, he leaned down and gave her a soft kiss. "Please."

She sighed. "Okay."

As they walked along, they chatted about nothing in particular and looked in shop windows. Isabella was fascinated with the masks and their colorful feathers, stopping to look at every storefront that had them in the window.

She stopped again outside a small candy store. "The antique store is next."

"You said you could feel something if we walked by—will you know for sure if the mirror is in there?"

"It depends. I didn't feel anything specific at Mr. Pantenburg's, just that I knew we had to go in."

"Okay, let's walk by."

Isabella nodded and they walked up to the shop, looking in the window, feigning interest at the items displayed. Reece saw a few antique mirrors on a wall, but nothing that looked like the first one.

"I can feel it, this is it."

"Let's go." As they walked slowly by, Reece noted the shop hours on the door. "They open up at ten tomorrow morning."

She tugged on his hand and made a point of showing him her watch on the other wrist at him. "It's only three p.m. What are we going to do until tomorrow morning?"

He grinned and decided it was time to switch tactics again. "We're going to play tourist and have some fun."

She squinted at him as if she'd never heard the word *fun* before. "What kind of fun?"

"Oh, you'll see." Still holding her hand, he turned them around so they were heading back toward Canal Street. He'd only ever been to New Orleans once before years ago. But he knew his bakeries and just where to take her.

When they reached the bakery he'd had in mind, Isabella grinned at him. "You're going to love this," he said, pulling open the door with his free hand. The place was long and narrow with the pastry counter on one side and small tables along a lengthy bench seat on the other. It was airy, with a vibe that was somewhere between Art Deco and a nineteen-fifties diner.

"Do you know what you'd like to drink or do you trust me to order for you?" he asked her when they walked up to the display case.

The serious expression she'd worn so much over the last couple of days dropped away when she smiled at him.

"Well, if I can't trust a bakery owner, then who can I trust?"

"Fantastic." He rubbed his palms together in exaggeration at his delight and she laughed. Switching back to a softening her up approach was the one he preferred and it was work-ing. It gave him the opportunity to show her both sides of him.

A bakery clerk finished with a customer and walked up to them smiling. "Did I hear you say you own a bakery?"

"Yes, Sweet Magic in Blue Mountain, Colorado."

"Oh my god! I've heard all about your bakery. My cousin was there last month and said the cupcakes are to die for!" Reece felt a sense of pride that even with his illness in the last year, his bakery was still making a name for itself. Their comments also gave Isabella another glimpse into him; he wasn't just another muscular body—he was also a successful business owner.

The woman turned and called out to someone in the back, and a man sauntered out, wiping his hands on a cloth. "Honey, he owns Sweet Magic in Blue Mountain, the bakery my cousin was talking about last month."

Reece shook the man's hand when he extended it across the counter. They spoke about the baking business in general for a few minutes before he was able to divert the conversation. It wasn't the conversation he minded—he'd talk about his bakery all day—but he was worried Isabella would feel left out.

When he started to give his order, the woman waved a hand at him. "No, let me, please. I'll pick out something you'll both love."

"Thank you, that'd be great." Reece wasn't sure if he was excited to get the owner's picks or disappointed that he wouldn't be able to choose something for Isabella himself.

They picked up their coffees and desserts and said their goodbyes before moving to the back of the shop. There was one open table left at the end of the long line. Isabella scooted onto the banquette and Reece took the chair opposite her. He would have loved to sit beside her but there wasn't room.

She picked up her drink and took a tentative sip. "Mmm,

yum. The owner said this was a café au lait and not a latte; what's the difference?"

Reece took a sip of his own before answering—it was made to perfection. "There are different ways to make a café au lait but usually it's some form of coffee and heated milk combo. A latte is made with espresso, steamed milk, and milk froth. Although ordering a latte in an Italian café will get you a glass of plain milk, as the correct term is café latte."

She chuckled. "I'll have to remember that."

They sipped their coffees for a moment and then Reece picked up a beignet. "Take a bite," he said, holding it near her mouth and not giving her a chance to take it from him.

He watched as she bit into the pastry and then groaned as she chewed. Powdered sugar stuck to her lips, and if they were anywhere else, he would have licked it off himself.

Isabella used her tongue to lick off the extra sugar and Reece shifted in his seat, adjusting his pants. "Delicious," she said.

He needed to stop thinking about her lips. So as they drank their coffees and ate the pastries, he regaled her with the history of beignets and other pastries.

They waved at the owners and thanked them when they finally left, heading back out onto the street. Taking her hand in his again, he led them along the sidewalk to the hotel he'd had Jack book for the night.

When she stopped to look at another storefront with masks, he tugged on her hand and pulled open the shop's door with his other. "Come on."

Isabella tugged back, her expression wary. "No, no, we don't have to go in there."

"Yes, we do." She didn't put up any more resistance as they walked into the shop and were greeted immediately.

"Can I help you find something?" the woman asked.

Reece gave her his most charming smile. "Yes, we're looking to buy a mask."

Isabella tugged on his hand again and went on her tiptoes. "No, it's okay, I don't need one," she whispered as she leaned into him.

"Excuse us a moment," he said to the shop clerk and turned his back on her. He placed a soft kiss on Isabella's lips. "Sometimes need doesn't matter. I'd like to buy you one."

She nodded and glanced around the shop. "Can we look over there?"

"Of course." The clerk took them over to the section that Isabella had pointed to and pulled some masks down. As the clerk described the masks, giving the origin of each design and where they were made, Isabella tentatively touched one like she was in awe.

Isabella finally picked one out and he purchased it for her, refusing her offer to pay. She settled on a purple lace swan mask with side feathers. He wanted to see her wearing it with an elaborate dress at a costume party while she danced with him. The thought of seeing her like that in his arms had him making a mental note for Meredith. When everything with Maverick was over, he'd convince Meredith to start a new tradition of a yearly masquerade ball.

Several times on their way to the hotel, Isabella held up the clear bag holding the mask and glanced at it, a wistful look on her face.

The mask hadn't been expensive, and because magics could conjure most of what they needed, many had lots of money in investments. Although they hadn't spoken about it directly, Reece had heard Isabella talking to Morgana about what she charged her clients, so he knew she was not strapped for cash. So, why hadn't she wanted him to purchase it for her?

"Cupcake?" He pulled her out of the throngs of people. "Why did you hesitate so much to let me buy the mask?"

She looked down at the bag again before meeting his gaze. The smile he expected to see was gone, her expression serious. "I don't have a place to wear it."

"You don't need one. Put it on a shelf where you can see it and remember drinking café au lait and eating beignets."

"I don't have a shelf… I mean, I haven't had one. Not for a long time. I have some things in a storage unit back in San Diego, but it's been ages since I've even been there. For years, I've gone from place to place looking for Mateo while seeking objects for my clients. I pretty much live out of my backpack and conjure or buy whatever else I need."

The thought of her not having anywhere or anyone to call home saddened him. The idea for a third vow came to him. He wanted so much to change her situation and tell her that she'd always have a home with him and his family. But he didn't. Not yet. "Well, right now you have a shelf in your apartment, so you can put it there."

She smiled, but it didn't meet her eyes. As soon as he felt it was time, he'd make that third vow to himself.

17

Reece pulled back from Isabella, his hands caressing her arms as he gave her one more soft kiss on the lips before letting her go. "I'm going to give Jack a call to fill him in on what we're doing. I won't be long."

Isabella watched Reece go into their hotel suite's bedroom and finally moved away from the door.

Walking over to the spacious parlor, what Reece had called the sitting area when they arrived, she sat on the sofa. Absently fanning her fingers over the expensive material on the seat cushions, she looked around the room.

They were staying in a historic luxury hotel in the French Quarter. The light fixtures in the suite were chandeliers, and all the accents were gold, including the frame around an ornate-looking mirror. A light, yellow-colored wallpaper in vertical stripes covered the walls, and everywhere she looked screamed opulence.

When they were almost at the hotel to check in, Reece had explained that he'd asked Jack to book a suite. There was a separate bedroom and fold-out sofa, which Reece told her he'd take. After she'd propositioned him once and then had their little rendezvous in the gym yesterday, the fact that he hadn't assumed anything would happen between them spoke a lot to his character. He was not the muscle-bound himbo she'd accused him of being.

She winced as she remembered what she'd said in front of his friends and family. Definitely not her finest moment. Reece was so much more than he appeared, and he was a gentleman.

Before arriving at the hotel, he had conjured a small suitcase for each of them. He said he wanted them to appear as a loving couple getting away for a night. Although he hadn't said it, she knew he didn't want people to get the wrong impression of her. That she wasn't the type of woman a man took to a hotel just for a quick rendezvous, no matter how luxurious the venue was.

After they'd checked in, they'd each taken a shower and conjured clean clothes before heading back out for a late dinner. Reece took her to Bourbon Street and employed the same trick he used at the apartment building to get them on the reservation list. He was constantly full of surprises.

They'd feasted on jambalaya, and he'd entertained her with stories of growing up with his sister and two female cousins. As if by unspoken agreement, neither of them mentioned their brothers.

When they'd returned after a late dinner, they had only managed to get inside the room and shut the door before they'd reached for each other.

"I let Jack know that we're going to head back to the antique shop in the morning," Reece said as he walked back in, shaking her out of her thoughts of earlier in the evening.

She smiled when he came over and took her hands, pulling her to her feet.

"I want to do something."

She raised an eyebrow as her lips curved upward. "Oh really? And what is it you want to do, Mr. Williams?"

Bending down, he ran his tongue over the seam of her lips, and they parted for him as if they had a mind of their own. "If I'm reading you right, I want that, but not yet," he said. He laughed when she pouted.

It had been years since she'd been this teasing, almost carefree person. If it weren't for entries in her journal that showed this person had existed, she would have thought she'd suddenly transformed into someone new. For so long, she'd been serious and focused.

"I think you're going to like this," he said, lightly rubbing his knuckles along her cheek. When they were together, he was constantly touching her. If someone had asked her two months ago if she'd like someone touching her all the time, she would have said no. But then, she hadn't yet known Reece. "There's a rooftop pool, but it's closed for the night. I want you to flash up there. When you were taking a shower earlier, I checked it out and there aren't any cameras." An image of the rooftop in broad daylight floated into her mind. "Can you see it?" he asked.

"Yes. Now?"

He rubbed his knuckles on her cheek again and she practically melted into him. "Yes, I'll meet you up there."

Isabella flashed, making sure she landed off to the side so she didn't end up in the pool. Reece arrived at the same time and took her hand in his, leading her across the space. "I want to show you the city at night."

Her main concern had been avoiding getting wet so she hadn't yet looked around her. Skirting the lounge chairs lined up in rows, he led her to a wrought-iron railing that looked out over the city.

Moving behind her, his front cradling her back, he wrapped his arms around her waist.

"It's beautiful," she breathed out in a whisper. The view was amazing, but it was the feel of Reece around her, making her feel like she mattered, that made her breath hitch. They stood quietly for several minutes before she turned in his arms. "Thank you for showing me this... and for today."

"You're welcome, cupcake."

She went on her tiptoes and brushed his lips with hers. It was a slow kiss, a thank you kiss.

He pulled back and smiled, what she was coming to think of as his mischievous grin. "I didn't bring you up here only to see the lights." Taking a step back, he bowed in front of her, causing a giggle to bubble up. Then he swept his arm forward as if he was an old-fashioned courtier. Big band music started playing. "Will you give me the honor of having this dance, Ms. Flores?"

Putting her hand in his, she let him pull her into his arms. Reece started to dance, gliding her across the stone floor just as Frank Sinatra sang "The Way You Look Tonight." Isabella felt a swelling in her chest and knew she would remember this evening for the rest of her life.

As Reece held her and guided her over the makeshift dance floor, she soaked in the lyrics. When Sinatra sang about there being nothing but his love and how she looked, Isabella wished that was how Reece truly felt. She didn't want it to be just a random, romantic song he'd chosen.

With one of her hands in his and the other draped over his shoulder, she let her head rest on his chest. The entire world fell away, and she focused only on the feel of being in Reece's arms.

She felt cared for and protected in a way she never had before she'd met him. She would never have wished for her brother to have gone missing, but because he had, she'd ended up here. It made all her sacrifices over the last nine years worth it because they had brought her here, to this moment.

As the end of the song faded out, she dropped her hand from his shoulder, but Reece tightened his hold on her. "Not yet, cupcake," he whispered against her head. When the music started again, she put her hand back on his shoulder, and this time Elvis Presley crooned "Can't Help Falling in Love with You."

During the first song, she'd figured out the music was coming from Reece's phone in his back pocket. He'd been able to manipulate his phone without having to touch it, as she'd seen him do with several objects over the last couple of weeks. Not many people had the type of magic he did, but in that moment, she couldn't think about how special it was. Instead, she focused on the man himself, and how special he made her feel.

When she leaned in closer to him, soaking up the feel and scent of him, he held her tighter. Her eyes welled with tears and she blinked rapidly to keep them from falling. If Reece asked why she was crying, she'd be too embarrassed to explain they were tears of happiness because of how he made her feel loved. Whether he truly felt like they were meant to be and he was falling in love with her like Elvis crooned in the song, it didn't matter. He made her feel that way and like she could let go just a little bit because someone was there for her.

When the song ended, he tipped her chin up with his finger and leaned down. The kiss was passionate and held promise of so much more than she'd ever expected of a man. She kissed him back with a feeling she'd never put into a kiss before. Not ready to name the feeling, she hoped he'd feel it and understand.

"Are you ready to go back?" he asked softly.

She nodded and they both flashed back to their suite. Her

feet had barely touched the carpet when Reece stalked toward her. A small squeal escaped her, and then a laugh, when he put one arm behind her back and one under her legs and lifted her. Wrapping her arm around his neck, she laid her head on his chest for the short walk to the bedroom.

Standing in front of the bed, he didn't move. She thought something was wrong until she looked into his eyes. The emotion there matched what she was feeling, but neither spoke of it.

When he slowly dropped his arm under her legs, she slid down his body, feeling how much he wanted her. He captured her cheeks lightly in his palms, and she couldn't have looked away even if she'd wanted to. Not because of his hold, but because of the intensity she saw in his eyes.

"Cupcake, I want all of you—your emotions, your thoughts, and your body. This isn't a roll in the hay for me. I need you to tell me you know that."

"I know," she whispered. A small voice in her head told her that Reece was still a distraction, yet he was even more dangerous than he'd been before. Whatever they were about to do was more than just sex. If they made love, and that's what it would be, whether she named it or not, could she walk away if she had to? If the opportunity to save Mateo presented itself and it meant leaving Reece behind, could she let him go? Could she walk away and leave him? She didn't have an answer to that. All she knew was that she wanted this moment with Reece more than she had wanted anything for herself in her entire adult life.

ALL THOUGHTS FLED Isabella's mind when Reece swept his tongue along her lips. His touch was almost feather light, and she opened for him, wanting more. Keeping his lips on hers, he gripped her waist and lifted her, settling her on the king-size bed. He followed her down to the mattress but didn't bring all his weight down on her.

Her hands roamed his muscles, loving the feel of them beneath her fingers. Fisting his shirt in the back, she pushed against him. "Please, Reece. I want to feel all of you." Those muscles had filled her daydreams for weeks. She wanted to feel all of him pressed against her.

"For you, cupcake," he whispered against her neck as he lowered his body the rest of the way to hers. She couldn't help the groan that escaped her lips. He felt so much better than any dream.

He continued to trail his lips over her jaw and neck as his hands moved down her sides. She arched up into him, needing to increase the pressure on her core. "More, Reece. I need you. I need to feel you."

He pushed against her, creating a friction she desperately wanted, but it still wasn't enough.

"No. More. I want you inside me," she begged him.

"Not yet."

A cool breeze ran across her chest—a sharp contrast to the heat building within her. He moved lower, his lips scorching a path across her chest. Her shirt was gone. He'd magically removed it—an excellent idea.

She waved her hands as far down their bodies as she could reach. Reece chuckled against her skin when she magically removed all their clothing, but he didn't stop. His lips captured one sensitive nipple in his mouth, while one of his hands kneaded her other breast. The contrasting sensations of his soft tongue and coarse facial hair drove her crazy with need. And when his other hand snaked under her and cradled her butt to tug her closer, she drowned in the exquisite sensations.

He journeyed down her body. His tongue swirled around her hip, and her breath caught in her throat. When he licked a trail from her inner thigh to her core, she cried out in pleasure. Her fingers gripped his hair and she thrust up. Rubbing against him, she tried in vain to increase the pressure. "Reece, I need you. Please. Now."

"Soon," he said, his hot breath caressing her sensitive skin. As he continued to explore, she writhed under him. The sensations were almost too much and yet not enough. She needed him in a way that was overwhelming.

"Please. Fuck. Reece, I need more," she begged.

Using both his fingers and mouth, he gave her the pressure she craved. His hand on her butt gripped her harder as he lifted her closer to his mouth and feasted. At the same time, he increased his fingers' movements and sucked her clit into his mouth.

Her body shuddered and then her legs tensed. She gripped his hair tighter as she screamed his name. Her orgasm continued to build before it shattered. An explosion unlike any she'd ever experienced before burst inside her.

When her breathing finally slowed down, Reece climbed up her body. He braced his hands on either side of her and leaned down. When he kissed her, she tasted herself on his lips, fueling her passion for him.

Feeling him lift away from her body, she opened her eyes. The sound of crinkling was brief and then he was bracing himself on one elbow as he hovered above her. He lowered again, their bodies flush, and he kissed her until she felt like she was melting yet also revved up for more.

"You're so beautiful, cupcake. I want you," he whispered as he looked into her eyes.

"Take me, Reece."

She felt the tip of him at her entrance. Then he braced himself on both his forearms and rocked into her slowly. A back-and-forth glide as her body accepted his. When he was in her fully, they both groaned. She reached her hand around his neck and pulled him down to her, kissing him with everything she felt but didn't say for fear of more of her armor cracking.

They continued to kiss, both a little sloppy, as they moved with each other, but it didn't lower the intensity. She scraped her nails along his shoulders and he shuddered. "Fuck, cupcake, you feel amazing."

He sped up, rocking in and out of her harder and faster, as she met him beat for beat. Another orgasm built and climbed like an out-of-control roller coaster until she flew over the edge. Reece pumped into her three more times, and then she felt his body shudder through his own orgasm.

When their breathing calmed, he moved over to her side. He disappeared the condom and pulled her half onto his chest. The sound of his heartbeat against her ear felt like the sound of safety and love. Even though she was still afraid to say those words out loud.

"Cupcake?"

"Hmm?" She propped herself on his chest and looked into his eyes.

"Thank you for the best night of my life." He kissed her forehead and pulled her back down onto his chest. She knew it was to give her a way out, so she didn't have to respond.

They lay there for several minutes in a comfortable silence until Reece lifted her up. "I just want to plug in my phone, in case someone tries to reach us." He picked up his pants from where they laid crumpled on the floor and pulled out his phone, wallet, and a necklace. After placing them on the nightstand, he conjured a cord to plug in his phone and climbed back into bed.

Once more, she lay almost on top of him, and his arms encircled her. Her gaze drifted to the nightstand and the chain on top of it and she felt her throat tighten. For so long the necklace had been her only connection to her brother. Now she had memories she wished she could forget.

Reaching across his chest, she picked it up, forcing him to loosen his hold. "This is mine. How'd you get it?"

"I needed something to find you when you sent me on that little trip to San Francisco." He gave her a sheepish look and then shrugged. "It was a way for me to find you, and I didn't want to give it back because it gave me a connection to you. A way I'd always be able to find you if you needed me."

She dropped the necklace back on the nightstand and laid her head on his chest once more. He wrapped his arms around her again and she knew her armor had more than just cracked—a whole piece had fallen off.

"Is the chain special to you?" he asked softly.

"Yes." She'd responded automatically, and then a vision of Mateo attacking them in the alley came to her. "Well… it used to be. Mateo gave it to me for my birthday when he was ten. He'd used his own money to buy it and was so proud." She could still picture his face when he'd given it to her.

Reece placed a kiss on her forehead and his arms tightened more snuggly around her. "It doesn't matter what's happening now. It was precious at the time he gave it to you and that means something."

She lifted her chin so she could look him in the eyes. "I want you to keep it. Like you said, you'll always be able to use it to find me."

"Thank you. But just know, necklace or no necklace, I'll always find you when you need me to, cupcake."

A sense of belonging flooded her, and she swallowed against the lump in her throat. Instead of trying to express it with words, she moved fully on top of him, and as she leaned down and kissed him, she guided his length into her. Slowly lowering herself, she took him into her body and showed him what he meant to her.

Just before they finally drifted off to sleep, she hoped once more that she'd never have to choose between Reece and her brother. She pushed aside the thought that no one who'd claimed to love her had ever stayed.

Isabella was quiet that morning, but she hadn't completely withdrawn back into her serious mode after last night, and he wasn't going to let her. When they'd woken tangled in each other's arms, she'd tried to pull away. He kissed her until she melted into him. After making love to her again, he'd wanted to shower with her, but she just shook her head and locked herself in the bathroom. Good thing he could be patient when needed.

They checked out of the hotel and walked out the back entrance. In the empty hallway, they disappeared their suitcases before stepping outside. Since they'd eaten breakfast in the hotel, they were going straight to the antique shop.

About a block from the hotel, the hairs on the back of his neck stood up. "Isabella, can you feel that?" He tugged on her hand and pulled her into the doorway of a closed shop. Pushing her back against the door, he braced his arms on either side of her and leaned over as if to kiss her. "I think we're being followed," he said quietly against her lips.

Getting in on the game, she nuzzled his neck when she spoke softly. "How do you know?"

"I saw two men when we were leaving the hotel, and they're magic. They didn't have luggage, and although we didn't either, they seemed too aware of their surroundings to be tourists."

"That's pretty loose to base your suspicions on."

He took the opportunity to kiss her, just in case someone was watching. When he lifted his head, they were both breathless. "I know. That's why I didn't say anything, but I just saw the same guy in the reflection of a shop window. He looked a bit shorter than me, skinny, short dark brown hair, and was wearing a green jacket. I think he may have been with Eddie behind the library, but he was one of the guys holding me so I didn't get a good look at him at the time."

"He sounds like the guy who was on your right; he was wearing a green jacket too. I think we should trust your gut. What do you want to do?"

Reece chanced a glance over his shoulder. "I can't see them, but let's detour and see if we can lose them."

"Okay. But it's going to be pretty difficult around here unless we can hide in a shop." With no back alleys to duck into, nor parks to cut through, they were out in the open.

Reece took her hand in his and pulled her out of the doorway. "I've got a better idea. What do you think of cemeteries?"

"Wh—what?" she almost screeched before she caught herself and whispered.

"We need to lose these guys and we won't be able to do it walking around here. We don't want to put ourselves in a situation where we'll be trapped with only one way out." He met her gaze. "You trust me?"

She nodded, and he felt like he'd grown two feet in a matter of seconds. Still holding hands, he led them onto Conti Street, and a block later, turned onto Bourbon Street, going back in the direction they'd come from.

Taking a chance, Reece glanced over his shoulder and caught a glimpse of one of the guys pretending to look into a shop window.

As they walked down the street, he noticed two magics

walking together. They gave him a suspicious look and crossed the street, giving them a wide berth. A man in a business suit came toward them, and Reece knew he was magic as well. When he was within about fifteen feet of them, he glared at them, before ducking into a shop. As they walked past the shop, Reece peered in the window and saw the man standing there, staring out at them.

"Cupcake, have you noticed any weird reactions from magics we pass?"

"Like the guy who was just staring daggers at us from inside that shop? Yes. It happened yesterday too, but I thought maybe I was imagining things."

"I expect that a lot of magics are becoming suspicious of magics they don't know because of Maverick. He could have already spread more lies, and we just haven't heard about them yet. We need to get somewhere safe."

Picking up their pace, he led them back and forth for a couple of blocks. When he chanced a look, he noticed that the guy in the green jacket was still behind them.

He glanced around to see if there were any visible cameras. Finding none, he used his magic to open a wooden gate between two buildings and pulled Isabella inside. He pushed an image into her mind. "Can you see the cemetery?"

She frowned. "How did you get that?"

"I remembered it from when I was in the city before. Can you get there?"

"Yes."

"Good. Flash now. I'll be right behind you." True to his word, Reece flashed as soon as Isabella disappeared.

When Reece's feet touched the ground, he took Isabella's hand and looked for a place to hide. Numerous tall tombs stood in rows that would be good cover to hide behind. But many of them were spaced far apart, leaving lots of room for someone to see them if they walked down an aisle near them.

They needed a tall tomb that was packed tight next to another one.

"What cemetery is this?" Isabella whispered as he found two tombs close together and snuck in between them, pulling her with him.

"It's called St. Louis Cemetery No. 1. and it was established in the late eighteen hundreds."

Reece stood upright, not wanting to lean against a tomb out of respect, and cuddled Isabella into his chest. "You can only see the cemetery with a guided tour… well, unless you do what we did." She huffed out a quiet laugh against his chest and he tightened his arms around her. "According to their website, the tour groups depart every fifteen to thirty minutes. If we need to, we can fall in with a tour and hope they think we just got separated from another group. But that wouldn't be my first choice—it could call attention to us. I'd rather flash out of here."

For the next twenty minutes, they stayed in each other's arms and didn't talk. At one point, they heard voices and what sounded like a tour.

Reece was beginning to think they were safe and snuck his head out between the tombs. The man with the green jacket was walking slowly down the row, heading toward them.

He whispered in her ear. "They've found us. Go that way," he said, pointing between the tombs, the opposite way of where they'd come in. Isabella went first, and it was a tight fit for Reece, but he managed to follow her.

They detoured between tombs and had to backtrack twice when they heard a tour guide drone on about the cemetery's history. When the tour moved in the opposite direction, Reece once more pulled Isabella between two tall tombs.

"Why don't we flash to Brandon's shop?" she whispered.

Wrapped around each other, he spoke into her neck. "I thought of that, but I don't want to lead the guys there in case they're magically tracking us. That's our one guaranteed place to use to be able to flash out of the city and I don't want to compromise its safety."

Nodding against him, she was so trusting, thinking he could keep them safe. She was a strong, confident woman who had been on her own for years, and yet she'd put her trust in him today. It didn't matter that she'd pulled back this morning because trust didn't come all at once, and he was willing to continue earning hers.

Her pulling back could mean she didn't trust that he wouldn't distract her from her goal of helping her brother or because she was afraid to rely on someone other than herself. Her parents had let her down and she hadn't been close to anyone else in years. There was no way he'd let her down. He would die to keep her safe.

Isabella shifted on her feet, easing the pressure in her legs, and leaned further into Reece. He tightened his arms around her and kissed her forehead. Tilting her head up, she kissed him softly. Kissing in a cemetery was probably a bit strange, but she couldn't resist him.

"I don't hear anyone," he whispered against her temple. "How do they keep finding us?"

"They followed us from the hotel."

"Yes, but one, how did they find us at the hotel when we didn't even see them yesterday? And two, we flashed here, so how did they know to check out the cemetery?"

Reece was right; it didn't make sense that they kept finding them. "If I had tagged you, I could have found you. And I thought of that, but it wouldn't have lasted if one of them had somehow tagged you."

He pulled back so he could look into her eyes, and she had to force herself to think and not get lost in their depths. "How long does a tag last?"

"That depends," she said. "On an object, it can sometimes

last a couple of days, but on a person, usually only an hour or two." Resting her head back on his chest, she breathed in his scent and tried to empty her mind. When she was able to do that, her mind sometimes came up with the answers she was seeking.

A few minutes later, voices outside the tombs where they were hidden called to each other, startling her out of her semi-conscious state. "They're this way," one of the voices called.

Reece put his finger on her lips and grasped her hand, tugging her to the right. Leading them away from the voices, Reece wound a path through the tombs, stopping several rows away and pulling her down into a crouch. He leaned over and whispered in her ear. "They must be tracking us somehow, or they would have given up by now."

"When could anyone have put a tracker on us?" she asked as softly as she could.

"In the alley behind the library."

She shook her head. "But that was three days ago. I've never had a tracker last that long."

"But could it last longer for someone else?"

"Someone with the same type of specialty as me, you mean?"

Reece nodded. "Do you think–" He stopped talking and tilted his head to the right as the voices became louder. She followed him through a row of tombs again until they came to the end. In front of them was a wide open space with no place to hide.

He moved in behind her and put his mouth to her ear. "See those large tombs over there?" he asked, pointing just off to their right. "Flash there."

She nodded and then flashed, landing behind the taller of the two tombs. Flattening herself against the stone, she hoped Reece had enough space to land just as his feet touched the earth. He missed landing on her by only an inch or so. This game of hiding in the tombs was getting really tiring.

Reece moved so his back was against the tomb and pulled her into his arms so she was facing him. "Do you think someone could get a tag to last for days?" he asked, picking up their earlier conversation.

"I honestly don't know."

"What about your brother?"

She looked up into his eyes, a shadow from the tombs falling across his face. "You know for sure he has the same specialty as me?"

Reece frowned. "You didn't know?"

"I could only guess because he left home before he'd come into his full magic."

"I'm sorry, cupcake. I wish I didn't have to tell you, but yes, he has the same specialty, and he used it to lead someone to an FBI agent."

She gasped. "You're talking about Javier? I heard that Drew beat him up; is that how Drew found him?"

Reece nodded. "Yes, your brother tagged him for Drew."

Isabella closed her eyes and leaned into Reece. Suddenly, she felt chilled to the bone and shivered. Reece must have felt it because he rubbed his large hands up and down her arms. A warmth seeped into her, and she knew he was using his magic to chase away the cold. Going up on her toes, she kissed him. "Thank you."

He grinned. "Anytime, cupcake."

Continuing to take comfort from Reece's closeness, she thought about her specialty. "What if Maverick's new power enhanced Eddie's specialty? Maybe he can make tags last longer than I can."

"That's what I'd been thinking. Although I think Eddie's tags lasted longer than a couple of hours before Maverick got the magic from the box. We think Eddie tagged Javier in his apartment when they knocked him out and they were still able to track him over the next few days."

She nodded against his chest. If that was the case, then Eddie's magic was far more powerful than hers.

Reece continued. "Since the extra power enhanced Eddie's strength, it seems plausible that it could do the same for his magic and make the tags last even longer. But wouldn't you have noticed if he tagged one of us behind the library?"

"Yes, I usually…" She stopped when she ran over the scene in her mind, trying to remember everything that had happened. "We thought it was weird that Eddie didn't have a purpose besides beating you up, right?" When Reece nodded, the pieces of the puzzle started to fall into place. "Maybe that was his purpose. With you on the ground and me focused on you, he could have tagged you. When you were unconscious, he crouched down beside you and laid a hand on your shoulder. He said, 'Thanks for the fun.' I thought it was just some sick game he was playing. But what if he took that opportunity to tag you?"

Reece dropped his arms from around her and turned sideways. "Which shoulder?"

"Ah… your left."

Turning the other way, he presented his left shoulder to her. She ran her hands over his shoulder. "I can't feel anything." Desperation clung to her voice, audible even through her whisper.

Reece faced her and ran his knuckles over her cheek. "Try again, cupcake. You can do this." He kissed her lips softly and presented his shoulder to her again.

When they'd made love the night before, she'd had her hands all over his shoulders and hadn't felt anything. Lifting her hands to him again, she blinked when she realized he'd magically removed his shirt. Feeling his warm skin under her palms, she closed her eyes and moved her hands up and over his shoulders. Still nothing. She tried again, moving slower this time. When she still couldn't feel a tag, she moved her hands to the top of his shoulder, but instead of bringing them down over his shoulder blade, she moved her hands to the side. Trailing them down his arm, she felt a tingle in her palm and had to bite the inside of her cheek from shouting with glee.

"I found it," she whispered. Once she had the edge of the tag, it was easy for her to find where it ended. She positioned both her palms across the area, just in case it covered a larger area than her tags usually did. Although not visible, its presence was only detectable to people with her specialty, like an essence that spoke to her.

Closing her eyes, she concentrated and pushed her magic into it. The tag dissolved underneath her hands, the essence disappearing to wherever it came from. "It's gone."

Reece turned around and took her into his arms, then his lips found hers. When she felt him shiver, she pulled back.

"A little chilly," he said as he replaced his shirt. "I knew you could do it. Now, let's flash into the back of Brandon's shop. We can go to the antique store from there."

Finding the tag wasn't difficult once she knew to look for it. But it terrified her knowing that tags could last for days and go undetected. When she flashed away, she wondered if she needed to include her brother in that category of things that terrified her.

"AFTER THE LOOKS we've gotten from some magics, I'm going to go in first. Okay?" Reece asked Isabella as they stood outside the antique shop.

She gave him a sly smile. "Yes, but only because you don't think I'm weak and need protecting."

"Oh, cupcake, I know you can take care of yourself." Leaning down, he gave her a chaste kiss before turning to the shop.

Enormous glass windows on the wide storefront flanked a double glass door framed in wood. Reece opened the door on the right, feeling Isabella right behind him.

A bell over the door chimed and the smell of furniture polish assaulted him. Then the bright lights of dozens of chandeliers hanging from the ceiling caused him to blink as they shone in his eyes. More lamps, all lit, stood between pieces of furniture. Surfaces gleamed underneath statues, clocks, china, and other smaller assorted antiques.

Nothing seemed out of the ordinary. Turning back toward the door, he took Isabella's hand in his. He kissed her forehead, giving him a chance to whisper without looking suspicious. "Anything?"

"It's here, I can feel it."

"Can you sense if it's out front or hidden somewhere?"

When she closed her eyes, he knew she was feeling for a deeper sense of the object. "No, just that it's here."

Straightening, he smiled and pitched his voice louder. "Okay, cupcake, let's look around."

They hadn't gotten very far into the crowded room when an older magic woman in a slim black dress, her hair in a bun, approached them. "Can I help you find anything?"

"Hello," he said, offering his hand to the woman. "I'm Ryan, and this is my beautiful wife, Isa. We're looking for a large mirror for our front hall." Reece couldn't quite say what made him lie. Even with nothing setting his nerves on end, his gut told him not to tell the truth, and his gut hadn't been wrong yet.

"We have some beautiful mirrors near the back of the store. Please follow me."

Still holding Isabella's hand, they followed the woman. When they were almost at the back of the shop, Isabella tugged on his hand.

Not back here.

Isabella had never spoken to him telepathically before. There was an intimacy to it with Isabella that he hadn't felt with others. It occurred to him that neither of them had done it when they'd been trapped in the cemetery. It hadn't even crossed his mind then. But they'd been close to one another, and there hadn't been anyone to question them when they whispered, unlike now.

Stepping back, he brought her alongside him and wrapped his arm around her waist. *Take over.* After throwing the thought into her mind, he waited for her to take the lead.

"Oh, that's so lovely," Isabella gushed and stepped closer to inspect the mirror.

"Excellent choice," the clerk said, probably calculating her commission. "The one on the left is a Baroque gilt-wood mirror, from eighteenth-century France." She gave more details before describing the one on the right.

"Honey…" Isabella drawled and flapped her hand behind her, as if reaching for him but not turning to look.

Reece had to bite the inside of his cheek to not laugh at the movements that were so unlike his serious Isabella. *His?* He'd never been the possessive type before, but something in her made him want to be, and he was okay with it. Taking her hand, he let her tug him closer. "Do you see something you like, cupcake?"

Isabella pointed to two ostentatious, oval mirrors on the

wall. Both were trimmed in a gold color and looked nothing like the one they'd found in Boston. "What do you think, honey? Would either of those work?" she asked, biting her lip as if undecided.

Taking his time, he pretended to seriously consider the mirrors. "Hmm… I'm not sure. I thought we were going to go with something simpler. But if they're what you want, cupcake, we can get them."

Dropping his hand, Isabella put her hands on her hips and tilted her head. "No, I think I'd like something rectangular and longer. And you're right, honey, something simpler. I hadn't meant for it to be the centerpiece, after all." She turned to the clerk. "I think I'd like something not so ornate."

The clerk turned around slowly, as if mentally assessing her inventory. "I thought I had something like that…" She wandered to the front of the store, still talking. "I don't see it out here, but I can't remember selling it." Turning back around, she spoke directly to Isabella. "I think I might have what you're looking for. Would you like me to check the back?"

"Oh yes, please." Isabella clapped her hands together with what looked like glee. "If it's not too much trouble."

"No, I'd be happy to look. Just give me a moment." The clerk excused herself and headed through a doorway behind the counter.

Taking Isabella into his arms, he kissed her, just because he wanted to. It wasn't a long kiss, but it was still a claiming.

Her face was flushed when he let go. She glanced toward the counter. "Here she comes."

"Showtime." Reece planted a soft kiss on Isabella's forehead before taking her hand and leading them toward the woman.

The clerk placed a long mirror lengthwise on the counter.

Isabella ran her fingers along the frame. "This is perfect, exactly what we were looking for. We'll take it."

"Perfect. Let's ring it up and then I'll wrap it for you." When she mentioned the price, Reece thought she had probably padded her commission. The mirror looked like it had been found at a garage sale, and it definitely didn't look like it was worth a couple of thousand dollars. He pulled out his wallet just as the clerk held up her hand.

"Excuse me a moment, please," she said, moving back to stand in the open doorway of the room she'd gone to for the mirror.

She pulled out her phone and called someone. Her eyes became wider as she stared at him and Isabella while listening to the person she'd called. "Yes… Yes, sir… I understand, sir."

Red flags were waving in front of Reece's mind's eye, warning him something was terribly wrong. Answering a phone call while with a customer was one thing, but something or someone had triggered this woman to *make* a call.

When she hung up the phone, her features looked pinched. "I'm sorry, but I can no longer sell you the mirror."

Isabella leaned forward, placing her palm flat on the mirror. "Oh, that's horrible. Why not?" she said, sticking her bottom lip out in an exaggerated pout.

"I just can't," she said. Then, in a split second, her eyes unfocused, like she was staring off, unseeing into the distance.

"We'll double the price," Isabella said. "It's perfect for our foyer, and we've been looking for just the right mirror for a long time."

The clerk's expression wavered from neutral to sad, like she was waging an internal war with herself. She blinked repeatedly before she looked directly at Isabella. "No, it is not for sale."

As the clerk reached for the mirror, the bell over the door chimed and she looked up.

It's him. As Isabella's message was thrown into his mind, Reece whipped his gaze to the door. The thug with the green jacket stepped into the store and the door swung closed behind him.

19

Isabella felt Reece move in right behind her, his hand on her hip. Pushing her magic into her fingers, she prepared for the worst.

Green Jacket waved his hand behind his back, and Isabella knew what he'd done, even before she'd heard the telltale click of the door lock.

He stalked toward them, and her feet felt planted to the floor. Only Reece's warmth and touch made her feel like this time wouldn't end like it had in the library's alley.

"You can't sell the mirror to them," Green Jacket grunted to the store clerk when he reached the end of the counter.

"I… I… no," she said as her hand fluttered to her chest.

When the man turned toward them, the sneer on his face sent a shiver up Isabella's spine. At least this time they weren't outnumbered.

"You gave us the slip earlier, but not again." He shrugged as if it had been no big deal.

Reece took a step back and pulled Isabella more firmly into his chest. "How did you find us?" he asked. Isabella wondered if Reece was trying to confirm whether or not they had anything to do with the clerk making a sudden phone call.

"Easy. Take this as a warning that it's useless to fight us. You'd do well to cooperate because we can find or make people do whatever we want them to. All we had to do was let the big boss know to send a message out to shop owners in the area and give your descriptions." He puffed out his chest like he was proud of himself. Good for him, but Isabella was fed up with his shit, and the guy was really getting on her nerves.

Isabella needed to figure out how to get the mirror out of the shop. Using her magic to send it to Kate's forge was an option, but it might drain all her magic and then she wouldn't be able to flash to escape.

Ideas? she asked, throwing the question into Reece's mind.

Bluff.

That was not the plan she'd been looking for, but maybe he had something else up his sleeve. She placed both hands on the mirror and looked at the thug. "It's just a mirror. We want it for our foyer and it's perfect for the space we have in mind. Surely there's another mirror here your boss would be interested in." The bluff sounded weak even to her, but lying on the spot wasn't her forte. She preferred the truth and wanted to tell the guy where he could stick his attitude, but that wouldn't get them anywhere so she held her tongue.

He huffed out a breath like he was losing patience with her. "Yeah, right." His palm came down on the glass and the metal frame wobbled on the counter. "I'm going to take it."

"Not if you break it first, asshole," she spat out.

He leaned forward, and Isabella forced herself not to push back into Reece to get away from the thug.

"Think you're tough, do ya?" His eyes flickered up to Reece. "You guys weren't so tough in the alley the other day, were you? You're gonna let me take the mirror or you'll get a repeat of that." He flicked his hand out and energy shot from his fingers, pushing her and Reece back several feet.

Stumbling sideways, she shot her hands out to catch her fall and braced for impact. Reece's arm clamped around her front, and he hauled her up against him, preventing her from falling.

The thug laughed at them and picked up the mirror. "You should just give up," he taunted.

They'd come too far to lose the mirror. Reece hadn't said anything to her after the bluff didn't work, so if he had another plan, she had no idea what it was.

Sending her magic to her fingers again, she lifted her hands and called the mirror toward her. He hadn't been expecting the move, and the mirror flung from his grasp, shooting toward Isabella. Just as she was wrapping her fingers around the frame, it was ripped from her hands.

"You can't have it," the clerk sneered at her, holding the mirror.

The thug leaned over the counter, stretching his arms toward the woman. "Give it to me."

"No," the clerk said and hugged the mirror to her chest like a child with a favorite stuffie.

"For fuck's sake," the goon yelled before flashing behind the counter and grabbing the mirror out of the woman's hands.

"What's taking so fucking long?" asked a new voice.

Isabella turned to see the other thug who had been following them standing by the door. He must have flashed inside the shop but hadn't come too far inside because of the furniture taking up most of the space.

When he stalked toward them, Isabella feared they were going to lose the mirror.

"We don't want it anyway," Reece said from behind her. "It's not worth it. We'll find another one."

The thug's expression was comical as he looked down at the mirror. "Don't you need it?"

"That's not it?" the newcomer asked from only a few feet away.

Isabella looked up at Reece. *Is this your bluff?* she asked in his mind.

No. Be ready.

Not knowing what Reece meant, she called up her magic so she would be ready for anything.

Reece took a step toward the counter. "The mirror is useless. It's just a pile of ash."

"No, it's not, asshole," the thug said, "I'm holding it right h—"

The mirror dissolved in the man's hands, and a small mound of ash landed on the counter.

"The fuck!" the man yelled.

"Jesus Christ!" the newcomer said.

The clerk burst into tears.

Flash! Reece yelled into her mind.

Isabella didn't hesitate and flashed outside the shop. Taking a quick look up and down the street, she wondered where to go next. She didn't want to lead the thugs to Brandon's shop, and the thugs might assume she'd go back to the cemetery, so that was out.

Using her magic to blur her image, she flashed to the alcove behind the gate they'd hidden in that morning.

As Reece had hoped, Isabella's disappearance distracted the men. He opened the small resealable bag he'd conjured and with a simple pull on his magic, the ash transferred to the bag.

He had it sealed and sent home before the thugs realized it was gone. Then Reece flashed away.

Later, the clerk would find cash sitting on her desk in the back room and a note explaining it was compensation for the mirror.

Worried about bringing the thugs to Brandon's shop if they were magically strong enough to follow a flash signature, he'd known he couldn't go there. And since the idiots might assume they'd go back to the cemetery, it was out too. Right before he flashed, he pictured Jackson Square from when they'd passed it yesterday.

Landing amongst a small clump of trees and shielding himself with a blurring spell, he could only hope he hadn't been seen.

Stepping out of the patch of trees and landscaped gardens, he put on an air of nonchalance. At least, as much as he could muster while his heart felt like it was beating a hundred miles a minute. He strolled out of the trees. On the other side of a low, well-manicured hedge that stretched for yards, was a wrought-iron bench that ran across its length.

Several people sat at different points along the bench, talking and soaking in the nice weather. Reece moved nearer the far end and sat, resting his arm along the back. Hoping that he looked like he was enjoying the scenery and waiting for someone, he did just that. His connection with Isabella had grown and he was counting on her being able to find him. Unlike Jack and Meredith, Reece and Isabella could only telecommunicate over short distances like most magics, so finding her that way wasn't an option.

Five minutes later, he finally felt like he could take a deep breath and relaxed his shoulders when he heard her in his mind.

Walking toward you.

Not wanting to wait any longer, he stood and headed to

her. She didn't stop and walked right into his arms when he opened them. He kissed the top of her head and then took her hand in his and tugged her with him until they were off to the side, his back against a tree.

"Cupcake," he whispered right before he captured her lips with his. Her apricot and vanilla scent calmed something inside him. When they finally pulled apart from one another, he ran his knuckles over her cheek, loving the feel of her skin. "I knew you'd find me."

Emotion swam in her eyes and then she blinked and looked steady. "The mirror? Is it gone?"

He chuckled. "No, I temporarily dissolved it. I sent the ash home so I can restore the mirror to its original form. I can manipulate objects, remember?"

"I didn't know you could do *that*!"

"I'm not just a pretty face," he teased.

Her expression sobered. "I know."

Reece wasn't sure what about his comment caused her to turn so serious, but this wasn't the place to get into a deep conversation. "How about we get out of here and head home?" After her comment yesterday about the mask and lack of having a shelf, he knew she didn't consider the Williams's buildings home, but it didn't matter. It was his home, and he wanted her there with him.

A small furrow appeared between her brows. "It's a long way and we've expended a lot of energy in the last few hours."

"True. But our little jaunt through the cemetery feels like a long time ago already. We'll make it, and then we can refuel at The Magic Plate."

"Sounds good. As much as I like this city, I want to leave." She pointed to a patch of trees. "Let's walk over there."

"Sure. And I'll throw up a cover spell." At the trees, he

protected them from view. "Okay, we're good. I'll meet you there."

She went up on her tiptoes and kissed him before flashing away.

As he flashed away, he knew their priority was getting some food, and then he'd restore the mirror. His lips curved up on one side as he thanked the stars for his magic being strong enough in the antique store to save the mirror and themselves. In the last twenty-four hours, he'd learned that being magically strong wasn't always going to fix all his problems, but this time it had. And he hoped he'd never be in a situation again where it wasn't.

20

*E*xhaustion pulled at Isabella from the flash but showering off the sweat and the feeling of the cemetery beat food on her list of priorities. Hungry and not wanting to keep Reece waiting, she took a quick shower and changed into clean jeans and a long-sleeved shirt.

She flashed to the back of the restaurant where there was a designated flash point for magics to come and go. When she pushed through the door into the dining section, she heard Reece's voice and a sense of calm blanketed her. It was seeing the people he was with that made her think about leaving. Could she turn around before he saw her?

Reece stood by a table already occupied by some of his cousins and friends—many of them having had run-ins with her brother. After the day they'd already had, she wasn't sure she had the energy to face them. What her brother had done was easier to ignore when she was only hearing accounts secondhand. But now that she'd had a taste of it herself, she wondered if they would consider her guilty by association or because of her and Mateo's shared DNA.

Before she could turn around, Reece looked up and

extended his arm, calling her over. It was too late to hide, so she metaphorically pulled up her big girl panties and walked over to Reece. When he slid his arm around her, some of her hesitation fled, but not all of it.

Pasting a smile on her face, she hid her surprise at his physical display of affection in front of the others. It also helped cover her nervousness. The prospect of facing all these people when they'd likely heard about what her brother had done to Reece was daunting. Her nerves didn't seem to care that she was helping them.

"Cupcake, I was telling everyone about the mirrors. I've restored the one we just got and it's at Kate's forge. I decided not to wait."

She nodded but couldn't find her voice to say anything.

"You know everyone, right?" Without waiting for an answer, Reece launched into introductions. "You saw everyone the night we created the spell and some at the council meetings but I think you were the only new person so there hadn't been introductions. We've become a big family…" He laughed and the others joined him.

"I know everyone. Except we haven't been formally introduced," she said, turning to Javier. Holding out her hand, she projected a level of confidence she didn't feel. Although she'd seen him around and he seemed friendly, she didn't know if he harbored any resentment toward her, considering her brother had left him for dead.

He stood to shake her hand. "I'm Javier," the man said. "I'm an agent who works with Jack."

"Nice to formally meet you," she said, forcing the corners of her mouth to lift in a semblance of a smile.

"Likewise."

"Please join us," Connor said. "We can make room." He moved over to sit beside Rowena, who had Sam on her other side.

She and Reece sat across from them with Javier beside her as everyone joked about all the connections between them, whether they were from being related or working together. They were familiar enough with each other to have inside jokes, even Sam who'd only been rescued a short while ago.

A server came over and passed her a menu as the conversation carried on around her. Feeling more out of place than she did when she'd walked in, she buried her face in the menu for a moment. During her time in Blue Mountain, she'd started to feel a little like she belonged, but she knew her biggest connection to them was what her brother had done.

Maybe they wouldn't bring up her brother, she thought, as she and Reece ordered. Everyone else's meals were brought out since they'd ordered before them. With the time differences between New Orleans and Blue Mountain and the late hour, it was almost dinner time for her and Reece. Isabella's mouth watered at the amazing aromas wafting up from the dishes. When her meal arrived, she'd eat and make a quick escape, saying she was tired, and hopefully avoid all mention of her brother.

While the others dug into their meals, Reece launched into the story about their escape at the cemetery, finding the tag, and then what happened in the antique store.

"Have you found anything about Mirek yet?" Sam asked. Rowena squeezed Sam's hand and the two women shared a look that Isabella could only read as hope.

Isabella shook her head in answer and was thankful when the server brought her meal, giving her a reprieve from the conversation. Heartache and guilt warred within her. Mateo had been in Mexico at some point during Sam's captivity, but Isabella didn't know the details about what he'd done. Her lingering seed of hope that he hadn't been involved in holding people captive refused to die. Hope that he had been coerced into doing the unspeakable acts she'd heard about and hadn't had a choice. When they'd been in the alley and he'd attacked Reece, he'd been under Maverick's influence, which meant he wasn't acting as himself.

"… have to be close. We will find them," Reece said, his words pulling Isabella out of her thoughts. "We've seen Isabella's brother, Eddie—er, Mateo—and we know he was with Mirek and Dylan—er, Rocky." He gave a humorless laugh. "Fuck, there are too many names."

"Tell me about it," Sam said dryly, and the others laughed. Isabella knew her name had been changed while she was in captivity. Her real name was Julia Davis, but since she'd gone by Sam for most of her life, she was keeping it.

"I'm just going to stick with Rocky and Eddie." Reece turned to her and lowered his voice, even though everyone was close enough to hear. "You okay with that, cupcake?"

"Yes." She sat up straighter, deciding to stop hiding. They were going to talk about her brother whether she wanted them to or not, and it was time she stopped cowering. That wasn't her. She looked around at everyone. "I get it. Rocky and Eddie works, and no, you all can't start calling me cupcake."

Her comment elicited the laughter she was going for.

"Right, that name's just for me," Reece said and leaned over, kissing her temple. She felt her face heat, but only a little this time—maybe she could get used to PDAs from Reece. "Anyway… Since Eddie is after the mirrors and he's been with Rocky and Mirek, we think we'll run into them soon."

"Be careful," Connor said. "He's extremely dangerous."

Isabella put down her fork, suddenly not very hungry.

Reece wrapped his arm around her shoulders and pulled

her into his side. "We know. I told you we had a run-in with him not too long ago."

"Hey, I don't want to be negative here," Javier said, leaning around her so he could see Reece. "But Jack and I were talking about your attack and wondering what Eddie's motive was because it seemed like he was just playing with you. Since you mentioned he tagged you, it makes sense now that the attack was just a means to an end. With power from Maverick, he's even stronger than he was when he attacked me and he was damn powerful then. I would have died from what he did if Frank hadn't found me."

"The same with Rowena. Eddie pushed her car off the side of a cliff, and if it wasn't for Taren, she would have died too," Connor said before wrapping his arm around Rowena's shoulders.

"Isabella," Sam said. "I know he's your brother, but he might not be the young boy you knew." She paused and glanced at Rowena before meeting Isabella's gaze again. "After all, he killed Taren."

"I thought Taren saved Rowena." Isabella knew that who saved Rowena wasn't really the point, but she was grasping at straws to avoid the real issue. She looked between the two women for answers.

"Taren was my younger brother, and Sam is right, Eddie killed him," Rowena said. "I can talk to ghosts, at least sometimes. Taren is a ghost now and he was able to use energy, not really magic—I'm not sure—but anyway... he pushed my car back up the cliff. Because Eddie had pushed it over the mountain in an attempt to kill me."

Some part of Isabella recognized that Reece pulled her tighter to his side and that the conversation had moved on. But she didn't participate. A numbness had settled into her with the knowledge of everything her brother had done. The tiny hope that she could save her brother—the one she continued to cling to—shrunk to almost nothing.

"I'm missing something." Isabella turned around and threw up her arms. "I know it's here somewhere but I can't find it."

She grunted her frustration. The sound turned Reece on, although it didn't take much for that to happen when he was with her. He'd been semi-hard watching her all afternoon as she paced back and forth, bent down, and stretched up as she reached for different books.

Pushing aside the book he was looking through, he got up and walked over to her.

She put her hands up like she was warding him off, but a small smile played at one corner of her mouth. "No, no kissing. And no anything else. You can't distract me."

He grasped her hips, pulling her against him, and moaned softly as the feel of his hard length pressed against her. "Just a little distraction," he whispered before his mouth captured hers.

When he finally let her go, they were both breathing hard, and his dick felt like he could hammer nails with it. Not his smartest move, but he was becoming addicted to her. He'd needed an Isabella fix, even if it was a small one.

"I need to figure this out." She pushed her long hair over her shoulder and turned back to stare at the bookshelves. "I was so sure that coming to the library again would be the answer. I can just feel that it's here somewhere."

"You'll figure it out."

She turned back to face him. "And what if I don't? What if Eddie and Maverick take over more people? Do you know the damage they could do?"

He could see how she carried the weight of the magic world on her shoulders from the stress lines etched on her face. Her skin was pale, and she looked more tired than he'd ever seen her. He grasped her upper arms but didn't pull her flush against him like he wanted to. Rubbing his hands up and down her arms, he sent his magic into her, warming her. "I believe in you. If you say it's here, then it is."

She nodded and turned back to the shelves, forcing him to drop his hands. Ever since they'd spoken with his family in The Magic Plate yesterday, she'd been withdrawn. It wasn't like before when she'd shut him out and did her own thing, but she wasn't fully present either. When they'd gone to his apartment after the meal, he'd had to repeat himself several times because she'd been too lost in her own thoughts to hear him.

Twice she'd mentioned going back to her own apartment, but each time he'd talked her out of it. When they'd finally gone to bed, he'd made love to her slowly, cherishing every inch of her. He hadn't forced her to talk, just shown her with his touch what she meant to him.

They'd both woken early, and she'd been even quieter, but he hadn't let her withdraw completely inside of herself. He coaxed her into a shower where he'd slowly washed her and given her pleasure until she was calling out his name.

Over breakfast, she'd declared they had to go back to the library, and that's where they'd been for hours. They'd filled Viktor in on what had happened over the last week and then they'd brainstormed.

Viktor prophesized that since Isabella's magic kept calling her back to the library when the books weren't yielding results, maybe it wasn't a book she needed. He suggested that it could be a different object or even a person in the library.

Isabella said that people had led her to objects in the past, but this time she said her magic was continually drawing her to this room. They were the only two people there but it wasn't either of them calling to her magic.

Reece had his head back in a book when he heard the door open. Turning, he saw Viktor walking in before the door shut softly behind him.

"Isabella, I have two more books for you to look at. I know you said that it's something in this room, but these books are usually kept in here. They were shelved incorrectly by a new staff member and he'd only just discovered this mistake." Viktor placed the books on the table and then he and Isabella sat back in their chairs.

"Thank you." She pulled the first book in front of her and laid both her palms on the soft, worn leather.

When she closed her eyes, her shoulders relaxed. Reece had seen her do this many times now, feeling for a sense of something—anything that could tell her whether the book held secrets.

After a few minutes, she opened her eyes and shook her head. "Sorry, nothing. I'll try the other one."

It didn't take long for her to know that the second book wouldn't help them either.

Viktor let out a sigh and pushed his chair back. "It was worth a try."

"Thank you, Viktor. The answer is in this room, I know it. I'm constantly drawn to the shelves on the back wall, but when I touch the books, I find nothing."

"You will," Viktor said, repeating Reece's earlier words. "I will go back to my desk but let me know if you need anything."

Reece turned back to the book in front of him. When the older man cried out, Reece jumped to his feet and spun.

Eddie had a knife to Viktor's throat and was pushing him back into the room. Somehow, likely from the power given to him by Maverick, Eddie had managed to sneak up on them, flashing into the room without them sensing him.

Mr. Green Jacket and Reece's college buddy from the alley followed them in and shut the door behind them.

"Keep them apart," Eddie ordered, looking at College Buddy and flicking his chin toward Reece and Isabella.

Before Reece could move, College Buddy flashed behind him and grabbed his wrist, yanking him out of his chair. Reece didn't fight the hold on his arm because as long as Eddie had a knife to Viktor's throat, Reece wouldn't do anything to put the older man's safety at risk.

Green Jacket had hauled Isabella out of her chair and now they were the three points of a triangle with Eddie at the head.

Now.

As soon as Viktor threw the thought into Reece's head, he reacted without thinking, using a technique they'd practiced. He splayed his fingers on the hand of the arm College Buddy was holding and brought his opposite leg across his body while he twisted toward the guy. With his open hand, he grabbed Buddy's forearm and brought it down and back, taking the guy off balance. At the same time, Reece brought his free hand up, and, putting a bit of magic into his fist, he punched his opponent in the jaw. College Buddy dropped like a lead weight.

Reece spun in time to see Viktor and Isabella take out Green Jacket, his limp body falling to the floor.

Eddie jumped to his feet and held up his hands, the blade still in his fist. "Hey, you didn't have to take out my guys. I just wanted to talk to my sister."

He turned to her and lowered his hands but didn't drop the knife. "Isabella, I just wanted to talk to you. You're my big sister—I need your help."

21

For years Isabella had longed to hear those words.

Just like the first time they finally saw each other after years apart, she'd imagined what he'd say to her. And just like the first time she saw him again, this scenario was nothing like she'd imagined.

"What do you want, Mateo?"

"The other day in the alley, I was wrong. I should have let you help me."

Watching his face, she saw none of the distaste he'd shown her before. He didn't smile, but he didn't sneer either. She was still wary but craved the connection with her kid brother, and hoped this was the real Mateo shining through. Maybe this was him trying to let her know that he really had been coerced and now he was reaching out. "How did you know we'd be here?"

His lip kicked up in a bit of a smile then, like he thought he was winning her over. "I knew I'd fucked up the other day—"

Her anger flared at the way he brushed off what he'd done to them. Even knowing she shouldn't test his patience, she couldn't hold in the rage at his comment. "Really? That's what you're calling breaking our bones?"

"I know you're staying at his buildings," Eddie said, jerking his chin toward Reece and ignoring her question. "But I wanted to meet you on neutral ground. I regret what I did, and I've had someone watch the library, waiting for you to show up."

"Isabella." She took her eyes off Eddie to look over at Reece when he said her name. He hadn't moved and the guy was still at his feet. "Your brother's playing you. He wants something from you." *The mirrors.*

She didn't need Reece to say the words into her head because she already knew. Eddie had beat up Reece and tagged him. Then sent his thugs after them and almost managed to get the second mirror. She threw a thought back to him. *I know.* She looked back at her brother.

"Mateo, I need to know what you want my help with."

"Aww, sister, I'd tell you, but I can't with others around. It's a family matter."

"Family?" That was the last thing she'd expected him to say, and she wanted so much to believe him. "If it's a family matter, have you spoken to our parents?"

When he hesitated, she knew Reece was right—Eddie was playing her. She waited to see how he'd phrase the lie.

"Yes, I talked to them. And they wanted me to find you. I need to talk to you in private. You know what they're like. They wouldn't want their business spread to strangers."

Mateo spoke the truth about their parents. They were so private, they'd covered up what had really happened, not telling anyone that their son had disappeared. They were so determined to keep it a secret that they hadn't even gone to the police for help. They had truly believed that anyone finding out Mateo had left would have tarnished their image of being upstanding citizens and outstanding parents. As if they even were. Instead, they hid the truth and blamed Isabella.

She didn't believe he was telling the truth, but deep down she wanted to. Everything she'd heard at lunch yesterday came back to her. All the horrible things they said her brother had done, how he'd murdered an innocent, and a child at that, was front and center in her mind. She wanted to help him, but she couldn't trust him. At least not yet.

"Hey, Eddie," Reece called to him. "I know you've got my brother and cousin—Rocky and Mirek. Where are they?"

Eddie's attention shifted from Isabella to Reece, but she could still see his face clearly. A change came over her brother as stark as the difference between Dr. Jekyll and Mr. Hyde. Eddie grinned, but it wasn't a happy expression. It was as if his mask had slipped and all the evil inside of him suddenly shone through. "You don't have to worry about them. They're right where they need to be."

"Are they alive?" Reece asked. Isabella could hear the pain in his voice and imagined what it had cost him to ask that question.

Eddie snorted a laugh. "Oh yeah, and they're having the time of their lives."

Reece took a step toward Eddie. "Take me to them."

"I don't take orders from you, asshole." He turned to Isabella, and she backed up. Viktor moved so he was beside her and it gave her some security. It was three against one. Reece would kill Eddie before he'd let him hurt her.

"Are you going to come with me?" Eddie's earlier attempt at a smile became a sneer as he dropped all pretenses.

"No." She stood her ground and met his stare.

"Wrong answer," Eddie spat out.

Before she could respond, Eddie had flashed to her side and grabbed her arm.

"Isabe—" She heard Reece start to scream her name as Eddie took her in a flash.

"Isabella!" Reece screamed her name and flashed to her. Extending his arms, he prepared to grab her but stumbled when he only hit air. Neither his strength nor his magic had been strong enough—she was gone.

He stared down at his empty hands as a feeling of utter helplessness swamped him.

"Stop!"

Reece lifted his head and met Viktor's gaze, having forgotten for a moment that he was there. "Stop what?"

"Whatever garbage you are feeding yourself right now. Stop. It was not your fault. Eddie is a terrible person."

"Yes, and now he has her." Reece scrubbed his face with his hands for a moment as he replayed the last few minutes. "It never crossed my mind that he'd be able to flash with her. Council leaders are the only ones I know of who have the power to do that for more than a couple of feet." Remembering the other two men, he spun around and realized they were both gone.

"Eddie took the men with him too. Maverick has to be behind this. Even Meredith and Jack can't flash with three other people, so something else is going on."

Shoving one hand into his pocket, Reece pulled out Isabella's chain and ran it between his fingers. "I'm going to find her." Clutching the necklace, he picked up a notepad from the table and recited the locator spell. The address appeared on the paper, and he knew it was the same building he and Isabella had visited. Only it listed a different floor.

He disintegrated the paper so Viktor couldn't alert

anyone to where he was going or try to stop him. Stupid maybe, but if it came between saving his brother and Isabella, he'd choose her, and no one was going to stand in his way. His brother would understand because he'd already made the same choice when Simon offered to help him. Without giving it any more thought, Reece flashed.

He landed in the hallway outside the apartment where Isabella was being held. There were only two apartments on the entire floor, which could mean there were lots of rooms, and Isabella could be in any of them.

Not knowing where she was, Reece pushed his magic out to get a sense of the space. When he felt nothing, he eased the door open with some magic to the lock.

The door opened into an empty foyer, with nothing to indicate that anyone lived there. No table for keys or shoes in the front, only a wide-open area with dim lighting. Since the area in front of him had a similar open floor concept to the apartment he and Isabella had visited, he hoped the rest of the floor plan was the same.

Keeping the magic in his fingertips at the ready, Reece walked across the barren room and turned down the hallway. Just past the first doorway—a room with two twin beds and nothing else—he heard voices.

"Williams, get the fuck in here!" Eddie yelled.

Since there was no point in being quiet now that Eddie knew he was there, Reece sped up until he reached the room where Eddie was holding court.

The room was a massive cavern, big enough to be a ballroom. Isabella stood to one side, her hands in front of her, wringing a cloth between her fingers. *You hurt?* he asked her telepathically. When she shook her head, he let out a breath and then sucked in another.

"You are so fucking predictable," Eddie spat at him. "I

knew if I took Isabella, you'd come for her. And now you're both going to find the fucking mirrors for me."

Reece heard Eddie but didn't respond, his gaze locked on what felt like a ghost. It was the first time he'd seen his brother in over twenty-two years. Simon had been right. Looking at Dylan, or Rocky, was like looking in the mirror. It would have been different before he'd bulked up after his coma, but now they could be twins.

He glanced at the person beside Rocky, and at first, he didn't recognize him. His cousin Mirek was the same age as his brother, but now he looked like a frail man who was many years older. Mirek leaned against a wall as if he didn't have the strength to hold up his own weight.

"I should have made a cake," Eddie said, sarcasm dripping from his words. "It's a fucking family reunion. Oh, except that poor, weak little Taren is missing."

Baiting Reece into reacting rashly wasn't going to work. Yes, Taren's death had left a permanent hole in his family; they'd never fully recover from losing him. But, for them, he'd been gone a long time. Yet Reece didn't miss the way Mirek's face tightened at the mention of his younger brother.

As much as he wanted to tell Mirek about Taren's ghost helping them, it would have to wait. Figuring out what game Eddie was playing so he could get them all out of there was his priority.

Directing his attention at Eddie, he kept his voice low, devoid of confrontation. "We don't have the mirrors. I'm sure your little soldiers told you what happened to the mirror in New Orleans."

"They said it turned to ash, but how do I know you didn't do something to it?"

"I didn't." He didn't usually like lying, but he had no problem lying to this asshole and bully.

"I don't fucking believe you." Without warning, Eddie

snapped up his hand and flung it toward Reece's brother. A soundless cry erupted from Rocky. Clamping his hands on either side of his head, he dropped to the floor like a marionette with severed strings.

While Rocky writhed on the floor, the corner of Eddie's lip lifted proudly. "That's another little trick I got from Maverick. He calls it the silent death. A person can't call out, and eventually their brain will implode. I can't wait to see it happen." Eddie's laugh filled the room as Rocky continued to flail.

"Stop." He didn't yell, his throat tight with seeing his brother in pain, regardless of the years that had separated them.

"You want me to let him go? Then you find the mirrors."

Reece nodded and Eddie waved his hand toward the floor. Rocky sucked in a ragged breath as he flopped onto his back, spread eagle. Walking over to his brother, he crouched. "You okay?"

Rocky only nodded but took Reece's proffered hand when he stood. It was the first time he'd touched his brother in decades. His instinct was to pull him into his embrace, but Rocky moved back. Out of a habit of self-preservation or because of Eddie's volatility, he didn't know. Glancing over at Mirek, Reece wanted to embrace his cousin as well. Maybe Mirek sensed it because he nodded at Reece and then jerked his chin to the side. Getting his drift, Reece backed away from them, moving closer to Isabella.

"When your sister and her stupid boyfriend were here, I realized that Rocky was a fucking traitor. Ain't that right, Rocky?" Rocky remained silent. Eddie must have taken it for agreement because he continued to spout off. "He helped Lucas escape. So I had to put a tight rein on my boy Rocky here."

Eddie walked over to Rocky and cuffed him on the side of

his head using a backhand. Rocky didn't react, and once more Eddie continued to drone on. "But a lot of good your helping did him, huh? He's still dead." He gave a dark laugh as he waved his hand at Rocky again. Once more, his brother's mouth opened, but no sound came out as he fell to the floor, thrashing about.

"Stop! Eddie, please stop!" Isabella pleaded. "I'll do what you want. Just stop hurting him."

Reece had been an idiot. The realization hit him as clearly as Eddie's hand had hit Rocky. He'd been an idiot for not wanting Viktor to know where he was going so he couldn't call in the cavalry. Reece hadn't wanted anyone to stop him from saving Isabella.

The truth had been staring him in the face all along. Physical and magical strength alone weren't always enough. Seeing the power Eddie wielded didn't make Reece envy his strength; it made him pity the guy.

Releasing Rocky, Eddie stood over him as Rocky struggled to get to his hands and knees, sucking in air. Eddie sneered as he lifted his eyes to meet Reece's. "I've had to teach your dear old brother here a few lessons to keep him in line. If you don't want me to do the same to you and my sister, you'll find me the mirrors. Now!"

As soon as Eddie held his hand out toward Isabella, Reece knew it was time to call for help. Reece didn't care if it made him look weak; he'd give anything to save the people he cared about.

Knowing Jack would be able to hear him, he reached out telepathically. *Need hel—*

His message was cut off when he was hit with a searing pain unlike any he'd ever felt before—like hundreds of knives slicing open each nerve in his brain simultaneously. A soundless yell erupted from his lips as he grabbed his head and crashed to the floor.

ime slowed down for Isabella as she watched Reece's face contort as he screamed but didn't make a noise. He fell to the floor, holding his head as Rocky had done.

Turning to her brother, she yelled, "Stop hur—" then cut herself off. The sound of her voice was like a bullhorn in the silent room. Seeing Reece's pain had looked like he should be crying out loudly, so she'd raised her voice, wanting to scream over the cacophony of suffering she was witnessing. Reining herself in, she lowered her voice. "Please, Eddie, stop hurting them."

"Fuck no. I want you to see that you're causing their pain."

Isabella walked to Reece and dropped to her knees at his side. She reached out to him but didn't know where to touch him. Pain marred his features as he writhed on the floor, his limbs hitting the hardwood with small thuds.

"Let him go!" she screamed over her shoulder at Eddie, no longer caring about lowering her voice.

A movement caught her eye. Looking across the floor, she

saw Rocky and Mirek thrashing on the floor like Reece was. "Stop!" she yelled.

No, not again. She couldn't let another person slip through her fingers like she had her brother. A fleeting thought that she hadn't saved her brother whispered through her mind, but she shoved it aside.

When Eddie didn't boast or strut his power, she looked over her shoulder at him again. He wasn't there.

Jumping to her feet, she spun and saw him heading toward the door. "Let them go," she pleaded. "Please, stop this."

"No. I'm going to leave them like this and you can watch. Maybe then you'll be more cooperative when I come back." He turned away from her and then stopped and turned back. "On second thought…"

Eddie stalked toward her like a lion hunting prey. Staring him in the eyes, she refused to cower. When he laid his hand on her shoulder, she couldn't help the involuntary flinch. He squeezed her shoulder, but there wasn't any love in the gesture. She felt a twinge, as if her clothing had rubbed against her the wrong way.

"Be ready to help me," Eddie said. The lock on the door clicked and he was gone in a flash.

Isabella dropped to her knees again and laid her hand on Reece's shoulder. With him squirming so violently on the floor, her hand slipped off. She tried again, this time laying it lightly on him so it moved with his body. Pushing her magic into her fingers, she sent a cooling breeze out to him, hoping it would help. "Reece, can you hear me?"

His eyes flung open and then snapped closed and his body's jerking movements increased.

Patting her back pocket for her phone, she remembered she'd left it in the library. *Jack!* she threw into the council leader's mind. When he didn't immediately respond, she tried reaching Meredith. *Meredith!*

After several attempts, she knew they hadn't heard her. Never having telecommunicated with either of them, she figured the protection spell was preventing her from getting through.

Moving to sit on her butt, she reached out to Reece, trying to cradle his head in her lap. For a moment, she was able to stroke his hair before his thrashing became more violent, knocking her over. She wiggled out from under him and stood.

It pained her to see him suffering. She didn't want to leave, but they needed help. She went to the door and pulled on the handle, but it didn't budge. Sending her magic into the door, she tried to unlock it. Again, nothing.

Next, she tried to flash, but she stayed exactly where she was.

Something or someone was blocking her magic. Likely it had something to do with the twinge she'd felt from Eddie's hand. Although she'd never heard of someone taking away magic like that before, it didn't mean it wasn't possible. Especially with all the new power Eddie possessed. And yet, she'd pushed cooling into Reece. Or maybe she only thought she had.

Clenching her hands, she banged on the door with her fists. "Let us out! Eddie!" she yelled over and over again until her voice was raw and hoarse.

"You ready to help me now?"

She turned around to see Eddie standing on the other side of the room. "Unblock my magic!"

Eddie let out a dark laugh. "You noticed that, huh?" He waved his hand at her. "Sure, you can have it back since you won't be able to escape anyway."

Isabella felt a tingle run through her body followed by her magic stirring within her. "Let them go. Please."

The man in front of her still looked so much like her brother, only older. Yet this person was cruel and hard. Was it just because of Maverick's magic? Did he have any compassion left in him at all? Or did he never have any? Did she and her parents not give him enough love as a child? Maybe he'd developed armor like she had, but he didn't have anyone to help him crack it.

He waved his hand toward Reece and the others, and Isabella heard their intakes of breaths. Ignoring Eddie, she ran to Reece and dropped to his side, pulling his upper body into her lap. "Are you okay?" She trailed her hands along the sides of his face, searching his eyes for an answer.

"Y—y—yes," he said, struggling to speak, and she saw him swallow. "Rocky? Mirek?"

Isabella looked in their direction and saw they were both sitting up. "They're okay."

Reece jerked in her arms and she looked down, seeing Eddie's feet. He kicked Reece's leg, causing him to jerk again. "Get the fuck up. It's time for you to find me the mirrors."

TRYING his best to ignore the lingering pain in his head that threatened to consume him, Reece stood, offering Isabella a hand.

You okay? he asked her telepathically. The question had become far too common for them lately. Looking over at his brother, he raised his eyebrows in question. Rocky nodded. His brother was tremendously strong, physically and mentally, to have endured that torture over and over again, which he guessed had started months ago after Eddie suspected Rocky of being a traitor. And now with Eddie's new power from Maverick, punishments had likely become worse.

"About fucking time," Eddie said, lifting his chin toward the door behind Reece. Grasping Isabella's arm, he took several steps back, closer to Rocky and Mirek, pulling her with him. When he saw Eddie's thugs from the library step into the room, he made sure Isabella wasn't in their line of fire.

With Eddie's enhanced magic, even with four of them against one, it hadn't been a fair fight. Now the odds were even worse. Asking someone else to come into this fight didn't seem fair either, but they needed help. Reece was willing to bet that Jack could help level the playing field.

Before Reece could telepathically reach out to Jack, a voice entered his mind. *Pass me some magic.* Hearing his brother's voice in his head temporarily froze him. Rocky grabbed his hand, pulling their joined hands out of sight behind his back. *Now.*

Trusting his brother had a plan, Reece pushed his magic down through his hand into Rocky's. When he felt the connection between their magic, Rocky dropped his hand.

Protect the girl. Rocky's words landed like a shout in his brain. Reece lunged at Isabella, jerking her into his arms as he flung them both backward against the wall.

At the same time, Rocky pointed his arms toward the floor, directing his magic about three feet in front of them. A floorboard lifted. Another pulled free after that one. Then one after the other, in rapid succession, were released from their moorings and stacked on their sides on top of each other to form a wall. The ballroom-size floor gave Rocky lots to work with as he continued to maneuver the planks. Rocky stacked them up to the ceiling as Eddie and his goons shouted from the other side.

"Flash now!" Rocky yelled at him. "I can't hold them for long."

Reece knew it was their only hope if any of them were going to escape. He nodded to his brother, hoping Rocky knew it was a promise that Reece would come back for him and Mirek.

He turned to Isabella just as she disappeared, flashing after her.

He landed in his apartment's foyer, but Isabella wasn't there. Flashing again, he arrived three floors lower in Isabella's apartment. She stood there, unmoving, as if in shock.

In two steps, he had her in his arms. Breathing in her scent, he held her tight, thankful she was safe. At the same time, his heart felt heavy for leaving his brother and cousin behind. Reece had vowed he would find them, but now he knew that wasn't the promise he should have made. Closing his eyes as he held Isabella, he amended his vow—he would bring them home.

Isabella pushed at him and stepped back. "We have to tell Jack. Eddie's magic is so strong he could get into the building."

She was right, but he'd been so wrapped up in his relief that she was safe and his worry about Rocky and Mirek that he hadn't been thinking clearly. *Jack?*

Here.

Isabella's apartment. Reece said, telling Jack where to come.

A moment later, there was a knock on the door and then Jack walked in. Meredith was with him. "What's going on?"

Reece filled them in on what had transpired. It was hard to believe that it had only been an hour. Their lives had changed so much in just one afternoon.

Meredith hugged Isabella and then him. "I'm glad you're alright," she whispered in his ear. When she let him go, there was a determination in her gaze. "I'm going to tell Rowena and Sam that Mirek is alive." She flashed away.

When considering the span of a lifetime, it had been such a short time that he and his sister and cousins had been using magic. Yet it was now an integral part of their lives. But Reece couldn't forget the damage it could do as well. Almost as a reminder, a slight headache still lingered from whatever Eddie had done to him.

He tried to shake off the pain and turned to Jack. "Can you let everyone in the building… well, all magics, know to be on the alert?"

"Yes, and Meredith and I will do one better. We'll cast a spell on the buildings that will last the night so that no one can come or go. During the day, everyone will just have to be on alert." Jack paused and then looked at Isabella. "You'll keep looking for the third mirror."

Reece heard the command in Jack's voice; it hadn't been a question. As much as he wanted to find the mirrors, Isabella still had a choice, and she'd been through so much today. "Jack—" he started to warn his friend when Isabella stopped him.

"It's okay." She rubbed her hand along his arm. "Jack's just doing his job. Yes, Jack, we'll go back to the library tomorrow. I'm sure the answer is there."

Jack nodded and disappeared.

Reece turned away from where Jack had flashed to see Isabella rubbing her hands over her face.

He gently pried her hands away. "Hey, cupcake. Talk to me." They both had so much to process, but right then, he wished they could go back to their perfect night in New Orleans.

Looking up at him, her eyes were red and brimming with tears. Waving her hand in front of her face, her eyes were dry once more. "Sorry," she said, looking up at him. "Everything just hit me all at once. I'd seen Eddie before now, but what he did to you guys—" She choked on a sob and lost her battle with her tears.

Pulling her into his arms, he held her as they stood in her apartment's entrance and she cried. There weren't any words to erase the conflicted feelings she must have about her brother. For years she'd searched for him, holding out hope of finding him and bringing him home. His fear for her was that they hadn't yet seen Eddie's worst side.

When she finally stepped back and magically dried her eyes again, he had a burning desire to give her some comfort.

Conjuring a glass of wine, he handed it to her, and her eyes became wide. "I look like I need alcohol?"

He chuckled. "It couldn't hurt. Why don't you sit at the island and I'll get us something to eat."

"Are you going to cook?"

After walking to the other side of the island, he took out plates and cutlery. "I'm going to conjure." Teasing her, he held up his hands as if to hold off any comments. "But I'm not going to conjure just any old meal. I'm going to conjure one of the best meals you've ever tasted. You'll eat until you're beyond full, and then you'll be begging me for the recipe."

"Really?"

"Yes. Wait until you taste my mother's meatloaf recipe."

"Meatloaf?" She raised her eyebrows as if she doubted the meatloaf could live up to the hype.

"Oh yes, ye of little faith. Just wait."

Since he didn't need time to cook, he made a big show of laying out place settings on the kitchen island and pulling out a large serving dish.

"To start..." He conjured two side salads first and then a bottle filled with red liquid. "Plus, the best raspberry vinaigrette dressing in the world," he said as he poured it over the greens.

"You're making a lot of big claims, you know. I've already had some pretty tasty salad dressings in my lifetime."

Taking the stool beside hers, he picked up his own fork and loaded it with spinach, purple onion, and crumbled goat cheese. He watched as she took a bite of her own salad.

Closing her lips around the mouthful, she slowly pulled the fork backward between her lips. He wished he was that fork; it was the first time he could ever remember being jealous of an inanimate object. She groaned as her eyes fluttered closed and he watched as she enjoyed her first bite. The sight was almost as good as watching her eat one of his cupcakes and licking her lips.

"Yum. You were right. I think that was the best raspberry dressing I've ever had."

"Good." They finished their salads without talking, a comfortable silence falling over them.

Disappearing their salad dishes, he rubbed his hands together and grinned at her. "Now for the main course."

"Meatloaf."

A laugh rumbled through his chest. "Oh, I hear the skepticism in your voice, but just wait." He conjured the meal just the way his mother had made it for so many years. A steaming plate landed in front of each of them. "That's my mother's amazing meatloaf with a side of vegetable pilaf."

He couldn't tear his eyes away from her as she picked up her fork and took her first bite. When she groaned, he felt a sense of satisfaction at providing her pleasure, even if only with a meal.

"You're right again. This meatloaf *is* amazing."

Digging into his own meal, they ate, and he regaled her with stories about growing up with a family restaurant.

Isabella hadn't asked for seconds, but she'd eaten everything on her plate before she pushed it away from her. "Oh, I'm full, but it was so good."

He used his magic to refill both their wine glasses and then picked up his, taking a sip. "After my mom and aunts spellbound me, Jo, Meredith, and Rowena—"

"The Little W's," she said with a chuckle. "I heard that's what you're all called. Although I was told you've now dropped the *little*. It's a great moniker."

"Yes, us W's... Looking back, I don't think the moms stopped using their own magic. Although they would have had to do it in secret."

"Why do you think they never stopped?"

"There were just too many things they made happen at the last minute. As kids, we didn't question it, but now, again, looking back, I see so much more. Such as always having homemade cookies when we needed them for school even though we didn't mention it until the morning of because we forgot. Or when kitchen staff called in sick but our moms got all the meals out to the customers, as if they had a full contingent of chefs."

"I always knew we were magic, and my parents used their magic to make life as easy as possible. I don't remember them ever cooking. Conjuring? Yes. But cooking? No. I think it would have been fabulous to grow up in a family where the mom taught the kids to cook."

Reece watched as the joy from their earlier conversation slid from Isabella's face. From what she'd told him, thinking of her parents probably didn't bring happy thoughts.

He stood and offered her his hand. "Come on, it's late." Without asking, he picked her up by her waist and she let out a small squeal before wrapping her legs around him. "I know just what you need," he said as he walked to her bedroom and dropped her onto the bed.

"I can only imagine," she said, the light back in her eyes.

"No, not that… well, not yet." Yes, he wanted to make love to her, but he wanted to make her feel cherished as well.

Kneeling beside her on the bed, he looked down at her. "Do you trust me?"

"Yes." The fact that she didn't hesitate made him feel ten feet tall.

Using his magic, he closed the drapes and dimmed the overhead light. Then he removed her clothes and had them land in a neat pile on the chair in the corner.

"Ha, I thought you said not that?"

"Once again, ye of little faith. You wait." Putting his arms underneath her, he cradled her, moving her up the bed, and then turned her onto her stomach. Getting on the bed, he straddled the backs of her thighs, careful not to put too much of his weight on her small frame.

He conjured massage oil directly onto his palms and rubbed them together, heating the oil. When he placed his hands on her back, he worked up to her shoulders. She groaned, and the sound was everything he needed to hear. He kneaded the muscles in her shoulders before working his way down her back. Time wasn't important as he continued to work, eliciting more sounds of pleasure from her.

As his hands massaged her, his mind wandered back to the day's events. Even though he'd known his brother was likely alive, seeing him and his cousin was still a shock. Instead of being physically or magically strong enough to save them himself, it was his brother who'd done the saving.

Another shock was realizing Eddie's reliance on power was its own weakness—it'd been a wake-up call for Reece. Because of it, he didn't begrudge his brother for being the one to save them. Reece just hoped that he'd be able to return the favor.

Isabella hadn't stirred in a while, so he leaned forward to look at her face. She'd fallen asleep and looked peaceful;

none of the usual stress lines bracketed her mouth. He moved off her and stripped, placing his clothes in a pile next to hers.

Crawling into bed beside her, he conjured a blanket and laid it over them both instead of trying to get her under the covers. When he pulled her back to his front and held her, she stirred, pushing closer into him.

His last thoughts when he drifted off to sleep were that she was everything he'd ever wanted. And would she forgive him for what he might have to do if it came down to a fight between them and her brother?

$\mathcal{I}$sabella sighed and looked across at Reece. "It feels like last time. Something is calling to me, but I can't find it."

"You'll find it, cupcake. I believe in you." Reece flashed to her side. Hauling her out of her chair, he kissed her in a way that said he wanted to devour her. Letting her hands roam over his shoulders and back, she sank into him and felt another piece of her armor fall off.

When he finally pulled back, she grinned up at him. "What was that for? Not that I'm complaining."

"You just looked like you needed a little break." He walked back to his chair and she flopped into hers. "I like that this room is private," he said with a wink.

Looking back down at the book in front of her, she tried to concentrate on the page, but she couldn't focus. They'd been in the library for several hours and she still hadn't found a clue to help find the last mirror, but she knew it was there somewhere.

This morning she'd woken up to Reece pleasuring her, his

hands running over her body as he moved lower. He'd brought her to orgasm with his mouth and hands before he'd moved back up her body and kissed her. Tasting herself on his lips was more erotic than she ever could have imagined.

She wasn't inexperienced, but her sexual exploits hadn't been vast either. Reece had given her more orgasms in the past week than she'd ever had before. When she'd reached between them and guided his length into her, she'd felt like he'd been made just for her. It was cheesy, but she couldn't think of another way to describe how he filled and fulfilled her. She felt the corner of her lips tip upward as she replayed what he'd done to her before they'd gotten ready for the day.

"What's the smile for, cupcake?"

Heat spread over her cheeks as she met Reece's gaze. "Uh… oh, nothing."

He sat back and grinned. "Thinking about this morning?"

"Maybe."

"I'd be happy to wake you up that way every morning."

"Okay." Who was she to argue?

When he just chuckled, she looked back down at the book.

An hour later, she still hadn't found anything. Gathering the books she'd already gone through, she got up and shelved them. She stood facing the shelving unit and closed her eyes, pushing her magic out.

Her magic was still telling her something was there. And her frustration was building by the hour as she went through book after book but found nothing. Picking two more random books, she took them back to the table.

"What if I don't find something soon?" she asked, looking at Reece.

He reached across the table and took her hand in his. "You can only do what you can."

"But this morning when we met with Jack and the other council members, he said they were getting more reports of people being controlled. He didn't say it, but you must have heard the worry in his voice."

Letting go of her hand, Reece flashed to her side of the table and took her into his arms again. He rested his head on hers as she snuggled into his chest. "You can't take all this on by yourself. You're only one person and you're doing everything you can." He pulled back and looked in her eyes but kept his arms around her. "You've already found two of the mirrors. That's a feat in itself."

"I know what you're saying, but the first two mirrors are useless without the third. And if we don't find them and close the box, how many more people is Maverick going to control? And then what will he do?" She didn't wait for Reece to respond as the feelings of failure at not finding the third mirror mounted within her. "Plus, we can't keep spelling the buildings at night and hope that no one comes after us during the day. Eddie already took me from here yesterday. We don't even know if the spell you put on this room will be enough to keep him out if he comes again."

"You'll find the third mirror, I believe it. As for the rest, we will find a way to stop Maverick and help the people he's controlling. And we will spell every room and building for as long as we need to."

She wanted to believe him but worried that the magic Maverick and Eddie were using was too strong for them to maintain control over it for long. Reece kissed her softly and went back to his seat.

"I'm going to use the restroom."

"I'll go with you."

She smiled at him. "I know." He'd gone with her when she'd used the restroom before they'd conjured lunch. Since

Eddie and his goons were still out there, she was totally fine with it.

"Did you find something?" Viktor asked when they walked out of the back room.

"No, not yet. I just need to use the little girl's room." She pointed to the back of the library, as if Viktor didn't know where it was, and then dropped her arm, feeling silly.

"I didn't tell you about the closer one? I was sure I did the first day you were here. I am sorry, Isabella. I must have forgotten because it is not for the public so I am not used to mentioning it. Go back into the small room and through the door on the far side of the back wall."

Isabella shrugged, not wanting Viktor to feel bad. "You may have told me, but then I forgot. When I saw the door earlier, I just assumed it was a closet."

"No, it leads to a few rooms in the back."

"Thanks," she said to Viktor and turned to Reece. "If you spell the room again, no one will be able to flash in. I'll be fine on my own."

Isabella left Reece talking to Viktor. Opening the door at the back of the room, she looked into a brightly lit hallway and laughed to herself. She'd been facing the shelves on the back wall for hours, on three different days, and didn't know there was a hallway behind them.

When she took a step into the hallway, her magic tingled like it did when she faced the back wall, especially on the right side. But the hallway opened up to the left side of the room.

Giving herself an internal shake, she looked for the restroom. It was two doors down on the left. When she finished and headed back to the private room, her magic felt like it was screaming at her.

There was a door with only a number on it, but no label.

Since no one was around, she tried the knob, only to find it locked. She was tempted to use her magic to open it but didn't know what she could be walking into.

"Did you find it?" Viktor asked when she walked back into the main library.

"Yes, thanks. There was another door to the right as soon I walked into the hall. It just had the number two on it. What's in there?"

Viktor frowned. "Just a storage room, why?"

"Can you open it?"

"Sure." He grabbed a set of keys and she and Reece followed him.

"You felt something?" Reece asked when they reached the storage room.

"Yes. You know how I kept thinking my magic was calling the strongest when I was at the bookcase at the far right of the back wall?" When Reece nodded, she continued. "What if it wasn't the back wall, but what was behind it?"

Viktor unlocked the door and held it open after flicking on a light. "Look all you want."

Metal shelving units lined each side of the long and narrow room from floor to ceiling. There was a musty smell in the air and a layer of dust sat on the boxes she passed. Boxes labeled Christmas ornaments, Halloween decorations, and other holidays were crammed onto the shelves. Cardboard cutouts and discarded clothing looked like afterthoughts, shoved into available spaces amongst the boxes.

The further she walked into the room, the more her magic called to her. The tingle had turned into a full-blown scream, telling her something was there.

At the end of the shelving units, there was a space about two feet wide before the wall. On both sides of the room, the spaces were stuffed with more items. Isabella turned to the space on the right, the one closest to the library's back wall.

Isabella lifted a white sheet draped over something but hadn't anticipated the amount of dust she would let loose. She bent over coughing, trying to clear her lungs.

"Hey, cupcake, let me help." Reece gently moved her to the side. He didn't have to direct his magic with his hand, but within seconds, the dust in the air had cleared. The white cloth lay folded on the end of the shelving unit and a stack of chairs blocked the small space.

"Could you move those?" she asked him, determined to find out what was behind them.

"Sure."

When the chairs were gone, Isabella went after one item at a time, pulling them out and handing them off to Reece and Viktor. She pulled out an old, framed movie poster, a painting, a large Christmas wreath, another poster, and a plastic skeleton.

Reece made a few jokes with the skeleton, like he was a teenage boy with too much time on his hands. She laughed before turning back to the hidey-hole of abandoned objects. As she pulled out a cardboard sign advertising a bake sale, she wondered when she went from thinking Reece wasn't serious enough to loving his ability to make her laugh.

He'd shown her he could be dedicated and focused when it was called for, but he also had a way of knowing when to not take life too seriously. That was something she'd never been taught, certainly not by her parents.

Thoughts of her parents fled as she reached for the final object in the corner, and her magic lit up inside her like a Christmas tree on steroids.

Taking a note out of Reece's playbook, she used her magic to clean the sheet of dust before she touched it.

Giving the corner of the cloth a hard tug, it fell to the ground, revealing the third mirror.

REECE SENT the mirror to Kate's forge, feeling when the object arrived. The forge was close enough that sending the mirror the short distance didn't take the use of much power.

"Did you feel it arrive?" Isabella asked, biting at her lip.

He rubbed his thumb on her lip to release the poor thing from her teeth's clutches. "Yes, I did."

She nodded and they followed Viktor back into the private room. He excused himself, going back to the front, while they cleaned up the books they'd strewn over the table.

Isabella flopped into a chair. "I can't believe we found it."

"*You* found it. I knew you would." And he had. Once she'd started to focus, he had faith that she'd find all three mirrors. Now they had to hope that Kate could forge the lock. And that Jack and the others could figure out how to get the magic out of Maverick, or rein him in. They still hadn't come up with a plan as to how they were going to close the box. But after that, there was the matter of releasing his control over other magics.

Mentally listing off all the things that had to take place was enough to make Reece's head spin. But right now, he wanted to take a short pause.

"That's the last one," Isabella said, shelving the last book. "Ready to go?"

"Yes. Meet me at my place?"

"Shouldn't we go to Kate's forge?"

He flashed to the other side of the table and took her lips in a soft kiss but kept space between their bodies. After their morning together, he'd been semi-hard all day, and if he touched her now, they might never get out of the library. "We will," he said and then caressed her lips with his tongue once more.

Putting her hands on her hips, she pursed her lips. "What are you up to, Reece Williams?"

There was both teasing and suspicion in her glance. It was one of the many things he loved about her—Isabella had a prickly side, but underneath the seriousness, there was also a caring and sensual side. That was the part he wanted to bring out now. "You'll have to meet me at my place to find out, cupcake."

He saw her struggle to stay serious as a corner of her lip lifted before she disappeared.

Reece didn't waste any time and took off right after her.

They both landed in his foyer at the same time.

"So what did—"

Cutting her off by placing a finger on her lips, he took her hand and pulled her into the living room. Standing in front of her, he gripped the bottom of her shirt and lifted it so his knuckles grazed the bottoms of her breasts. Her inhale told him all he needed to know.

Instead of magically removing her clothes, he had decided to do it the regular way to heighten the anticipation. Lifting her shirt higher, he watched her eyes, making sure she wasn't going to object. When she lifted her arms, he pulled her shirt all the way off and threw it onto the chair beside them.

She was so beautiful; he wanted to kiss every inch of her, and he would, but not then. Later he'd show her how much he loved her. And yes, he meant love. He figured he'd been falling in love with her since the first time she'd given him the cold shoulder. Or maybe she'd just been a challenge then.

Reaching behind her, he undid her bra and let it fall to the floor. Leaning down, but only letting his lips touch her, he sucked one of her perfect nipples into his mouth. She inhaled again and he wanted to hear her call out his name as she came.

He gave both breasts attention, loving the sound of her

shallow pants before he dropped to his knees and undid the button on her jeans.

Little by little, he'd seen beneath the rigid armor she showed the world, and he wanted to strip away the rest of her layers. On a rooftop while Elvis crooned out of his phone, he'd known he wanted to spend the rest of his life with her.

He loved everything about her, from how she ate cupcakes, to the loyalty she felt for her family even though they didn't deserve it, to the way she tackled everything head-on. From an alley to a boardroom to a cemetery to a face-off with her brother—she was a fighter and he wanted her to fight by his side.

When he pushed down her jeans, he took her panties with them. She stepped out of them, using his shoulder for support, and he tossed them to the side. Gripping the backs of her thighs to hold her still, he ran his lips up her legs. Her breath hitched when he let his hot breath linger over the apex between her thighs.

He tilted his head back to look up at her. "Cupcake?"

When she looked down at him with passion shining through, he almost changed his plans. She deserved to be loved and cherished. Something she'd been missing for so long. Yet he knew he didn't have to go slow to love her. "Do you remember what you said the last time we were in this position?"

A glint came into her eyes and she didn't shy away. "I think it was something like, 'I don't want to talk. I want to fuck.'"

"It was, with the name 'muscles' thrown in there."

She gripped both his shoulders and leaned forward, her breasts dangling in front of his face. "Well?"

Not being able to resist, he took one nipple into his

mouth and bit lightly before switching to the other. At the same time, he snaked his fingers down her body and grazed her labia but didn't enter her. She pushed into his hand, likely trying to get more friction.

Lifting his head so he could look into her eyes, he cupped her butt cheeks with both hands and pulled her flush against him. "You deserve to be cherished, cupcake. Every time I'm with you, I want to take it slow so you feel special, but I also have a driving need to fuck you until you scream my name."

"Yes. Yes, that," she said, breathless.

With just a thought, his clothes were in a pile on the floor beside hers. Gripping her hips, he manhandled her until she stood at the end of the couch. "Put your forearms on the armrest and don't move."

She did as he ordered, her ass in the air presented to him like a special gift. "You're so beautiful." He grabbed his shaft and stroked to the tip, giving himself a squeeze so he wouldn't come from only how she looked bent over. Holding out his hand, he used his magic to retrieve a condom from his bedroom and sheathed himself.

He rubbed the tip of his cock against her wetness, and she pushed back against him. Using one hand, he pushed her back down, holding her in place. "You want me to fuck you, cupcake?"

"Yes, Reece, please! Stop fucking teasing me. Tease later."

If he hadn't been so turned on, he would have continued to tease so she'd beg for more and he could stretch out her pleasure. But he was just as impatient. He rubbed himself against her again, feeling her wetness coat the tip of his cock. Bending to compensate for their height difference, he positioned himself at her entrance and pushed into her so she enveloped the head of his cock.

"Brace your hands on the armrest." His order came out as

more of a bark than a request, but she didn't hesitate. Gripping her hips, he lifted her so her feet no longer touched the ground as he sunk the rest of the way into her. They groaned together and then he started to move, pumping in and out of her. He wasn't fast, but neither was he gentle as he pounded into her. Her body gripped his cock as eased back out before driving his cock home again.

By pushing a little magic into his arms, he was able to firm up his grip as he rocked into her over and over again. The meeting of their flesh and their heavy breathing spurred him on.

"Yes! Uh… yes, yes. Harder!"

He lifted her hips higher, adjusting his angle to make sure he was giving her what she needed.

"Uh… yes!" she yelled, her core tightening around his dick. It took everything in him not to come.

Leaning back to alter his angle a little more, he pumped into her faster. When she screamed his name and her orgasm milked his cock, he let go. His own orgasm ripped from him, forcing his eyes closed as he felt it to the depth of his core.

When he finally came back to reality, he eased out of Isabella, disappeared the condom, and lowered her feet to the floor. She turned around and went on her tiptoes, weaving her arms around his neck. "Wow," she said against his lips.

"Yeah, definitely wow." He kissed her back but had to pull away when he swooped her up into his arms and sat on the couch. Turning so she was straddling him, their mouths played, nipping, and licking each other.

What could have been only minutes later or might have been longer, she snuggled with her face in his neck. Neither one of them rushed to get dressed as they held each other.

The ringing of his phone a few minutes later brought reality crashing in. Holding out his hand, he used his magic to retrieve it. "It's Kate," he whispered to Isabella as he answered the call.

"Hi, Kate. We just had something to do," he said and felt Isabella giggle against his neck. "We'll be over in a few minutes."

"You need to get here now. I don't have good news, Reece."

24

*I*sabella flashed to Kate's forge, Reece right beside her. The forge was a cinderblock building on several acres, surrounded by trees.

From the open double garage-type doors, Kate walked toward them. At probably five foot six or seven, she towered over Isabella. Yet, compared to her brother's massive build, she looked petite. Add in her slender frame and long, strawberry-blond hair, and the two siblings looked nothing alike.

Isabella had met Kate a few times at the family dinners and had felt an affinity with her right from the start. With the love that Kate's family and friends surrounded her with, their backgrounds were poles apart. Yet, like recognized like, and Isabella saw herself in the way Kate held herself—a chip was firmly planted on her shoulder, like she had something to prove. Isabella didn't know the woman's background, but she knew something had made her this way.

For years Isabella had built armor up around herself. It had taken Reece chipping away at it for her to realize that instead of protecting her heart, it was keeping her from finding love.

She now walked over to where he had walked up to greet Kate. Without turning to her, he held out his hand and she put hers in his much larger one. Hand-holding was a simple gesture, but their connection wasn't.

Kate put a sword down on a side bench and her expression was grim when she faced them. "I've checked all three metals and there isn't a magical thing about them."

Isabella sucked in a breath. "That can't be. They called to me." She didn't want to accuse Kate of making a mistake, but she had. This couldn't be the end. Not only because of everything they'd gone through to get the mirrors, but because it was their only way to stop Maverick, and she knew what she had felt.

"Yes, they're just plain old ordinary steel—simply iron mixed with carbon. I checked each one and there isn't anything special about them, let alone magic. I even tested the paint covering the steel, and it's regular enamel paint with a primer."

"Did you use your magic?" Reece asked her.

"Of course, and nothing."

She looked between Kate and Reece. "What am I missing?"

"I can feel emotion in some objects—mostly metals. Again, I got nothing from the metal frames."

Isabella couldn't wrap her mind around the possibility that she had failed. Again. They had focused on the mirrors because she'd been so sure they were the object that had been foretold to close the magic box. If the mirrors weren't the answer, then Isabella had sent herself and Reece on a wild goose chase. Chases, actually, and wasted precious time. "Could there be a spell on the frames? Something concealing what's really there?"

"I hadn't thought about that, but if there is one, I don't

know how to check for it." Kate turned to Reece. "Do you think Jack or Meredith might know?"

"I'll ask." Reece's eyes became unfocused for a moment before he blinked. "They'll be here in a minute."

"I wish one thing would go our way," Meredith said from behind them.

Isabella turned around as Meredith and Jack walked toward them, hand in hand. "I agree. I'm not yet ready to believe the mirrors are useless." Isabella turned to Kate. "Sorry, no offense, Kate."

"Hey, none taken," Kate said, holding up her hands. She turned to Jack and Meredith. "Can you guys tell if they're spelled?"

Kate had put all three mirrors on a long workbench. Meredith laid her hand on one of the mirrors. After a moment, she shook her head. "I don't feel anything." She then checked the other two before turning to face them. "Sorry, nothing. But that doesn't mean they aren't spelled. After all, the spell on Morgana had been undetectable until Isaac sensed something."

The small ember of hope within Isabella that never seemed to extinguish flamed to life. "Could Isaac check the mirrors?"

"I doubt he'll sense anything since his magic works with people, not objects, but we can ask," Kate said before pulling out her phone.

"Don't bother texting him," Jack said. "I've already reached out."

Kate smirked. "I keep forgetting you and Meredith are 'enhanced,'" she said, putting air quotes around her last word.

"I wouldn't call us enhanced," Meredith said with a laugh. "But it does come in handy to reach out telepathically over long distances. And we don't have to worry about someone not answering their phone."

"You called?" Isaac said as he walked up beside Kate and placed a kiss on her temple. She stiffened for a moment but didn't say anything. Isabella figured she'd have to corner her friend sometime later and ask what that was about.

"Do us a favor and check the mirrors for a spell," Jack directed.

"Objects aren't my specialty, but sure." Isaac walked over to the mirrors and placed both his palms on the glass of the one closest to him. When he shook his head and moved onto the next one, Isabella felt the ember of hope inside her dim once more.

"I don't feel anything," Isaac said as he came back over to them. "But don't take my word as gospel. Again, I work with people, not objects."

"Thanks for checking," Jack said. "Anyone have any ideas?"

"What if there was more than one magic object?" Reece threw the thought to the group. "I mean, there are rumored to be seven books, even if we only know of two. And the seer said there was a key for each book. That could mean that when the box was created and the object was made as a countermeasure, more than one object could have been created."

Jack nodded. "I'll check with our seer. In the meantime, let's lock up the mirrors. They might be useless, but we don't know that for sure."

"You can lock them up here," Kate said. "I've got a locker I've been storing them in. You can spell it too."

After the mirrors were stored and locked up, Jack and Meredith left. Isaac pulled Kate aside, and since it looked like an intimate conversation, Isabella turned to Reece. "I want to go back to the library."

"Okay, but it's late and it'll be closed. We can go in the morning. I'll let Viktor know that we'll flash into the back room before the library is open, so he can make sure we won't trigger an alarm."

As much as she wanted to find an answer to the mirrors right away, she wasn't disappointed that they would wait until the morning. It had been a long day already with her emotions taking a roller coaster ride. "Okay…" Insecurity swamped her when she thought about what this meant. Did he want time away from her?"

As if he could read her mind, he leaned down and kissed her softly on the lips. "Let's go back to my place. We can have meatloaf and then give my arms another workout."

"Workout?" She grinned when she realized he was referring to the couch and not the gym. "Meet you there."

Reece sat back in his chair and rubbed his neck, using some magic to heat and loosen his tight muscles.

"Stiff?" Isabella asked.

Dropping his hand, he smiled at her. "Yeah, but not too bad. How about you?"

"I'm good. I just feel like we've done this before."

He huffed out a laugh. "We definitely have. This private library room is becoming a second home, but not in a good way." Flashing over to her side of the table, he sat in the chair beside her and then pulled her into his lap. Her soft squeal made him smile, but then he silenced her with a kiss. The entire world and all their problems fell away when he had her in his arms. The problem was that eventually the world always intruded.

Her head rested on his chest and he nestled his lips against her neck. Soaking in her sweet smell of apricot and vanilla, he pressed his lips against her soft skin. "What are you thinking, cupcake?"

"Yesterday, when we found out about the mirrors, I was devastated. Then after some more of your mom's meatloaf and some sexy times…" She lifted her head and grinned up at him. "I was refreshed and ready to tackle this again, but now…"

"Now?" he prompted.

"I don't know that I'm devastated so much as disheartened. We've been back at this for two hours and I haven't found anything."

"You will." He had to believe it. The thought that they wouldn't save his brother and cousin, or that someone like Maverick could control all magics, was too much to even think about. There had to be a way for them to win.

"There is something that's been puzzling me."

"What's that?" he asked.

"Why did the book tell us to find the mirrors if they weren't the answer? I mean, they don't contain the metal we're looking for, but there has to be a reason that the prophecy said to look for them to begin with."

He thought about all the magic he'd studied since coming out of his coma. Most of the spells were straightforward, but some had been more like info dumping. Sometimes one spell was actually a clue that led him to the correct spell.

Lifting Isabella off his lap, he jumped to his feet. "You're right. I don't know why I didn't see it earlier." It was like a thousand-watt lightbulb had suddenly been switched on in his head.

Remembering what Jo and Simon had told him about combining spells, he headed to the door.

"Wait. Reece, where are you going?"

"I'll be right back."

When he walked into the main part of the library, Viktor looked up. "You find something?"

"Not exactly, but I think you can help us."

Viktor stood and gestured to the back room. "You lead, I follow."

Back in the private room, Isabella was standing, as if she'd been planning on following him. "Reece, what's going on?"

He pulled up a chair beside her and she sat in hers. Viktor sat across from them. They both looked at Reece as if he had all the answers and he hoped he did. Or at least a clue to finding one.

"Just before Jo and Simon found the ancient book, I'd been put in a magically induced coma…" Isabella put her hand on his lap, and he pushed all thoughts of the coma aside and focused on the present. "Later, they explained that they had to combine some spells to find the final clue to the book. And then Jo said it was like they had to prove they were worthy of finding the book before it would even present itself."

"Yes, I remember," Viktor said. "When you first came here, I said the first spell they found was a dud. But later, they combined part of it with another."

"Exactly," Reece said, his excitement amping up because he was sure he was on the right track. Turning to Isabella, he saw a hint of hope in her eyes. "What if the prophecy told us to find the mirrors, but we haven't yet proven we're worthy of what they're hiding?"

Her eyes widened as recognition dawned. "You mean like we thought yesterday? That we need to find a spell that will unlock the metal?"

"Yes, or we'll discover that the mirrors are only a clue to the object we need to find."

"I don't mean to be a downer, but we've looked through

everything. How are we going to find the right spell and how will we know when we do?"

"The first book," Viktor said as he stood and walked to one of the shelves. Pulling out a book, he placed it on the book cradle in the middle of the table and stepped back. Reece and Isabella walked around the table to stand beside him.

Reece glanced at the book's cover. "That's the one where we found the prophecy?"

"Yes, but it also holds the first spell Jo and Simon found."

Isabella frowned. "Wasn't that the one that was a dud?"

"On its own, yes," Viktor said. "But they did use part of it to help them find the final clue."

"You think that's what we need to do? Combine two spells?" Isabella let out a huge sigh. "How will we find the other spell?"

Reece lifted the book's cover. "I don't think we'll need another one. Will we?" he asked, looking over his shoulder to find a grinning Viktor. "You think this one will be enough?"

"I do, yes. There's just something about the words in the spell that seem right. Float the original prophecy in a bubble and then we will do the same to the spell Jo and Simon found," Viktor said and then dimmed the lights.

When Viktor had done it the first time, Reece had asked Viktor to teach him how to do it too. Anything extra Reece could add to his magic arsenal, he did, never knowing when a particular spell could come in handy. Turning to the page with the prophecy that told them of the mirrors, Reece used his magic to float the words in a bubble.

Viktor came over and turned to a different section of the book. "This is the spell Jo and Simon found." Like he'd taught Reece, he floated the words into a bubble beside the first one.

"Cupcake, why don't you read them?"

Isabella nodded and read the verses aloud.

"Looking glasses with secrets they confide,
Reflections of fate, they must abide.
Hidden from all eyes,
Thrice divided under safety of skies.
Entwined they decree,
Unveil what's meant to be."

She shifted over a foot until she was standing in front of the second bubble and continued.

"For all the magics seeking within be worthy of this book.
To know thine self to know that worth is the right look.
"For the spells of magic herein have been undertaken.
Only by the most rightful and honest will they awaken.
Evil that lies in wait be gone now, abate.
Reveal thyself to be true and end this wait."

Reece hadn't realized he was holding his breath until a third bubble floated beside the first two.

"It worked," Isabella whispered in awe. Without waiting, she read the passage.

"A trio shall be,
To unlock secrets for all to see.
Looking glasses align, as lights dance,
A story whispers as if in trance.
Secrets unfold as magic flows.
Reflections echo and treasure unveiled,
A hidden object detailed."

Isabella faced him, her mouth open in shock. "It's not the metal at all! We'd assumed that from what we were told, but it's the mirrors themselves, isn't it?"

"Yes, I think it is." Reece looked at the words still floating in a bubble. "I think 'looking glass aligned' means we need them to face each other. The 'reflections echo' must mean that when the three reflections intersect, it will open a portal or something."

"We did it!" She bounced against him, weaving her arms around his neck, and planted her lips on his. When he picked her up, she wound her legs around his hips and kissed him like he was her lifeline.

She slid down his body after they finally broke their kiss. They'd been so caught up in each other they hadn't noticed Viktor had left and the bubbles were gone.

After putting the books away, they popped out to the main room to thank Viktor. Since they'd flashed into the private room early in the morning before the library opened, they would leave the same way. Reece wanted to avoid back alleys and limit their chances of running into Eddie.

Isabella had suggested they flash right to Kate's forge as it wasn't even noon. She hadn't given much thought to what the object made from the metal would look like, but now she was pumped to see it.

25

*I*sabella smiled, the endorphin rush from finding the answer still vibrating through her, as she landed in the forge's enclosed back porch.

Reece arrived at the same time, and he took her hand as they walked around to the building's garage doors.

When they reached the front, he tugged her hand, pulling her back around to the corner of the building. *Something's wrong.*

Dropping her hand, he lifted his in front of him. She did the same, pushing magic into her fingers as she responded. *How do you know?*

The doors.

It wasn't until he pointed to the doors that she noticed one was hanging on its hinges.

Sending her magic toward the building, she felt for malevolence but sensed nothing. "Sense anything?" she whispered.

"Nothing out of the ordinary. But someone is in there." They walked toward the doors, both ready with their magic.

With one door hanging from its hinges and the other

thrown wide open, they had a clear view inside once they rounded the corner. "Kate!" Isabella screamed and ran toward the woman lying on the ground.

Reece flashed ahead of her to Kate's side and kneeled beside her prone form. Isabella dropped down as well, barely feeling her knees hit the concrete floor. "She's bleeding. Did you message someone?"

"We're here," Jack said as he came up behind them before Reece could answer. Isabella got to her feet and moved back to give Jack and Meredith room to see to Kate.

"What happened?" a deep voice asked, and she recognized Isaac as he knelt by Kate's head. He ran his hand over her forehead and hair, the blood and cut disappearing as he did.

"We don't know," Reece said, pulling Isabella back into his front and wrapping his arms around her. "When we got here, we noticed one of the doors was off its hinges and put out some feelers but didn't sense anyone inside."

Jack hovered his hands over Kate. Worry for her friend collided with a feeling of security as she stood in the warmth of Reece's arms.

"Bruises and a hit to the head, but I've healed her. She'll be fine," Jack said as he waved his hand over Kate one more time.

Kate moaned and her eyes flung open. "Wha—" She struggled to sit up, but Isaac reached her before she could. Taking a seat on the floor behind her, he pulled her up so she could lean against him.

"I'm fine." Kate batted one of Isaac's hands away and pushed forward to sit up before wobbling backward.

Issac pulled her higher onto his lap, his arms around her waist. "For Christ's sake, woman. You were unconscious; give yourself a second."

Several expressions flitted across Kate's face before she leaned back into Isaac. Isabella understood those expressions as like recognized like once more. Kate was worried about leaning on Isaac, and not just in a physical sense, because it could be seen as weakness. She expected that Kate also felt guilty for letting whatever had happened get the better of her.

"Kate, can you tell us how you got hurt?" Meredith asked.

"Someone came up behind me. I was using my power hammer, so it was loud. I didn't notice anyone was there until someone grabbed my arm. When they spun me around, I used my magic to grab a blade and I jabbed at the guy but missed. It was like he had superspeed."

"You should have flashed away," Isaac said close to Kate's ear, the accusation still loud enough for everyone to hear.

Seeing Kate bristle, she knew what was coming next and almost smiled. If the situation wasn't so serious, Isabella would have teased Isaac about saying the wrong thing. Instead, she watched, waiting for the explosion she knew was coming.

"Flash away? Are you crazy?" Kate's voice rose an octave as she twisted in Isaac's lap so she could see him. "My forge is my life! I wasn't just going to leave all my equipment and let a bunch of assholes do whatever they wanted! And what about the mirrors? Did you just want me to leave them too?"

"No, of course not," Isaac said with sarcasm. "But instead, you let them almost take your actual life!"

Isabella bit the inside of her lip as her smile threatened again. Watching the interaction between Kate and Isaac was fascinating. But she expected it wasn't so dissimilar from what she and Reece must have looked like not too long ago. Like Kate, Isabella's chip on her shoulder and her fortified armor had put everyone in danger because it stopped them from finding the mirrors sooner. It was a sobering thought.

"Why are you here, anyway?" Kate asked, glaring at Isaac.

"I was having lunch with Jack and Meredith when Reece messaged."

"You didn't have to come," Kate said again.

"What? You think—"

"Kate," Jack said, stopping the lover's spat. He hadn't barked her name, yet authority dripped from the one word. "Tell us the rest."

Turning in Isaac's arms, Kate looked at Jack. "There were three of them. The guy who grabbed me, a woman, and another guy. The third guy didn't come near me, but he was definitely in charge."

Isabella felt like her stomach was constantly in knots lately, and she felt another one form. "What did he look like?"

"The boss guy? His head was almost shaved, and he had olive-toned skin. The backs of his hands were covered in tattoos, but I couldn't make any of them out."

"Eddie," Isabella said and felt Reece's arms tighten around her. She loved that he was trying to comfort her, but it wasn't enough to ease the growing knot in her gut. "That's my brother. Reece and I have already had a couple of run-ins with him. Was he looking for the mirrors?"

"I don't know if they got them!" Kate struggled to get up but Isaac didn't loosen his hold on her.

"Kate—"

"I'll check," Jack said as he stood and walked to the back of the forge.

Isabella didn't have to look to know they were gone, but she did anyway. The mirrors were the only explanation as to why Eddie would have been there.

Jack pulled on the locker door and it swung open. The locker was empty.

"The door was still locked, but someone dissolved the spell," Jack said as he walked to them. "Only someone with Maverick's magic could have destroyed the spell I cast.

Which means that the spells we're using on the buildings at night aren't going to be enough to keep out Maverick and his people."

Meredith grasped her husband's hand. "Plus, we still have to figure out how to close the magic box since the mirrors didn't work."

Isabella felt Reece straighten behind her as she remembered their discovery. She'd been so distracted by Kate that she hadn't thought to share it with them. "We found the answer!" All eyes turned to her. "It wasn't the metal frames we needed to find. It's the mirrors!" Her earlier excitement flooded back into her. It didn't matter that they didn't have the mirrors anymore; they'd get them back. Due to the type of magic they were facing, she had no idea how. But with everything they'd been through, she couldn't give up hope now.

Reece dropped his arms from around her and took her hand, coming up beside her. "We'll get the mirrors back," he said as if reading her mind. "We know where Eddie hangs out."

"What help do you need?" Jack asked.

"Some kind of backup, but I don't know yet. Isabella and I should go in first since Eddie will be expecting us."

Jack furrowed his brows. "Then you'll need more people."

Reece gave her hand a squeeze and she squeezed back. They were on the same page. "Jack," she said, "I agree with Reece. Eddie will be expecting us, and he has Rocky and Mirek. He won't hesitate to hurt them if too many people show up." As much as she felt ashamed to reveal more about her brother's weaknesses, these people needed to know. The sudden realization that these people weren't just friends hit her. They were more like family to her than her own had ever been. "If Eddie feels threatened, he'll want to flaunt his superior power. And he won't hesitate to do it. Reece and I have already seen him do just that."

Jack nodded. "Give us the address and we'll be close by, ready to help."

Reece squeezed her hand again and she knew he agreed. Never before had someone supported her the way he did. And with that, the last of her armor fell away.

"Let's all go to The Magic Plate. Isabella and I need some lunch. We expended a lot of magic this morning, and we still need to refuel. We can give you the address and explain the layout."

Jack and Meredith agreed, and Isaac said he'd stay with Kate. He ignored her protests, and this time Isabella couldn't stop her smile. Isaac chipping away at Kate's armor would be something to see. Though Isabella worried she wouldn't be around to witness it because she might be dead by the end of the day.

26

Reece looked up at the building before turning to Isabella. He expected Eddie would have kept his brother and cousin alive to use them, but Eddie was also a loose cannon, so he couldn't be sure. "Are you sure Eddie will be on the same floor?" he asked Isabella.

"Yes. In his mind, changing floors will make it look like he's hiding from you. He'll do everything he can to show his superior strength. I…" She shook her head.

Using his fingers to lift her chin, he looked her in the eyes. "Hey, cupcake. Talk to me," he said softly.

"I've been looking for my brother for years, but I still had this vision in my head of him as my cute and outgoing kid brother. How could I have been so blind?"

"Because you loved him." He touched his lips to hers in the softest of kisses.

"I did… I still do… or maybe I love who I thought he was."

"It's okay for you to love him, cupcake. He's your brother, no matter what he's done. That's a tie you can't sever."

"I know…" She looked toward the building before looking back at him, and he saw her resolve settle. "Let's go get your brother. And your cousin," she said, "And the mirrors." Her lips twitched with a small smile. "We have our work cut out for us."

"We do... but wait," he said before she could flash. When he clasped her upper arms and faced her, she met his gaze. "Before we go in there, I need you to know that I love you, cupcake." Her breath hitched, but she didn't look away. "I love everything about you—your prickly side, your feisty side, and how you love with your full heart, even when someone doesn't deserve it. I love you, Isabella."

Before she could respond, he pulled her into his arms and kissed her like it was the last kiss they'd ever have. The possibility that it could be had crossed his mind more than once. If it came to be, he needed her to know how he felt. Not because he wanted her to say it back, but because he couldn't die with her not knowing how much she meant to him.

When they pulled back from one another, she cupped his cheek. "I love you too, Reece." She lifted to her tiptoes and gave him a quick kiss. "Now let's get this over with. I'm getting fucking sick of Eddie's shit."

"Same." During their planning, they'd agreed to flash to the far end of the hall of the floor below where they were held the day before.

Once in the hall, they didn't speak as Reece led them up the stairwell to the floor above. Since Eddie had sensed Reece yesterday, they knew it was a possibility that he'd be able to sense them now. But they didn't know how soon he'd be able to detect them.

Reece stopped at the door leading into the hallway and opened it, looking for Eddie's goon. The hall was empty.

"Get the fuck in here!" Eddie yelled when Reece had only taken three steps.

"I guess he's talking to us," Isabella whispered. He looked

down in time to see her roll her eyes and his love for her swelled. They were going to make it through this.

They passed the ballroom they'd been in the day before and found Eddie in the next room.

When they faced Eddie, doubts hit him for the first time.

Smaller than the ballroom, the room held furniture which further diminished the space. Two sofas, a coffee table, and two end tables with lamps perched on their surfaces made it the homiest room he'd seen in the apartment. Mirek was curled up on one of the sofas, his eyes closed. Rocky laid on the floor against the back wall, as if Eddie had flung him there.

One of the mirrors had been smashed into pieces, the shattered glass spread out on the floor near Eddie's feet; the frame, broken in two, lay off to the side.

"About fucking time you got here," Eddie said. "These mirrors are fucking useless, and you've been leading me in fucking circles." When he pointed at him, Reece moved in front of Isabella and braced himself for whatever Eddie was going to throw his way. "Find me the fucking object that closes the box!"

With Eddie's vocabulary deteriorating by the second, Reece knew his options for dealing with the man were limited. He hesitated for a moment, debating which approach to take with Eddie. He could stay calm, which could incite Eddie more, or he could be aggressive, matching Eddie's attitude without overdoing it. Reece chose the latter, taking a gamble that Eddie would consider anyone who didn't stand up to him to be weak. Reece widened his stance and put his hands on his hips as he spoke. "The mirrors were the answer, but you broke one, asshole."

"Then fucking fix it!" Eddie yelled, his face turning red.

Reece feared that as soon as he did just that, Eddie would kill them all. If he could get Eddie to explain Maverick's plan, it might help Jack and the others. It might also give Reece time to think of a way to get them out of there. "Why do you want them? If you can't get the object, then no one can, and the box is safe."

"Think you're so fucking smart, don't ya," Eddie sneered. "I'm not like that idiot Drew who wanted everything for himself. I know where the real power is. By getting the object for Maverick, he'll give me more power, and then I can do whatever I want."

"What *do* you want?"

Eddie's eyes widened as if Reece had asked him if he was a man. "Are you fucking stupid? I want what everyone wants. Power. Now shut the fuck up and fix the mirror."

Isabella grasped his wrist. "No, don't. If you do it, he'll never stop," she whispered, but she wasn't so quiet that Eddie wouldn't have heard her.

"Shut the fuck up, Isabella. If he won't fix it, I'll make him." Eddie turned to one of his goons standing in the at-ease position a few feet away and lifted his hand. The goon clutched his throat and gasped for air but didn't make a sound. When Eddie lifted his hand higher, the man rose in the air. Suspended about a foot above the ground, the man struggled to release the invisible clasp on his neck as his feet thrashed in the air.

"See what I can do?" Eddie taunted. "And that's not all." The man's face turned red, and his feet flailed.

"Stop! Eddie, stop! Don't kill him!" Isabella screamed.

Reece stepped in front of Isabella again but didn't yell at Eddie. There was no point—he was power-hungry and nothing was going to stop him from displaying it.

It didn't take long for the man's face to turn blue and then his struggles ceased. Eddie dropped his hand and the man hit the ground with a thud. There were no gasps for air. He'd already been dead when Eddie released him.

Turning back to them, Eddie pointed in their direction. "Are you going to fix the fucking mirror now?"

Glancing at Rocky and Mirek, Reece still had no idea if they were even alive. But with no doubt that Eddie would attack Isabella if he didn't repair the mirror, he had only one choice. "Yes, I'll fix the mirror for you." What Eddie didn't realize was that he'd just taught Reece a lesson, and it wasn't about power. No, Reece realized that physical and magical strength meant nothing without compassion and morals.

ISABELLA STARED at the man's body on the floor. One moment he'd been alive and the next he was dead at her brother's hands. As if the man's life hadn't mattered.

So many times over the last few weeks, she'd tried to reconcile the sweet little boy she used to know with the man she just saw carelessly take a life. Yes, she knew now that she'd put Mateo on a pedestal. After all, little boys were cute and meant the world to their big sisters, especially one like her, who had practically raised him.

Had she always ignored his selfish behavior and temper tantrums? Or was it only after he'd disappeared that she'd shoved all but the fondest memories to the recesses of her mind?

She half listened as Eddie ranted more about wasting time and a memory of Mateo when he was about ten came to her mind. She'd been called by Mateo's principal because the woman hadn't been able to reach their parents. Walking into the woman's office, Mateo had looked so small sitting in a hardbacked chair in the corner. As soon as he'd seen her, he'd rushed to her, wrapping his arms around her waist. He'd been small as a child and hadn't come up to her chin.

She'd asked him what he'd done, needing to hear it in his own words. Tears had welled in his eyes. "I didn't mean it, Izzy. They bullied me first." He sniffed as a tear trickled down his cheek. Hugging him, she'd kissed the top of his head and told him everything would be alright.

Leaving Mateo in the outer office, she'd had a private conversation with the principal. The woman explained that Mateo had bullied other children and taunted them, saying mean and spiteful things.

Searching her memories now, she tried to recall how she or her parents had punished Mateo for the acts, and realized they hadn't. They'd let him get away with it, just like always.

"Yes, I'll fix the mirror for you," Reece said, his words pulling Isabella out of her memories.

Tearing her eyes away from the dead man, she turned to Reece. Cupping one side of his face in her hand, she looked into his eyes. With Eddie in the room, she wouldn't voice her love for Reece and give Eddie more reasons to taunt them. But she pleaded for Reece to see it in her eyes. *Don't do it. Please.*

I have to, cupcake. He leaned down and kissed her forehead before turning to Eddie.

Walking closer to the glass on the floor, Reece raised his hands. Since he didn't need his hands to direct his magic, she figured he was doing it because he didn't want to show Eddie how powerful his magic really was.

The frame moved first, the two pieces sliding toward each other until they came together to form a rectangle. Next, the glass. The scattered shards melted like molten lava and oozed across the floor. Each bubble of liquid seeped under the frame and joined with its brethren. A few inches at a time, the mirror lengthened as the liquid bubbles melded together and solidified. Finally, the last fragment of liquid glass fused with the others—the mirror now complete.

"About fucking time," Eddie said, his hands on his hips like he owned the world. "Now get the object."

"We don't know how," Isabella said before Reece could speak up. She was sick and tired of Eddie bossing them around. But she knew there was no reasoning with him either. It was time to call in Jack and the others.

Keeping her eyes on Eddie, she threw a message to Reece. *Contact Jack.*

No response.

That wasn't what she expected. Jack had said he'd be on standby, and from what she'd seen and heard, the man was good for his word.

Eddie stalked toward her. "I'm done fucking waiting. Get the object."

She looked him in the eyes, and for a moment, she saw the little boy who had the same eyes she saw every day when she looked in the mirror. "I said I don't know how."

Standing in front of them, his eyes softened, and she wondered if it was a trick of the light. "Please, Izzy, I need you to get the mirror."

Hearing the nickname called to something inside her. She looked up into his eyes, wanting so desperately to believe that the brother she remembered was still inside him. Then, out of the corner of her eyes, she saw the dead man on the floor.

She'd never questioned whether Mateo's tears had been real. Only now she wondered if they'd been assisted by magic and had been one of many weapons in his arsenal that he used to manipulate people.

Lifting her chin, she locked her gaze with his. "Fuck you, Eddie."

Reece chuckled beside him, but she kept her eyes on Eddie. Taunting him had been the wrong thing to do, but she'd had enough of his manipulation. Pushing magic into her fingertips so she would be prepared for anything, she hoped Reece was doing the same.

Eddie grabbed a handful of her hair, forcing her onto her toes when he pulled her toward him. "Think you're tough, do ya? Well, look what you made me do." Twisting his hand, he turned her head and she gasped.

Reece lay on the floor, his mouth open in a silent scream as he thrashed around. "I'm the one in control, bitch."

Lifting her hands, she aimed her magic at Eddie, prepared to do her worst, when her throat squeezed shut. Clawing at her throat, she tried to release the pressure on her neck, but there wasn't anything physical to loosen. She felt blood trickle down her neck as her fingernails bit into her own flesh. Eddie's image swam in front of her as her vision blurred and a lightheadedness swamped her.

Her brother was going to kill her.

His image was gray now, a faded blending of his features.

Slowly, her eyelids closed, blocking out all light.

"I should kill you," Eddie said, his voice in her ear.

The pressure on her neck released suddenly and she fell forward. Bent over, her hands on her knees, she took in small gulps of air. Her swollen and bruised throat made breathing difficult, even as she desperately drew in air.

"Now find me the fucking object!" Eddie grabbed a fistful of her hair again and twisted her head back so she was forced to look at him.

"Release Reece and I will," she whispered.

"I told you, you fucking bitch. I'm in control here, not you."

She stared him in the eyes and didn't waver. "Release him or I won't help you."

He threw his hand back, letting her go, and she stumbled to stay on her feet. Spinning around, she dropped to her knees beside Reece.

When they were cuddled in bed the night before, Reece had tried to explain the feeling of Eddie's torture. He knew he could breathe, but the pain was so excruciating and all-consuming that it felt like every cell in his body had shut down. And because of her refusing Eddie, Reece had to feel that agony all over again.

"Reece?" She picked up his hand and kissed the back of it as she watched his chest heave up and down while he tried to take in air. "You're okay. You have lots of air."

She waited as his breathing returned to normal. It was hard to believe that it had only been the night before when she'd been in his arms, listening to him talk. It felt like a lifetime ago.

Eddie towered over them and kicked at Reece's feet.

"Stop it!" she screamed. So intent on Reece, she hadn't noticed Eddie swing his leg back. Pain bloomed in her hip and she fell over, skidding several feet across the floor.

27

Isabella's brother or not, Reece was ready to end this guy. "Enough!" he tried to yell at Eddie, his voice still barely above a whisper. "I'll help you. Just let me check on her."

"She's fine; I didn't kick her hard. Now hurry up."

Using the arm of a sofa, he pulled himself to his feet and glanced over at Isabella. *Cupcake?*

I'm okay.

That would have to be enough for now. *Jack?* Still no answer from Jack. Something was wrong.

"Move it," Eddie said.

Reece couldn't stall anymore and walked into the middle of the room.

"Oh, and don't think you can call your friends. Maverick is entertaining them." Eddie snorted at his own joke. "You've got five minutes to get the object or I kill someone. I'll start with your useless brother and then I'll move on to the bitch over there."

"I'll do it. Just give me a fucking second," he said, putting authority in his voice and hoping Eddie would respond to it, at least temporarily.

Behind him, Isabella cried out and he spun around. She was being dragged across the floor, her hair leading the way, but no one was touching her. Before he could do anything, she was pulled up onto her feet.

Eddie grasped her around the throat. "She can breathe—for now. Let's just say I thought you needed a little more incentive. And don't think I won't kill her."

Reece couldn't look Isabella in the eyes because if he saw her in pain, he'd lose it. With Eddie's immense power, fighting him would be useless. His only hope was that Jack would get free of whatever Maverick was doing and come help.

Using his hands to direct his magic as if he needed to use them, Reece floated the three mirrors toward him. They hung in the air, like they were laying flat on an invisible cloud. One by one, he rotated them until each mirror stood perpendicular to the floor. Bringing them to him and turning them all upright in one move would have been easy. But drawing out his actions as long as possible would give Jack more time and also help Eddie underestimate Reece's power.

Taking his time, he moved the mirrors a few inches each, one at a time, as if lining them up in a perfect circle.

I'm here.

Reece heard Rocky's voice in his mind, and it took all his concentration not to look in his brother's direction. He didn't know if Rocky had awakened or if he'd been pretending to be unconscious all this time. Whatever the reason, he was glad to have his brother by his side. *Okay.*

"Hurry the fuck up!" Eddie yelled.

Isabella cried out, and Reece jerked his head up. Her fingers were curled around Eddie's that were on her throat as she gasped for air.

Reece lowered the mirrors to the ground. "Loosen your grip, or I stop."

"I'll kill her," Eddie said.

They both knew Reece had the upper hand at the moment, although it wasn't much of one.

The only sign that Eddie had loosened his fist was Isabella's huge gasps for air. "Hurry the fuck up."

Reece picked the mirrors back up and went through the same process as before, once more taking his time. He didn't need Eddie questioning why he could go faster this time around.

The mirrors floated in a circle that was about ten feet in circumference, the space big enough for someone to walk into the circle and retrieve an object. Reece hoped they were close enough together.

When he couldn't stall anymore, he rotated the mirrors inward, guessing that once he did, the reflections would catch.

He stepped back, and within seconds, a light shot out of one of the mirrors, connecting with the one across from it. Then another light from the same mirror hit the third one. One by one, two lights shot from each mirror and connected them with the others.

Reece flung his forearm over the tops of his eyes, acting as a visor when the lights brightened to be almost blinding. The point of intersection of all the lights swelled until it filled the entire circle. Then, without notice, it burst like a supernova, filling the room with an intense flash of light.

Reece stumbled back, catching himself before he fell on his ass. Looking back at the mirrors, the light had dimmed. While still bright, it no longer felt like a laser burning his pupils.

Inside the circle lay a long broad sword, like one a Viking

would have used. Over three feet in length, it floated on a cloud of air.

"Holy fuck!" Eddie said as he stepped into the circle.

Reece didn't try to stop him. Their only hope now was to escape while Eddie was occupied. Jack and the others could figure out what to do about the sword later.

Eddie gazed down at the sword while his fingers hovered above it but didn't touch it. Admiration. That was the only word Reece could think of to describe the look on Eddie's face. The man could kill without remorse but stood in awe of a piece of metal.

Reaching for the sword with his right hand, Eddie hesitated, then looked over his shoulder to where he'd left Isabella.

"For years you've hounded me, and I've had to stay one step ahead of you. I can't have you stand in my way anymore." Flinging his arm up, he aimed his fingers toward his sister.

Eddie's magic flew out, hitting Isabella square in the chest.

Reece couldn't yell or scream, his feet frozen to the floor. He watched in disbelief, time slowing down before his eyes, as the magic hit Isabella.

Her eyes widened as she looked at her brother before the force lifted her off her feet. Flung up and backward, she hung in the air, suspended for only a moment before crashing to the floor.

As if his body was suddenly thawed from its frozen state, Reece flashed to Isabella. "Cupcake?" Dropping to his knees, he pulled her into his arms, wiping the hair out of her eyes. All the color had drained from her face, her skin too light a contrast with her dark hair. "Isabella? Can you hear me?"

"It's mine!" Eddie shouted.

Reece whipped his head around to the circle as Eddie's right hand grasped the sword. When his fingers curled around the hilt, his back arched unnaturally and his body went rigid. A bloodcurdling scream followed. Like shards of glass to Reece's ears, it sent a shiver down his spine.

Eddie's scream felt like it went on forever as it echoed through the room, bouncing off the walls. Then it stopped.

Eddie fell backward, his hand charred and his eyes open and vacant.

Not sparing him another glance, Reece looked down at the woman who had captured his heart, now laying lifeless in his arms. He didn't say a word because there were none that would make this right. His tears fell and hit her cheek as he rocked her.

"Reece!"

The harsh tone registered first, then the hand on his shoulder. Somehow, he knew it was Rocky, but he couldn't tear his gaze away from Isabella. Her eyes were closed, and he wanted to believe she was just asleep.

"Reece, lay her down."

Startled by the voice, Reece looked forward. Mirek knelt in front of him, gently pulling at his arm to release Isabella.

Lowering her to the floor, Reece picked up her limp hand and rubbed it between both of his, willing her to live.

Mirek hovered his hands over Isabella and then dropped them to his knees. When his cousin met his gaze, his eyes were tired and solemn. "To non-magics, she would be dead, Reece."

"What do you mean to non-magics?"

"Her body is dead, but her magic hasn't left her yet. As long as she still has some magic remaining in her body, she's still technically alive."

Too afraid to ask if there was hope, he pleaded instead. "Please, Mirek. Sam said you're an extraordinary healer."

"Sam?" The tiredness fell from Mirek's face as he sat up straighter. "You've seen her?"

"Yes, she's back home."

With those four words, Mirek slumped and hung his head.

"She said she loves you. Do you love her too?"

"I do," Mirek whispered, meeting his eyes.

"Then you'll understand what I'm feeling. I love Isabella, but it's more than that. I've never felt anything like this before. I need her. I'll give my life for hers. Please, you have to help her." Reece wasn't sure what was possible, but he'd read about some astounding accounts of healing in the ancient magic books. Maverick and his cohorts wouldn't have kept Mirek with them for this long if he wasn't a valuable healer. "Please, Mirek."

Lifting his head to Rocky, Mirek looked like he was asking a silent question. Then Rocky kneeled beside them and shook his head.

"What am I missing? What's going on?" He looked between his brother and cousin.

Mirek let out a long sigh. "There might be a way to bring her back since her magic is still with her. But it's fading fast."

"Then do it!"

"It's not that simple, Reece. There are risks. Plus, my power is almost drained. I've been like this for a long time. Eddie would drain my magic and only give me enough to heal. Before him, it was Snake. Before him, it was… it doesn't matter. I don't think I have enough."

Reece kissed Isabella's hand again, sending warmth into her. "But there is a way, right? That's why you both shared a look."

"Eddie is continually siphoning my magic, and Rocky gives me some when I need it to heal. But today he had to give me more than usual because Eddie got careless and almost drained me. I would have died if Rocky hadn't helped me." Mirek looked up at his cousin and an understanding passed between them. "I won't let him give me any more because it could hurt him."

"Take it from me." Reece could hear the desperation in his own voice but didn't care.

Mirek shook his head. "You're already weak from what

Eddie did, and if I take more, it could kill you. And there's no guarantee I can even heal her. Then you'd both be dead."

Reece looked down at Isabella again and knew there wasn't a choice. "Do it. I don't want to live without her." If giving up his strength meant Isabella would live, he'd willingly live out his days as weak as a baby. And if he died, he'd go knowing he'd done everything he could to save her.

"Hurry, then, her magic is fading. Lie down beside her."

Stretching out beside her, Reece kept her hand in his, still pushing warmth into her. He knew it likely wasn't helping, but he had to at least feel like he was doing something.

Moving to kneel in between them, Mirek laid one hand on Reece's stomach and the other on Isabella's.

Reece locked his eyes on Isabella and waited for any sign of her improving.

The draw on his magic was weak at first, just a tingling sensation in his core. He stopped pushing warmth into Isabella so Mirek could take all the magic he needed.

The tingling turned to an ache, but Reece didn't move or look away.

When the ache became painful, he felt his magic push against the sensation. It was like his magic was trying to protect itself. He let out a slow, long breath, forcing himself to relax and not fight.

Time had no meaning as he laid with Isabella's hand in his and breathed against the increasing pain.

"I can't do any more. I'll drain you," Mirek said, his voice tinged with shame. "I'm sorry, Reece. I'm just not strong enough."

When he felt Mirek start to lift his hand, Reece placed his own on top of his cousin's. "Drain me. Take what you need to help Isabella. She's all that matters."

"No," Rocky said, standing behind Mirek.

After the fire when he'd lost his brother, Reece had

dreams that Dylan wasn't dead and that he'd come back. In the mornings, he'd wake devastated, realizing it was never going to happen. Now, he had a chance to get to know his brother again, but it would mean nothing without Isabella.

"Pleas—" Before he could finish, his brother cut him off.

"Together," Rocky said as he placed his hands on Mirek's shoulders.

Mirek nodded and closed his eyes as he took power from both his cousins.

As Reece's power drained from him, his thoughts drifted. He remembered the first few days after coming out of the coma and feeling so disgusted with his weaknesses—both physically and magically. He didn't regret working hard to strengthen his body and his magic. It was the thought of how he would use those strengths that had changed since then. They weren't so he could prove he never had to rely on anyone again or so he could find all the answers and be seen as worthy by others.

All that mattered now was having the strength to give Mirek what he needed to save Isabella.

A gasp sounded from beside him. Isabella's eyes opened just as Mirek fell backward, caught by Rocky's legs.

Isabella felt a strange sensation inside her, like her magic had just recharged. Except it didn't usually feel that way. Someone squeezed her hand.

"Hey, cupcake."

"Hey." She smiled at Reece and then realized they were lying on the floor. "What happened?"

Neither of them tried to sit up, staying on the floor holding hands. "You put the mirrors together," she whispered. Rewinding time in her mind, she remembered Eddie hurting her. She had been sure that her brother was going to kill her.

"You put the mirrors together..." she repeated and then let her voice trail off as she rolled to her side and kissed him. Just a soft brushing of her lips against his, needing to feel more than only his hand.

Now also on his side, they faced each other. "Then what?" he asked prompting her.

"He choked me again and you put the mirrors down and waited for him to let me go before you started again." When he nodded, she had to think hard before continuing. After that, everything that had happened seemed fuzzy. "A portal formed. There was a sword."

She gasped when the pieces started to fall into place. "Eddie reached for the sword and then he turned back to me. He hit me with his magic." The first thing she'd felt was disbelief that he was really going to kill her. Even though he'd almost done it earlier, she'd convinced herself it was just a threat, and that he wouldn't actually act on it.

When he had the sword, it should have been enough, but it never had been with her brother. Then she'd felt a searing pain, like a red-hot poker right through her chest.

Looking down, she patted her chest and felt no soreness. Her shirt looked pristine. "He hurt me, didn't he?"

Reece nodded and pulled her to him, weaving one arm under her so she was cradled against him. "I thought I'd lost you," he whispered against her neck.

She felt him shaking and cuddled deeper into him as they laid on the hard floor.

When he calmed, she pulled back so she could look into his eyes. "Tell me."

"Eddie's magic—or whatever Maverick had given him— hit you square in the chest. You—" He choked on the word and blinked several times before he could carry on. "You died." He paused and kissed her forehead. "But your magic hadn't died yet, so Mirek was able to revive you."

Something in the way he rushed through the last part of his explanation told her that it hadn't been that simple. She could only imagine what it had been like for him to see her die, and yet she was still here. She didn't understand, and as much as she wanted to know everything that had happened, she'd wait and ask later.

"I love you, Reece."

He grinned at her, and it was everything she needed. "I love you too, cupcake."

When he pushed to a sitting position, he almost fell backward.

Sitting up, she steadied him. "What's wrong?"

"I'm fine, just a little weak."

More questions rested on the tip of her tongue, but she'd wait until they were somewhere safe to ask them.

"Need a hand?" Rocky asked, extending his hand to her.

"Thanks." He helped her up and then she turned to Reece, expecting to see him standing. Still sitting on the floor, he looked as if a light breeze would knock him over.

"Need a hand?" she asked, mimicking Rocky. When she offered her hand, Rocky did the same and they hauled Reece to his feet. He wobbled before placing a hand on her shoulder and steadying himself.

"Are you sure you're okay?"

"I will be, cupcake."

She turned toward where Reece had made the circle with the mirrors, but he stopped her with a hand on her arm, blocking her view. "Isabella, Eddie tried to take the sword, but it wouldn't let him."

"What do you mean?" It wasn't until then that she realized Eddie hadn't been hurting or taunting them. Deep in her soul, she knew why, but she needed Reece to say the words. She looked up at him, her eyes dry. "Tell me, Reece."

"Something in the sword killed Eddie."

Reece stepped aside, her view now unfettered, and the first thing she noticed were the mirrors. They were on the ground, as if they'd fallen backward, still arranged in a circle, but they hadn't shattered.

Eddie's scuffed chucks were the next thing she fixated on. Walking slowly toward him, her eyes scanned up his body. His right hand lay at his side, the palm black and charred, the fingers swollen.

She walked closer so she could peer down at his face. His eyes were closed like he was sleeping. He looked like he was at peace.

Reece walked up behind her and encircled her with his arms, resting his chin on her shoulder. "Eddie—uh—Mateo was—"

Spinning in his arms, she put her finger against his lips. "You were right the first time. That man was Eddie. I lost Mateo a long time ago. Or maybe I just never saw what he was really like. I'll mourn the young boy I knew. But that man had to be stopped. He'd hurt too many and he would only have hurt more."

Reece nodded and kissed the top of her head again before taking her hand and pulling her out of the circle of mirrors.

"Rocky," Reece said, calling to his brother who was sprawled on one of the couches. Mirek lay on the other, his eyes closed. Later, she'd ask Reece what Mirek had done to heal her so she could thank him properly.

After heaving himself off the couch, Rocky walked over to them. "Isabella, you need to turn around."

She raised her eyebrows at him in question.

"I need to move Eddie."

Having already seen Eddie's dead body, she didn't think

seeing him moved could be any worse, but she did as he requested. Thinking about everything they'd been through in the last couple of days, she realized that she'd never been introduced to Rocky.

They knew each other's names, of course, but had bypassed introductions and skipped to helping with dead bodies. She bit her lip to stop a hysterical laugh that threatened to burst free. Maybe someday she would have to invent a lie if her children ever asked how she'd first met their uncles.

A year ago, even a couple of months ago, the thought of children would have scared her. But not know. She wanted a life with Reece. If they had children, that would be great, but if not, she'd be okay, as long as they were together.

"You can turn around now," Reece said.

When she did, she couldn't stop herself from looking around the room. At the wall by the door were two human-shaped lumps covered with sheets. They must have conjured the coverings.

"What now?" she asked, looking between the two brothers.

"I think we've got two options," Reece said. "We take the mirrors back to Kate's and have the council decide what to do..." He trailed off as if waiting for someone to take over.

"Or we try to retrieve the sword and hope that Eddie was killed because of what's inside him and not because of the sword," Rocky said, supplying the second option. "Let's go for it."

Isabella felt torn. Risk someone being hurt or risk the mirrors being stolen again? Maybe even permanently destroyed this time. Both options were risky and she didn't like either of them.

"Dyl—Rocky, are you sure?" Reece asked.

"Yes, I need to try. Let me do something good for once."

"Rock," Mirek said from the couch.

It sounded like a warning, but Isabella didn't know why and didn't feel it was her place to ask.

Using the armrest for support, Mirek pulled himself up. Before he was fully upright, Rocky was there helping him. Slowly, they made their way to the middle of the room. "Rek, I have to do this."

Mirek didn't say anything, only nodded. "I don't have any strength to help, but I can watch and offer suggestions."

She remembered a comment from Simon when he'd realized that Reece and Rocky had to be brothers. He'd said that when Rocky helped him, he'd offered to help Rocky escape. He'd responded that he couldn't or he would have years ago.

There was history there that Isabella didn't understand.

Something between Rocky and Mirek, maybe more than just them having been in captivity together. Although that was big enough on its own.

Not wanting to get between the two of them, but wanting to help, she directed her magic toward the closest couch and pulled it over to Mirek. Moving something took less magic than conjuring a chair, and since all three men seemed to have drained their magic, she wouldn't waste hers. Just in case.

"Thanks." Mirek sat down and it seemed to spur Reece and Rocky into action.

Reece used his magic to lift the mirrors off the floor, but this time he didn't make a show of it or drag it out. He quickly got them in place and stepped back. "Ready?" he asked, looking at his brother.

Once more, she looked between the two brothers—Reece and Rocky physically looked alike, but their similarities didn't end there. They'd been separated for decades, and yet earlier, they knew what the other had been thinking. Nor did they argue about any of their next steps. Was that just from shared DNA? And what did that say about her and Mateo? Maybe she'd never really known him. It hurt to think that their connection hadn't been real. She would just have to trust that her good traits would be enough to keep her on the straight and narrow.

The bond that these brothers had with each other, even after years apart, was something she wanted. She'd do her best to be worthy of the Williams family.

Rocky nodded and Reece turned the mirrors inward. Isabella was prepared for the bright flashes this time. Just like before, one light shot out of a mirror, connecting it with another. When all three mirrors were connected, the lights brightened into a blinding array.

The lights' point of intersection swelled until it filled the entire circle. Isabella braced herself for the massive light explosion and squinted against the intensity.

Exactly like the first time, a long broad sword floated in the circle.

Rocky took a tentative step forward. What he was willing to do for all of them, not just for himself, hit Isabella deep in her soul. Whatever Rocky's reasons were for proving that he was worthy didn't change the selfless act he was doing now.

She glanced back at the sheet-covered forms against the wall. A feeling of shame hit her. Her brother had caused so much pain for the Williams's family, and yet here they were still willing to sacrifice themselves for what was right. Sure, they were getting justice for everything done to them. As well as making sure others like Eddie didn't succeed, it was how quickly the Williams's men jumped to do it that spoke to Isabella. They were good to their cores.

Turning back to the circle, she pushed aside thoughts of her brother.

Rocky's hand hovered over the sword, and she wondered if he was having second thoughts. He shouldn't have to sacrifice himself; there had to be another way. "Roc—" Just as she was speaking up, Reece's voice overrode hers.

"No! Rocky, don't!" Reece barked as he took a step forward. "You can't do it. We'll find another way."

Rocky dropped his hand to his side. "It's okay, Reece. Someone has to. You and Isabella have each other and Mirek is far too important. I'm expendable."

"Rock, don't." Mirek pushed to his feet, holding onto the couch for support. "Reece is right; there has to be another way."

Isabella watched the interchange between the cousins and sensed the kind of bond she'd only ever hoped to have. But instead of dwelling on what she'd lost, she was determined to be a part of this family. In order to do that, she needed to make sure no more lives were lost.

She remembered how Reece had manipulated the mirror in the antique shop. And again when he put the shards of glass back together. Rocky's specialty must be the same since he had manipulated the floor. "What if you manipulated the sword?" she asked.

Reece looked at her. "Manipulate it, as in change it?"

"I'm not sure, but you changed the mirrors, disassembling and reassembling them, and Rocky moved the floorboards. Could you do something with the sword so you don't have to touch it?"

Rocky stared at the sword. "Maybe, but I don't know how that would help."

Moving inside the circle, Reece stared at the blade too, as if it carried the answers. "We could try dissolving it, but to pour it into a container, we'd probably have to touch it."

Mirek walked toward the circle, and the couch behind it caught Isabella's focus. She'd used her magic to move the object—something she'd done a thousand times. What if... "Hey, guys. What if you used your magic to move the blade?"

"You think it could be that simple?" Reece asked.

"I don't know, but it's worth a try. If you can get it out of the circle, it might stay solid. Then we can figure out what to do with it."

"You're right, it couldn't hurt." Rocky looked at the sword and lifted his hands. "I don't need to use my hands to move it," he said, still staring at the sword. "But I thought maybe I could direct it that way." He dropped his hands and his shoulders slumped in defeat. "Nothing."

"I'll try." Reece moved closer to the blade, but it didn't budge. "Isabella, you want to try?"

"I can't manipulate objects the way you two can. Moving

a couch or something lighter than that is usually all I can do. But sure, I'll try."

Walking into the circle, she felt a sense of trepidation. Not because her brother had died in there, but because she might fail.

Raising her hands, she tilted her fingers up so her palms faced the sword. Unlike Reece and Rocky, Isabella needed her hands to direct her magic. "Here goes." Focusing all her magic, she directed it at the blade.

At first, nothing happened and then the blade wobbled in on its pillow of air. "It moved!" Her hope grew. Using her hands as a guide, she tried to direct the sword's movement, but nothing happened.

"Maybe it's the amount of power," Mirek said. "Three of you have the combined power of maybe one person."

"What do you mean?" she asked. When Mirek didn't answer, she turned to Reece. "Tell me, please."

He rubbed his knuckles against her cheek. "I gave my power to Mirek so he could save your life," he said softly. "It wasn't enough, so Rocky passed on some of his power as well. Yes, a lot of power went into you, but most of it was used to heal you." He turned to Mirek. "Right?"

"Yes. Even though I pulled power from both of you, I expended most of it healing Isabella."

Reece grasped her gently by the arms so she was forced to look back at him. "Cupcake, I have no regrets. I'd do it again in a heartbeat."

"Same, Isabella. I don't know you, but Reece loves you, so, no regrets," Rocky said.

Her throat tightened as she realized she didn't have to prove herself worthy of this family. She didn't need to earn their loyalty or cash in any chips for Reece's love, unlike with her own family. Swallowing against the lump in her throat, she passed her gaze over all three of them. "Thank you."

Reece took her hand and jarred a memory loose. "Rocky, when you moved the floorboards yesterday, Reece gave you his magic, right?"

"Yes. I'd been hurt…" He didn't need to say it was Eddie who'd hurt him; they all knew. She nodded for him to continue. "I wanted to make sure I had enough power to lift all the boards and hold them until you could get away."

"Oh my god, I'm sorry. We didn't get to say anything then, so thank you. And I didn't ask what Eddie did after that." She eyed him, waiting for him to explain.

He gave a one-shoulder shrug. "It doesn't matter. You're thinking we should combine our magic?"

"Yes." She held out her hands to her sides and Reece and Rocky each clasped one. "Let's move it to the right and see if we can lower it to the floor. On three. One. Two. Oh, wait. I can't move an object without my hands."

Reece chuckled. "That's okay, cupcake. We've got it."

"Okay. On three." She focused on pushing her magic into her hands. "One. Two. Three."

Her hands tingled as she felt the magic connection between the brothers. She'd never pushed her magic into someone else before. The sensation was unexpected, like she'd just main-lined caffeine—a sudden burst of energy filling her, but it didn't hurt.

She gasped when the blade moved. Flowing to the right as if pulled on a string, it crossed outside the circle. Each mirror fell to the floor with a soft *whoosh*.

When the sword was on the ground, Rocky dropped her hand. She turned and jumped at Reece, weaving her arms around his neck with the confidence he'd catch her. "We did it!"

He lowered his lips to hers and she got lost in his kiss until someone cleared their throat. Reece laughed against her lips before they broke apart and she looked back at Rocky. "Sorry, not sorry," she said, smiling at him.

"No worries." Rocky crouched on his haunches by the sword. "Now what do we do with it?"

"Wrap it up?" She turned to Reece. "Or maybe we can reach Jack now?"

"Let me check." Reece's eyes unfocused for a moment. He shook his head. "Still nothing. I couldn't reach Jack or Meredith."

"It's beautiful, isn't it?" Rocky asked, but she didn't know who he was talking to.

She looked down at the sword, and for the first time, noticed the intricate details that had been forged into the blade. "It is. I bet Kate will be excited to work with it."

Reaching toward the blade, Rocky's fingers came within millimeters of the sword. Reece jumped forward, pushing on his brother's shoulder, knocking him backward onto his butt. "What the hell were you thinking? We don't know if we can touch it."

Rocky scrubbed his face with his hands before pushing to his feet. "I don't know. I wasn't even aware of what I was doing."

"It's okay," Reece said. "Let's conjure something to wrap it in." Using their rapidly draining magic, they conjured three large leather cloths. As an added layer, they placed a protection spell on each of them and used their magic to wrap them around the sword, further draining them all.

"I'll carry it," Rocky said when they were finished. He lifted it without offering it up for debate.

Reece walked to Mirek and helped him up, then put his arm around the man's waist. "None of us can flash out of here and I still can't reach anyone. Should we Uber it?"

Isabella laughed. "Maybe not with a sword. Simon and Jo

said they were brought here in a large SUV. Is that still around?"

Rocky nodded. "This way," he said as he headed to the door with his bundle.

Isabella looked around the room and stopped when her eyes landed on the two white forms by the wall. "We need to take the mirrors too and what about them?" she asked, pointing to the bodies.

"I have a bit of magic left, so I'll spell the apartment, and if Jack gets freed up, he can come back tonight with some help, or we can come back tomorrow," Reece said. "Right now, we're all too vulnerable to stay here."

She nodded and took one last glance at the sheet-covered bodies before following the others out.

EPILOGUE

*I*saac heard Reece call his name. "In the last room," he called back and looked at the clock on the wall. Only fifteen minutes late. Not too bad; he'd expected them to be even later.

"I'm so sorry we're late," Isabella said in a rush when she walked in with Reece, carrying a plastic food container. "We didn't realize the time, we…" A blush started on her neck and moved into her cheeks.

"Hey, no worries. I didn't expect it."

Her eyes widened. "You did?"

Reece wrapped his arm around Isabella's waist and pulled her into his side. "We're like newlyweds, cupcake," Reece whispered against her head, but still loud enough for Isaac to hear.

She smiled up at Reece. "Right."

He swiveled on his stool, pretending to stack some papers to hide his smile.

Isabella huffed out a small "oh."

The two of them were cute together.

Spinning his stool back around, he observed them as

Reece sat on the adjustable tattoo chair and pulled Isabella up onto the end between his thighs.

"I almost forgot," she said, and the food container she'd been holding, floated over to him.

Isaac took it and saw four fancy cupcakes with yellow icing. "Lemon?" he asked, looking up at Isabella.

Reece grinned. "Not quite. You are one of the first to try my newest creation. The Isabella cupcake. It's apricot and vanilla with hints of lemon, so it's both sweet and tart.

Isabella blushed again and Isaac just smiled. "Thanks, I'm honored. I'm sure I'll enjoy them." He put them on his counter, knowing just who he wanted to share them with. Then he became serious. "Isabella, are you sure this is what you want?" he asked. "It's only been a week since..." Isaac didn't bring up what had happened, but it was common knowledge amongst the Williams's clan, which he was an honorary member of.

"Yes, I'm sure." She looked over her shoulder at Reece and he nodded. Isaac expected they were speaking telepathically, but it didn't bother him that they might be having a private conversation.

"Sorry," she said, looking back at Isaac. "I didn't know how much you knew, and I didn't want to say the wrong thing."

"It's okay. When Reece called yesterday, he said you were laying your brother to rest."

"Yes, we had a ceremony for the internment of his ashes yesterday. It was just supposed to be me and Reece. I..." She visibly swallowed and conjured a small cloth, twisting it in her fingers. "I didn't ask anyone to come, considering what Eddie had done to them all, but... they did. Damon and Morgana, Jack and Meredith, and Rowena and Connor showed up." She turned in Reece's arms and buried her face against his chest.

Isaac moved to his desk in the corner, giving them a moment of privacy. He understood what it was like to lose a brother. It was a feeling he didn't wish on his worst enemy. It left a hole that could never be filled.

He grabbed his tablet and worked on a design for a few minutes while Reece and Isabella whispered behind him.

"I'm okay now," Isabella said.

Picking up his tablet, he pulled his stool back over to them. "We can do this another day, you know. I'll always find time to fit any Williams or honorary Williams in."

"Thanks, but I'm good. I'm just still processing."

He nodded but didn't offer any platitudes—he knew they didn't help. "So, do you know what you want?"

"Yes, a small compass like you gave Meredith, Jo, and Rowena. I love the blue and red watercolors swirling around it."

Isaac didn't want to offend Isabella and needed to tread carefully. "Did they tell you why they picked that design?"

"Meredith told me the compass represented her mother who had been her true north and had passed the torch on to Jack. Eddie wasn't my true north, but without the years I spent searching for him, I wouldn't have wound up here."

Reece leaned forward and kissed her temple. Isaac didn't begrudge their happiness, but he wanted that for himself. If a certain stubborn female ever dropped the chip on her shoulder, he might get his wish one day. As he did a hundred times a day, he pushed thoughts of Kate to the side and concentrated on his client.

"Did anyone tell you that I might not be able to embed a memory within the tattoo? I have to listen to my magic, and I refuse to do something that I don't think is meant to be."

"Yes, Reece told me. How can you tell?"

"It's difficult to explain, but I get a feeling."

She nodded. "I get it, that's what it's like with me."

"Did you want the tattoo in the same spot as Meredith?" When she nodded, he continued. "Do you have something of your brother's?"

Reece pulled a chain out of his pocket and Isaac placed his tablet on the floor before holding out his hand for the chain. It was inexpensive with a butterfly charm.

"My brother gave that to me when he was younger."

Still holding the chain, he nodded and held out his other hand. "May I?" She placed her wrist in his palm and he gently closed his fingers around it, still holding the chain in his other hand. Closing his eyes, he let his magic flow, feeling the emotions in both Isabella and the chain.

His magic pulled back, rejecting the chain like an offensive gift. Opening his eyes he let go of Isabella's wrist and handed the chain back to Reece. "I'm sorry, Isabella."

She twisted the cloth again, then stopped and disappeared it. Her eyes were bright but dry by the time she met his gaze. "I understand, Isaac. I figured it was a long shot anyway."

"Would you still like the tattoo without the memorial?"

"Yes. The meaning of it doesn't change."

"Sounds good. But it doesn't have to be today, you know."

"I know, but I don't want to wait. I'm excited."

"Great. Let's draw up your design." His eyes met Reece's when he stood, and his gratitude was easy to read. Isaac gave him a nod and picked up his tablet.

It didn't take long to draw up the design as Isabella didn't want any changes to the ones the female W's all had. He transferred the design onto Isabella and when she approved the placement, he got everything set up.

The design was small and didn't take long, but after he cleaned up and gave Isabella after-care instructions, they moved to the front of the shop to continue talking.

"You haven't heard from them at all?" he asked, referring to Rocky and Mirek.

Reece shook his head. "Not since the morning after we brought them back here. They both took off, but Mirek did contact Rowena once and said he'd talk to her again soon."

"How's she taking it?"

He huffed out a humorless laugh. "As good as anyone in her situation, I guess. She lost both her brothers and then found out one's a ghost and the other was held in captivity for twenty-two years and now he's disappeared. At least she has Connor."

Isaac conjured a cup of coffee and held it up in question.

"Thanks, but I've got it." Reece conjured two mugs and passed one to Isabella. "Café au lait," he said.

She smiled up at Reece as she whispered thanks and Isaac could see the love between them.

"Speaking of Connor," Isaac said, picking the conversation back up. "How's Sam now that Mirek was rescued?"

"I had lunch with her a couple of days ago," Isabella said, "But she's not saying much."

"I gotta admit, there hasn't been a dull moment since I moved here. Unfortunately, there's been a lot of tragic ones, as well." A picture of Kate lying unconscious on the floor of her shop popped into his mind.

"Yes, and with Maverick still out there and taking control of more people every day, it's not over," Reece said.

"Has the council had any luck in locating Maverick?"

"Not yet," Reece said and smiled. "And speaking of the council… you're looking at the two newest members. We'll be going through the ceremony soon."

"Wow, congratulations."

"Thanks."

They chatted for a few more minutes and then Reece disappeared his mug and Isabella did the same as they stood. "We should be going."

Isaac stood to walk with them to the door.

"Oh, I should have asked earlier… I heard about Jack and Meredith, along with a few others being occupied by Maverick while you were rescuing your brother and cousin. Is everyone okay?"

Reece huffed out a humorless laugh. "Yeah, everyone's good. Maverick had created a diversion downtown by trapping a bunch of magics with a type of protection bubble that was soundproof. As soon as someone walked into the area, they were trapped inside the bubble as well. Then Jack and Meredith got trapped when they went to help. Jack said they were trapped for two hours before bubble dissolved. He thinks it was Maverick's way of giving Eddie time to get the blade, but we have no idea why he didn't send more people to help him. It's one of those mysteries that may never be answered, or we'll find out because he's set another trap. Anyway… everyone's fine and we're all staying alert."

They finally said their goodbyes and Isaac walked to the back of his shop. He still had a few minutes before his next client. Sitting on the stool at his desk he spun and looked at the drawings on the closest wall.

His eyes were drawn to the framed one in the top right corner, as they always were. He knew it so well he could have drawn it with his eyes closed. It had hung in his old shop, and when he'd moved here, he'd considered not hanging it, but he had to. It was a stark reminder that embedding memories in tattoos wasn't always the right choice.

He'd been right in refusing Isabella a memorial tattoo of her brother. At least she hadn't fought him on it. He never again wanted to be in a position where he had to make the decision of going against his magic. Causing one death was enough to last him a lifetime.

Thanks so much for reading *Love in Magic*!
NEXT IN THE IN MAGIC SERIES:
Kate and Isaac are explosive between the sheets, but when they must work together to defeat magic evil, there are sparks of a different kind. Find out what happens in
FORGED IN MAGIC
https://books2read.com/forged-in-magic/

ALSO BY KJ WARAWA

IN MAGIC SERIES

Lost in Magic

Truth in Magic

Found in Magic

Courage in Magic

Love in Magic

Forged in Magic

Forever in Magic

CURSED TO LOVE SERIES

Cursed to Love

Cursed to Dream

Cursed to Dream

ABOUT KJ WARAWA

Paranormal romance author KJ Warawa had worked every job under the sun, including swimwear seller, switchboard operator, legal secretary, sign language interpreter, soldier, massage therapist, and process improvement advisor, before settling into the career she'd always dreamed about: Author.

She still loves processes and spreadsheets, doesn't love massaging feet, and is currently living out her own love story in Alberta, Canada.

STAY IN TOUCH WITH KJ:
Join KJ's Newsletter at
https://kjwarawa.com/free-book/
to receive a FREE book, exclusive deals, special offers, behind-the-scenes info, and learn about new releases, plus more!
www.kjwarawa.com